Sabrina Jeffries is the *New York Times* bestselling author of 40 novels and 9 works of short fiction (some written under the pseudonyms Deborah Martin and Deborah Nicholas). Whatever time not spent writing in a coffee-fueled haze of dreams and madness is spent traveling with her husband and adult autistic son or indulging in one of her passions – jigsaw puzzles, chocolate, and music. With over 7 million books in print in 18 different languages, the North Carolina author never regrets tossing aside a budding career in academics for the sheer joy of writing fun fiction, and hopes that one day a book of hers will end up saving the world. She always dreams big.

For more information, visit her at www.sabrinajeffries.com, on Facebook at www.facebook.com/SabrinaJeffriesAuthor or on Twitter @SabrinaJeffries.

Praise for Sabrina Jeffries, queen of the sexy regency romance:

'Anyone who loves romance must read Sabrina Jeffries!' Lisa Kleypas, *New York Times* bestselling author

'Irresistible . . . Larger-than-life characters, sprightly dialogue, and a steamy romance will draw you into this delicious captive/captor tale' *Romantic Times* (top pick)

'Another excellent series of books which will alternatively have you laughing, crying and running the gamut of emotions . . . I guarantee you will have a tear in your eye' *Romance Reviews Today*

'The sexual tension crackles across the pages of this witty, deliciously sensual, secret-laden story' *Library Journal*

'Exceptionally entertaining and splendidly sexy' *Booklist*

'An enchanting story brimming with sincere emotions and compelling scenarios . . . an outstanding love story of emotional discoveries and soaring passions, with a delightful touch of humor plus suspense' *Titles*

'Scorching . . . From cover to *Reader*

'Full of a witty dial *Publishers*

By Sabrina Jeffries

Sinful Suitors Series
The Art Of Sinning
The Study Of Seduction
The Danger Of Desire
The Pleasures Of Passion

Hellions Of Halstead Hall Series
The Truth About Lord Stoneville
A Hellion In Her Bed
How To Woo A Reluctant Lady
To Wed A Wild Lord
A Lady Never Surrenders

SABRINA
JEFFRIES

THE PLEASURES OF PASSION

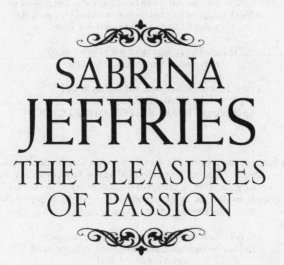

HEADLINE
ETERNAL

Published by arrangement with Pocket Books,
a division of Simon & Schuster, Inc.

First published in Great Britain in 2017
by HEADLINE ETERNAL
An imprint of HEADLINE PUBLISHING GROUP

1

Cataloguing in Publication Data is available from the British Library

ISBN 978 1 4722 4544 1

Typeset in 11.76/14.58 Berling LT Std by Jouve (UK), Milton Keynes

Printed and bound in Great Britain by CPI Group (UK) Ltd, Croydon, CR0 4YY

MIX
Paper from
responsible sources
FSC® C104740

Headline's policy is to use papers that are natural, renewable and recyclable
products and made from wood grown in well-managed forests and other
controlled sources. The logging and manufacturing processes are expected
to conform to the environmental regulations of the country of origin.

HEADLINE PUBLISHING GROUP
An Hachette UK Company
Carmelite House
50 Victoria Embankment
London EC4Y 0DZ

www.headlineeternal.com
www.headline.co.uk
www.hachette.co.uk

*To my lovely mother, who's as fierce as Lady
Pensworth when protecting those she loves.
I love you, Mom!*

THE PLEASURES
OF PASSION

Prologue

London
1823

Seventeen-year-old Brilliana Payne shoved the note from Niall Lindsey, Lord Margrave's heir, into her pocket. Then she slipped into her mother's bedchamber. "Mama," she whispered. "Are you awake?"

Her mother jerked her head up from amid the satin covers and feather pillows like a startled deer. Brilliana winced to see her mother's lips drawn with pain and her eyes dulled by laudanum, even in midafternoon.

"What do you need, love?" Mama asked in her usual gentle voice.

Oh, how she loathed deceiving Mama. But until her suitor spoke to his parents about their marrying, she had to keep the association secret.

"I'm going for my walk in Green Park." *Where Niall, my love, will join me.* "Do you need anything?"

Despite her pain, Mama smiled. "Not now,

my dear. You go enjoy yourself. And tell Gilly to make sure you don't stray near the woods."

"Of course."

What a lie. The woods were where she would meet Niall, where Gilly would keep watch to make sure no one saw them together. Thank heaven her maid was utterly loyal to her.

Brilliana started to leave, then paused. "Um. Papa said he won't be home until evening." Which meant he wouldn't be home until he'd lost all his money at whatever game he was playing tonight. "Are you *sure* you don't need me?"

She dearly hoped not. Niall's note had struck her with dread, partly because he rarely wrote to her. Usually he just met her at Green Park for her daily stroll when he could get away from friends or family. Something must be wrong.

Still, it shouldn't take more than an hour to find out what. And perhaps let him steal a kiss or two.

She blushed. Niall was very good at *that*.

Then again, he ought to be. He was rumored to be quite a rogue with ladies, although Brilliana was convinced it was merely because of his wild cousin, Lord Knightford, with whom he spent far too much time. Or so her maid had told her.

"I'll be fine," Mama said tightly. "I have my medicine right here."

Medicine, ha! It made Mama almost as ill as whatever mysterious disease had gripped her. The doctors still couldn't figure out what Mama had, but they continued to try everything—bleeding her, cupping her, giving her assorted potions. And every time a new treatment was attempted, Brilliana hoped it would work, would be worth Mama's pain.

Guilt swamped her. "If you're sure . . ."

"Go, dear girl! I'm just planning to sleep, anyway."

That was all the encouragement Brilliana needed to hurry out.

A short while later, she and Gilly were in Green Park, waiting at the big oak for Niall.

"Did he say why he wanted to meet, miss?" Gilly asked.

"No. Just that it was urgent. And it had to be today."

"Perhaps he means to propose at last."

Her breath caught. "I doubt it. He would have approached Papa if that were the case."

Gilly's face fell. "Then you'd best take care. 'Cause if he spends as much time with the soiled doves as I've heard, he might be the sort of fellow to take advantage—"

"He's not like that," Brilliana said. "Not with me."

Except for those lovely kisses, he was respectful. Besides, the gossips always painted a scandalous picture—that was why they were called gossips. But through weeks of secret meetings, she'd seen his character, and it was a good one. She was sure of it.

"Well, I daresay you're right about him then," Gilly said soothingly. "And he still might be proposing, you know. He might just have wanted your consent before he approached your papa." A hopeful expression crossed her face. "That's how all the gentlemen is doing things these days, I'm told. And only think what your mama will say when she hears you've snagged an heir to an earl!"

"I haven't snagged anyone yet." Besides, the word *snag* was too coarse for what she wanted from Niall—his mind, his heart, his soul. Since hers already belonged to him.

"There you are," said a masculine voice behind them. "Thank God you came."

Her heart leapt as she turned to see Niall striding up to them. At twenty-three, he was quite the handsomest man she'd ever known—lean and tall and possessed of the most gorgeous hazel eyes, which changed color from cedar brown to olive green depending on the light. And his unruly mop of gold-streaked brown hair made her itch to set it to rights.

Though she didn't dare be so forward until they were formally betrothed. Assuming that ever happened.

Offering Brilliana his arm, he cast Gilly a pointed glance. "I'll need a few minutes alone with your mistress. Will you keep watch?"

Gilly curtsied deeply. "Of course, my lord."

Normally her maid balked a little at that, but

she was obviously eager to allow Niall a chance to propose.

Indeed, his behavior did signal that today's meeting wasn't going to be like the others. Without his typical pleasantries, Niall led Brilliana into the woods to the clearing where they generally talked.

That dimmed her joy in their meeting a fraction. "You do realize how fortunate we are that Gilly is a romantic. Otherwise, she would never let us do these things."

"I know, Bree."

He was the only one to call her that, and she rather liked the nickname. It made her sound carefree when she felt anything but.

Halting well out of earshot of Gilly, he added, "And then I wouldn't get the chance to do *this*."

He drew her into his arms for a long, ardent kiss, and she melted. If he was kissing her, he obviously didn't mean to break with her. As long as they had this between them . . .

But it was over far too soon. And when he drew back to stare at her with a haunted look, her earlier dread returned.

"What's wrong?" she whispered.

Glancing away, he mumbled a decidedly ungentlemanly oath. "You'll be furious with me."

She fought to ignore the alarm knotting her belly. "I could never be furious with you. What has happened? Just tell me."

"This morning I fought a duel."

"What?" Her heart dropped into her stomach. How could that be? "I—I don't understand." She must have heard him wrong. Surely the man she'd fallen in love with wasn't the violent sort.

"I killed a man, Bree. In a duel."

She *hadn't* misheard him. Still scarcely able to believe it, she roamed the little clearing, her blood like sludge in her veins. "What on earth would even make you do such a thing?"

"It doesn't matter." He threaded his fingers through his hair. "It's done, and now I risk being hanged."

Because killing someone in a duel was considered murder. Her heart stilled. Her love was a murderer. And now he could die, too!

"So I'm leaving England tonight," he went on. "For good."

The full ramifications of all he'd told her hit her. "You . . . you're leaving England," she echoed hollowly. *And me.*

His gaze met hers. "Yes. And I want you to go with me."

That arrested her. "Wh-what do you mean?"

"I'm asking you to marry me." He seized her hands. "Well, to elope with me. We'll go by ship to Spain, and we'll wed there. Then my friends in Corunna will help us settle in."

She gaped at him. He was *serious*. He actually meant for her to leave her family and home and run away with him now that he'd gone off and *killed* a man.

But in a duel. Might it not have been done with good reason?

"Do you *have* to go abroad?" she asked. "Sometimes the courts will acquit a gentleman of the charges, assuming the duel was a just one."

"It was." His expression grew shuttered. "But I can't risk defending myself in court."

"Why not?"

"I can't say. It's . . . complicated."

"It can't be more complicated than running away to the Continent, for goodness' sake."

A muscle worked in his jaw. "Look, I've made a vow to keep the reasons for the duel quiet. And I have to keep that vow."

"Even from me?" She couldn't hide the hurt in her voice. "Why? Who demanded such a thing of you?"

"I can't say, damn it!" When she flinched, he said, "It isn't important."

"It certainly is to *me*. You want me to run off with you, but you won't even explain why you fought or even with whom you dueled?"

Letting out an oath, he stared past her into the woods. "I suppose I can reveal the other party in the duel, since that will get around soon enough. The man's name is Joseph Whiting."

She didn't know any Joseph Whiting, so that information wasn't terribly helpful.

"But that's all I can reveal." He fixed her with a hard look. "You'll simply have to trust me. Come with me, and I will take care of you."

"What about passports? How can you even be sure we can marry in Spain?"

"There's no reason we can't. And I have a passport—we'll arrange for yours once we arrive."

She didn't know anything about international travel, but his plan sounded awfully havey-cavey. "If you're wanted for murder here, surely no British consulate—"

"I promise you, it will all turn out well in the end."

"You can't promise that."

"Deuce take it, I *love* you," he said, desperation in his tone. "Isn't that enough?"

"No! You're asking me to risk my entire future to go with you. To leave my family and my home, possibly never to see either again. So, no, it is *not* enough, drat you!"

He squeezed her hands. "Are you saying you don't share my feelings?"

"You know I do." Her heart lurched in her chest. "I'd follow you to the ends of the earth if I could, but I can't right now." Certainly not without some assurance that he truly meant to marry her and not just . . . carry her off to have his way with her.

Oh, Lord, that was absurd. Just because he was heir to an earl and she the daughter of an impoverished knight didn't mean that Niall would stoop so low. She was sure of it. She'd heard of women being fooled into thinking they were eloping when really they weren't, women who were discarded after they'd served their usefulness to some randy lord. But Niall would never do such a thing. He was an honorable man.

Except for the fact that he fought a duel for reasons he won't reveal.

She winced. It didn't matter. He would never hurt her that way. She couldn't believe it. And for a moment, the idea of being his forever, of traveling abroad and seeing the world without their families to make trouble—

Families. That brought reality crashing in. "You know I can't leave Mama." Regretfully, she tugged her hands from his. "She needs me."

"*I* need you." His lovely eyes were dark with entreaty. "Your mother has your father."

"The man who spends every waking moment at his club or in the hells, gambling away my future and Mama's," she said bitterly. "She could die, and he wouldn't even notice."

Papa had never met a card game he didn't like. Unfortunately, he'd never met one he could win, either. But he spent all his time and money trying to find one.

Consequently, Mama spent much of *her* time alone with Brilliana or servants. Brilliana had hoped that when—*if*—Niall proposed marriage, she could persuade him to let her take Mama to live with them. But that was impossible if he meant to carry her off to the Continent.

"What about *your* family?" she asked.

He tensed. "What about them?"

"Do your parents know that you mean to flee London? Have you spoken to your father about . . . us?"

The stricken look on his face told her that answer. "He knows I'm leaving England. But no, he doesn't know about us, because I wanted to speak to you first. In case you . . . refused to go."

His reluctance to tell his parents about their courtship before approaching *her* parents had long been a topic of discussion between them.

She'd understood—really, she had. She probably wasn't lofty enough to suit his family, and Niall had been waiting until she had her come-out and his parents could meet her in a natural setting. Then he could ease them into the idea of his wanting to wed her.

But now . . . "You could still speak to *my* parents, gain their blessing and agreement to the marriage. Then you . . . you could get a special license, and we could marry before we leave here."

Though that didn't solve the problem of Mama.

"There's no time for that! Besides, it takes at least two days to acquire any kind of license. And my ship leaves tonight." He drew her close. "For once in your life, sweeting, throw caution to the wind. You love me. I love you. We belong together. I don't know how I'll bear it if you don't flee with me."

His words tore at her. She wanted *desperately* to go.

And apparently he could read the hesitation in her face, for he took advantage, clasping her head in his hands so he could seal his mouth to hers with breathtaking ardor.

Oh, Lord, but the man could kiss. He made her heart soar, and her blood run fast and hot. Looping her arms about his neck, she gave herself up to the foretaste of what their lives could be like . . . if she would just give in.

But how could she? Reluctantly, she broke the kiss, even knowing it might be their last.

His eyes glittered with triumph, for he could always tell how easily he tempted her. "I know this isn't the ideal way for us to start out, Bree, but I'll make it up to you. Father will continue to send my allowance, and my friends will take care of us until we're settled. I might even find work in Spain."

She wavered. It sounded wonderful and exciting and oh so tempting.

He cupped her cheek. "All we have to do is leave tonight, with the tide. You and I, together for the rest of our lives. Trust me, you won't regret going."

Ah, but she would.

She could handle travel to a strange country and everything that such an upheaval entailed. She could live on a pittance. And yes, she would even risk ruin if it meant being with him.

But she couldn't abandon Mama. Papa would never manage the doctors or sit wiping Mama's brow when she was feverish. Papa could hardly bear to be in the sickroom. And with money short because of his gambling, they couldn't afford an extra servant to tend to her mother night and day. Besides, she could never entrust Mama's care to a servant.

She pushed away from him. "I can't," she said. "I'm sorry."

His expression turned to stone. "You mean, you won't."

"If we could bring Mama with us, I'd go, but that's impossible. She's too ill to travel."

"Don't pretend that this is about your mother," he said harshly. "It's about your blasted caution. How many weeks did it take me to convince you to start meeting me in the park? To tempt you into a kiss? You're a coward at heart, and you know it."

The bitter words stabbed her through the heart. "Well, at least I don't recklessly fight duels and then run off to avoid the consequences!"

She regretted the words the instant he drew himself up, every inch a lord. "So that's how you see me, is it? Fine." He started to walk off.

"Wait!" she cried. "I'm sorry. I shouldn't have said that. I suppose you must . . . have had your reasons for dueling."

He let out an oath, then turned back to her. "I'm sorry, too. I don't think you a coward."

She stifled a sharp retort. That wasn't true. Men always wanted women to throw caution to the winds, but that was only because they had less to lose. A woman lost *everything* when she trusted the wrong man. Just look at Mama.

"Bree," he said softly, "I don't want things to end this way."

"Neither do I, but . . ." Frantically, she tried to think of another solution. "I—I could write to you once Mama gets better." Though she feared that wasn't going to happen. "Then you could send for me somehow."

"You would travel alone to meet me?" he asked skeptically.

"I'd find a way to get there." Tears filled her eyes.

"Don't cry, sweeting. Please, I can't bear it." Thumbing a tear away, he said, "I'm not giving up on you, on us. If you need to reach me—*when* you need to reach me—let my father know. I'll tell him to expect to hear from you. He can get a letter to me, and we'll arrange matters so you can follow me."

"I will, I promise." She gazed into the face she loved so well and fought back more tears. "But I can't go yet."

He nodded, as if he couldn't trust himself to speak.

"So I suppose this is farewell," she choked out.

"*Au revoir*," he said fiercely. "Not farewell. Never farewell." He brushed a kiss to her lips, then stared into her eyes so longingly it made her ache. "If you change your mind about going with me today, I'll be on the *Cordovan*. It sets sail shortly after sundown. Ask for Mr. Lindsey—that's the name I'm using abroad—and they'll direct you to me."

"Be careful," she whispered.

Then, before she fell apart completely, she walked out to where Gilly stood. And as she left the park, while Gilly peppered her with questions, all she could think was, *Will I ever see him again?*

Despite his insistence on *Au revoir,* she very much feared that she would not. And that realization shattered her heart.

The sun was setting over the Thames as Niall stood on the deck of the *Cordovan,* scanning every bonnet on the crowded dock in hopes of spotting Bree's face and chestnut curls. But the hollow feeling in his gut told him the truth—she wasn't coming. He was utterly alone.

Unbidden, the exchange he'd overheard between her and Gilly popped into his head.

Only think what your mama will say when she hears you've snagged an heir to an earl!

I haven't snagged anyone yet.

His hands clenched on the rail. Bree hadn't meant that the way it sounded, so . . . so calculating. If she'd been trying to reel him in, she would have agreed to go with him, for God's sake.

"The captain tells me that you should have a good voyage."

He stiffened. Father had come to see him off.

Facing the man who'd engineered his escape, he asked, "How is Clarissa?"

"Your sister is as well as can be expected, under the circumstances." His father's eyes sparked with futile anger. "I can't believe the girl was fool enough to trust that bastard Whiting, even for a few moments."

"It wasn't her fault. She fancied herself in love."

Just like Bree, who'd met *him* alone regularly because she'd trusted him not to hurt her. Because Niall had persuaded her he could be trusted, that his reputation as a rogue was greatly exaggerated.

Apparently Whiting had convinced Clarissa of the same thing. So Niall could hardly blame her for going off alone with the man. But he could damned well blame Mother, the worst chaperone in London. She should have done better in warning his sister about the dangers a devil like Whiting could present.

Last night, Clarissa had been raped. This morning Niall had killed her assailant. And he couldn't tell a soul, because the world knew only that he and Joseph Whiting had dueled. Clarissa's reputation and future were intact and would stay that way as long as everyone kept quiet.

"Were you able to convince Mrs. Whiting

to hold her tongue about why her son and I dueled?" he asked his father.

"For now. We're very fortunate that Whiting was hoping for a marriage to Clarissa and thus didn't tell anyone else why you two fought. Now that he's dead, no one will learn of it unless Mrs. Whiting speaks, and she swears she won't. She doesn't want her son's name dragged through the mud any more than we want Clarissa's ruined. But I can't guarantee that Mrs. Whiting will keep to her word if you're hauled before the court."

"One more reason I must leave England."

"Yes. Perhaps someday I can find a way to change the situation, but for now . . ."

It was highly unlikely that Niall would be returning. Yet he still didn't regret what he'd done, just that he couldn't reveal the truth to Bree.

He didn't dare. Not even to her. Clarissa now had a chance at a good life despite what had happened to her, and that was all that mattered.

Even if it meant he lost Bree.

No, blast it, he wouldn't lose her! He couldn't. Which was why he had to tell Father about her.

"There's a woman I'm leaving behind," Niall said. "I asked her to go with me, but she refused, on account of her sickly mother. She may, however, come to you in a few months asking that you send a letter to me, and if she does, I request that you treat her kindly and help her in any way you can." He met his father's gaze. "I promised to send for her when she's ready to join me. I love her. I mean to marry her if I can."

Alarm sparked in his father's face. "You didn't tell her about Clarissa, did you?"

"Of course not. I made a vow to you, and I intend to keep it."

"Thank God. If I'm not even telling your mother, you'd damned well better not be telling some adventuress you fancy yourself in love with."

Niall stiffened. Father still didn't entirely trust him. Not that Niall could blame him. Father was a gentleman through and through, with a strict code of honor. He had no truck with young men sowing their wild oats. Ever since Niall had done so a bit too enthusiastically in his salad days, his father always seemed to be expecting him to prove himself.

By God, what did he have to do to show he'd reformed in the past year? "I don't 'fancy' myself in love with her. I *am* in love with her. And she's not 'some adventuress.' She's respectable."

"Well, that's something at least." His father searched his face. "Who is she? Do I know her?"

Now came the hard part. "I don't believe so. Her name is Miss Payne, and she's the daughter of a fellow named Sir Oswald Payne. He's—"

"I know Sir Oswald." His father's face clouded over. "Damned wastrel has lost nearly everything gambling. I'm surprised he hasn't yet landed in debtors' prison. He has few connections and practically no money."

Niall sighed. This was precisely why he'd hesitated to tell his parents about Bree.

"And when the hell did you meet his daughter,
anyway?" Father demanded.

"Last summer, when you were too busy reno-
vating Margrave Manor to accompany Mother
to Bath so she could take the waters. While she
and I were there, so were Miss Payne and her
parents."

"Your mother never mentioned them."

"Because Mother never met them. Miss Payne
is not yet . . . . out."

"God help us," his father muttered. "So she's
what? Fifteen? Sixteen?"

"Seventeen," he said defensively. "She'll come
out next season. I happened to encounter her
in the park in Bath one day when we were both
taking a walk. We were introduced by a mutual
acquaintance."

"Ah." Father looked relieved. "So you haven't
even met her parents yet."

"No. I'd hoped to wait until her come-out and
have you meet her formally first, but—"

"Good, good, always best to be cautious in
these things. If Sir Oswald knew that a man of
your consequence was sniffing round his daughter, he'd be angling to gain any advantage from it.
At least you weren't so stupid as all that."

Niall bristled at Father's typically dismissive
tone. "I don't think I was stupid at all. I didn't
rush into my friendship with Miss Payne. I took

my time making sure she would suit me as a wife. And I truly believe she will."

"A wastrel's daughter?" Father shook his head. "Take care, my boy. There's a reason rank separates people. Look at your sister, taking up with that fellow Whiting. I should think you would be more cautious."

"*You* weren't," Niall snapped. "You married a rich Cit who proved flighty as a finch."

"Only because your grandfather gambled so much that he left me no choice," Father said irritably. "But you don't have to take such a chance in marriage. Fortunately you can marry a solid girl, someone with the right rank, breeding, and connections."

"Or I can marry for love. Which is what I prefer."

Father snorted. "Love? What you're feeling is lust, pure and simple. I take it this young woman is pretty?"

"Yes, but—"

"She didn't turn you down because of her ailing mother, I can assure you. She turned you down because you can no longer be her savior."

"What do you mean?"

The pity in his father's eyes sliced through his confidence. "What good would you be to her once you two are in hiding in Spain? She won't be able to lord it over her friends as a viscountess or show off her fine town house or prance about to balls on the arm of an earl's heir. And after I'm gone, she won't have the advantages of being a countess."

I haven't snagged anyone yet.

He thrust those words from his mind. "She's not like that. She only cares about being with me."

"Are you sure? She's lived her entire life with dwindling expectations, thanks to her idiot father. Suddenly, you come along and the world opens up for her. Until you fight a duel, and everything changes. So now she says she can't go with you because of her sickly mother. Has she said anything to that effect before?"

Fighting to ignore his father's logic, he gazed out at the river. "We've barely talked of marriage before. And yes, she has spoken of her mother's illness in the past." But she'd never hinted that she couldn't marry because of it.

Worry crossed Father's face. "Don't be a fool, son. The last thing you need as you head off to an uncertain future is to be saddled with a wife who's unhappy about your exile. She did you a favor, don't you see? Now you can start life over abroad without such a burden. You might do very well for yourself, if you just keep your wits about you."

His temper flared. "And if I have Miss Payne at my side. I need her."

"Pretty girls are thick upon the ground, in Spain as well as here. No reason you have to marry *this* one."

"I love her. That's reason enough. And I'm sure that she will come to meet me once her mother is . . . gone."

"I hope you're right. I hate to see—" He steadied his shoulders. "If it's her you want for a wife, then it's her you shall have. Just don't be disappointed if she proves to be . . . not what you think, all right?"

"That won't happen." Niall seized his father's arm. "So you will help her if she asks for it? You owe me that much."

A pained smile crossed his father's face. "Yes, I suppose I do."

"Do you swear it?" Niall persisted. His father put great store in vows.

Father sighed. "I do. But only if you swear to *me* that you will stop worrying about it and concentrate on your escape. You're not free yet, you know."

That reminder of his tricky situation sobered him. It would do none of them any good if he were captured and taken to court. "I swear," Niall said.

Though he wasn't sure that particular vow was one he could keep. Father could caution him all he liked, but Bree had imprinted herself upon his heart. Niall could no more stop worrying about her than he could stop breathing.

So it was going to be a long, hard trip to Spain.

One

Impatiently, Niall paced the drawing room of the Margrave town house, waiting for his mother to be ready so they could go to dinner at Clarissa's. This was his first time in town since his pardon and subsequent return to England a month ago, but some things never changed.

Mother still didn't know the meaning of being on time. And she was worse than ever now that Father was dead and Clarissa had married one of his childhood friends—Edwin Barlow, the Earl of Blakeborough. There was no one around any longer to reel Mother in.

His newly hired valet entered the room. "Begging your pardon, my lord, but when I was unpacking the trunk you shipped from Portugal, I found this envelope at the bottom." He held it out. "I wasn't sure if it was important."

As Niall took it and saw the script written in his father's hand, he wondered why he would have kept an old letter with his other correspondence. Only after he opened it and a newspaper cutting fell into his hand did he remember.

A few months after his arrival in Spain, Father had sent him the article from *La Belle Assemblée*, a ladies' magazine. It was the Provincial News section—a list of births, deaths, and marriages outside London.

And Niall remembered its contents word for word:

Cheshire

Married. At Chester, Mr. Reynold Trevor, son of Captain Mace Trevor, to Miss Brilliana Payne, of London, only daughter of Sir Oswald and Mariah Payne.

Father's accompanying letter had only said, *I thought you would wish to know.*

Bree had married within scant months after Niall's departure.

Niall felt the pain of the loss of her anew, the years having barely dulled it. Clearly Father had been right—Bree had merely been waiting for a better offer. Mr. Trevor might not have been heir to an earl, but he'd been wealthy enough to own an estate in good condition, and his father had some standing in society. Apparently those two things had sufficed to prompt Bree to throw Niall over.

If she'd ever even loved him at all.

Now, as then, Niall noted that Bree's mother hadn't been listed in the cutting as the *late* Mariah Payne. So Father had been right about that, too. All that nonsense about Bree not wanting to marry because of her sickly mother had been naught but an excuse.

"My lord?"

With a start, he realized his valet was asking him something. "Sorry, I'm woolgathering. What is it?"

"Is the letter to be kept? Is it important?"

In a surge of temper, he crumpled the cutting in his fist and tossed it into the fire. "It's naught but a bit of inconsequential old gossip."

Inconsequential gossip that had destroyed him after he'd read it. But he was past all that now.

Granted, Bree had taken him by surprise a couple of weeks ago when she'd shown up at Stoke Towers, Edwin and Clarissa's estate in the country, and then at the wedding of his cousin Warren to Delia Trevor. How could he have known that Bree's husband was Delia's brother? Or rather, *had been* Delia's brother before the man's tragic death a year ago.

Niall had practically fallen apart at his first sight of the widowed Bree—no, Mrs. Trevor now—looking lovelier than ever, with a lusher figure and a haunting sadness in her chocolate-brown eyes. She was even out of mourning, which meant she was available again.

He gritted his teeth. Not to him. She hadn't

sent him so much as a word in all these years. If not for Father, he wouldn't even have learned that she'd married. If not for running into her at the wedding, he wouldn't have known she was widowed and had a son. Clearly she didn't give a damn about him anymore.

If she ever had.

Niall's valet cleared his throat. "One more thing, sir. Shall I lay out different attire for when you return from dinner? Will you be attending St. George's this evening?"

Niall had been made an honorary member of St. George's Club by virtue of being Edwin's brother-in-law. And by virtue of what he'd done to protect his sister, though no one knew about that except Edwin and Warren.

"I may, if Edwin wants to. But if I do go, I'll just wear this."

"Very good, sir." With a nod, his valet left.

Niall glanced at the clock, then swore. Stalking out into the hall, he called up the stairs, "Mother! We were supposed to be at Clarissa's half an hour ago!"

"I'm coming, I'm coming," she grumbled as she appeared at the top of the stairs.

A lump caught in his throat. Mother might be flighty and prone to exaggeration, but he'd missed her. The separation from his family had been a particularly hard part of his exile in Spain and then Portugal. And he still couldn't get used to how much older Mother looked now.

"I don't know what you spent your time abroad doing," she added as she made her slow way down the stairs, favoring her bad hip, "but I swear it has turned you into quite the grump."

"Sorry, Mother." He hurried up to offer her his arm. "It's just that this isn't one of your society balls, where you can show up whenever you wish. This is dinner with your daughter and her husband. Whose company we both happen to enjoy."

Apparently madly in love, the pair were happily expecting their first child. And that made all the sacrifices of his last seven years worth it.

Even losing Bree.

He grimaced. He'd never really *had* her. He'd just thought he did.

"Don't be ridiculous," Mother said. "Clarissa knows how I am. She won't fret a bit over our being late. Besides, one always hears the best gossip late in the party, so there's no point in showing up early."

"Not *early*, Mother—*on time*. And is hearing gossip the only reason you go to dine with your daughter?"

"Of course not. I do enjoy a good meal, and Edwin's cook is exceptional."

God, he hoped so. One thing he missed about Spain and Portugal was the food there—excellent cheeses, well-spiced dishes, and exotic fruits. It had spoiled him for the usual British mutton stews; he'd give anything for a good dish of paella or *pulpo*. Hmm, perhaps he should look for a Spanish cook. . . .

"I also wish to hear how Clarissa is feeling these days," Mother went on. She shot him a sly glance. "She *is* carrying my first grandchild, you know."

That was Mother Code for *When are you providing me with a grandchild?*

Thankfully, she was easy to distract. "So, the best gossip comes later on, does it?"

A bright smile lit her face. "Oh yes! Why, we might even coax Lord Fulkham to tell us intimate details about the king's death." She leaned in with a conspiratorial air. "If anyone should know them, it's the undersecretary of state for . . . for . . ." She waved her hand. "Important things of some sort."

"For war and the colonies. But Fulkham isn't the sort to gossip. And why would *he* be at this dinner?"

"How should I know? But he accepted the invitation."

"There were *invitations*?" Niall had thought this was just an intimate family dinner. "Who else was invited?"

"Well, Lord Fulkham's sister-in-law, Mrs. Vyse, for one." She cast him a knowing glance. "A very pretty woman, you know. And quite an eligible widow."

He groaned. *That* was Mother Code for *When are you getting married?* He hadn't considered the possibility that Clarissa and Mother might use this dinner for matchmaking.

"Though sadly," Mother continued, "she's not rich. The widow you *ought* to consider is Mrs. Trevor—her aunt has provided her with a nice dowry, and frankly, you could use the funds for Margrave Manor."

Niall grimaced. God, was *she* invited to this deuced dinner?

"I haven't met her yet," his mother rambled on, "so I don't know if Mrs. Trevor is pretty enough for you—or young enough, for that matter. But—"

"Stop it, Mother. I don't want any more nonsense about how I require a wife. I need time to settle in. Besides, I prefer to pick my own, not have one shoved at me by you or Clarissa. Not even a rich widow."

"I'm only saying—"

"I *know* what you're saying. *I'm* saying to leave it be. If I need your help with finding my countess, I'll let you know." And that was *never* going to happen. Mother would choose him a wife based on rank alone, which was the last thing he wanted.

She sniffed. "Good heavens, but you're prickly these days."

His eyes narrowed on her. "So, Fulkham and Mrs. Vyse will be there this evening. Anyone else I should know about? How many is Clarissa expecting?"

"Ten."

"Ten!"

"Or perhaps fifteen." She tapped her chin. "I'm not sure, actually. I confess I wasn't paying much attention once she started rattling off names. Except for Fulkham and Mrs. Vyse, the others sounded dreadfully tedious. Sadly, it won't be the usual fun people. The Keanes are at their new estate in Hertfordshire. And Warren and Delia are still on their honeymoon in Italy."

He let out a breath. So none of Delia's family would be there. Thank God. Surely that meant Bree wouldn't be there, either.

Not that it mattered if she was. After the horrors he'd witnessed in Portugal during the ongoing bloody conflict between the British-backed liberals and the absolutists, he desired only one thing: peace. Not a two-faced female who wanted, as Father had said, "the advantages of being a countess."

No, this time round he would find a woman who actually cared about him, who could help him put the images of his exile out of his mind. This time he wouldn't fall into the trap Bree wove with her soft words and shy, entirely false smiles. Let the widowed Mrs. Trevor look elsewhere for a husband. He was out of the running.

Brilliana Trevor stood in the Blakeboroughs' drawing room, listening with rapt attention as

Lord Fulkham and Lord Blakeborough debated the merits of planting oats over barley. She wished she could take notes, but that just wasn't done at a dinner party.

Clarissa frowned at her husband as she passed by. "Honestly, Edwin, can't you talk about anything but estate matters? Poor Brilliana must be bored to tears."

"No, indeed!" Brilliana said. "Now that I'm managing Camden Hall, I'm trying to learn everything I can about how to look after it." Especially since she no longer had to worry about losing it to creditors.

"Very wise," Lord Blakeborough said. "I wish more ladies would take an interest. Even Clarissa has a broader knowledge of such matters than the average wife."

"Ah, but that's because you include her in your estate affairs." Bitterness edged into Brilliana's voice. "Even when I tried to get my late husband to involve me, he wouldn't. He always said not to worry my pretty head about it."

"It *is* a very pretty head, to be sure," Lord Fulkham said.

She stared him down. "Sadly, the prettiness of my head isn't much help when it comes to knowing what to plant or how to manage tenants. Sir."

A faint smile tipped up the corners of his lips. "Touché, Mrs. Trevor."

What an odd response. Other men were

offended when she wasn't flattered by their empty compliments.

Unsurprisingly, Clarissa said, "Lord Fulkham, I do hope you're not one of those gentlemen who think women are only good as ornaments."

"Certainly not. Though I do believe Mrs. Trevor would be better off hiring an estate manager than trying to acquire such extensive knowledge in a matter of weeks."

"I agree," Brilliana said. "But, sadly, I can't yet afford one. Besides, the more I learn, the more I can teach Silas when he's older. Camden Hall will be his one day, after all."

"Ah, yes," Lord Fulkham said. "I forgot you have a son. How old is he now?"

"Sixteen months. I'm hopeful that by the time he's old enough to assume responsibility for it, the estate will be self-sufficient."

Clarissa's husband, Lord Blakeborough, smiled broadly at Brilliana. "An admirable aim. I have some books I can loan you."

"Thank you. I'd appreciate that." How nice to have at least one man here who didn't assess her just by her appearance.

"And I'm always happy to answer your questions, too," he added. "Ask me whatever you wish."

"Or better yet," Lord Fulkham said with a veiled glance, "you should ask Margrave once he arrives. I daresay he knows plenty on the subject of estate management, since he's spent most of the past month trying to get his own property in order."

Brilliana's heart dropped into her stomach. Niall was coming here. For dinner. Oh, Lord. The least Clarissa could have done was give her some warning.

Fixing her with a hard look, Brilliana said, "I assumed that your brother was still at Margrave Manor in the country."

Clarissa's smile was suspiciously bright. "Oh, didn't I mention that he came to town yesterday? He and Mother are probably on their way now. Mother tends to be late to everything, you know."

Aunt Agatha, Brilliana's aunt by marriage, said, "I'm afraid I have not yet had the pleasure of meeting your mother."

Lord Blakeborough chuckled. "It's not so much a pleasure as an experience. The dowager is a cross between a whirlwind and a lunatic."

Clarissa tapped his arm with her fan. "I can't believe you're calling my mother a lunatic!" She shot Aunt Agatha a furtive glance. "You'll give Lady Pensworth the wrong impression, after I invited her expressly to meet Mama. I thought they'd enjoy each other's company."

"Why, because we're both old widows?" Aunt Agatha asked tartly.

But Clarissa wasn't flustered one bit. "Because you both have a wealth of knowledge about the inner workings of society. We younger ladies can benefit from your advice."

That seemed to mollify Aunt Agatha. "Well then. I am always happy to counsel young ladies. Especially ones who appreciate the value of age and experience."

Astonishing. No one else parried Aunt Agatha's jabs so effectively. But then, Clarissa had a wonderfully deft hand for managing people. Which made Brilliana even more curious to meet her mother.

Niall's mother. It dawned on Brilliana that she was about to meet the very woman he'd resisted introducing to her years ago.

Back then she'd resented that, but hadn't entirely blamed him for his caution. Of course, that was before she'd heard *why* he had dueled— because of some woman rumored to be his paramour. He and Mr. Whiting, known to be a notorious seducer, had apparently fought over this other woman's affections.

No wonder the wretch had refused to tell her the reason for the duel. He'd known she would then see him for the lying, cheating scoundrel he was. The whole time he'd been courting her secretly by day, he'd been bedding some lightskirt by night.

Not that anyone had told her about it directly, since young ladies weren't supposed to know that such women existed. She was lucky she'd managed to hear the gossip about the duel itself, and had it confirmed as true.

She had Niall's father to thank for *that*. The

late Lord Margrave, whom she'd turned to briefly after Niall's exile, had made it quite clear what sort of fellow his son was. She could only imagine what would have happened to her if she'd fled with Niall to Spain—a steady descent into ruin and degradation. At least she'd been spared that.

Just then the footman announced the arrival of Lord Margrave and the dowager Lady Margrave. Fortunately Brilliana was standing in the corner when they entered, giving her a chance to observe them without being seen.

This time she wouldn't be taken by surprise, as she'd been two weeks ago, when she'd seen Niall for the first time in seven years and had behaved like a blithering idiot, blushing and stammering.

No, she would be cool and collected, as if there were naught between them but their family connections. And she would be the same with his mother.

But Lady Margrave, a bubbly older woman with bright eyes, wasn't quite the dragon lady Brilliana had expected. And Niall . . .

He looked so delicious, making her fingers fairly itch for her sketchbook. His time abroad had cut away the boyishness from his features, leaving the strong cheekbones and firm jaw of a man in his prime. And Spain's hot sun had streaked his cedar-brown hair a wonderful gold and bronze, complemented by his smart tailcoat of chocolate superfine with gilt buttons.

"Sorry we're late," Niall said to Clarissa. "You know Mother. The word *punctual* isn't in her lexicon."

"Oh, pish-posh." His mother greeted her daughter with a kiss on the cheek. "Punctuality is for the dull. Just look at your sister; she's never on time anywhere. And she's always the liveliest one at every party."

"True," Lord Blakeborough said with obvious affection.

But Clarissa was glaring at her mother. "Mama, you're insulting every one of my guests who *was* punctual."

"Am I? I don't see how." The dowager blinked. "I haven't even met half of them."

Brilliana choked down a laugh. She was beginning to understand Lord Blakeborough's unusual description of his mother-in-law.

Clarissa winced. "Yes, well, we must remedy that. Mama, this is Lady Pensworth, Delia's aunt."

Aunt Agatha nodded stiffly. "I am one of the dull, punctual guests."

"Are you? Well, I'm sure you can't help it. Not everyone can be as lively as Clarissa and I."

"Mama!" Clarissa said. "I assure you that Lady Pensworth is quite lively."

Aunt Agatha gave a thin smile. "I don't believe anyone has ever classified me as—God forbid—*lively*. Don't fret, Lady Blakeborough. I'm quite happy to be considered dull." Pushing up her spectacles, she shot the dowager a pointed glance. "It's better than being considered a lunatic."

"Oh, I quite agree," Clarissa's mother said cheerily. "Lunatics are very difficult to manage. I used to know this one duke . . ."

As the dowager waxed on about the mad duke of something or other, Brilliana caught Niall scanning the room until he fixed on her like a hunter spotting his prey.

When a scowl knit his brow, she tipped up her chin. She had as much right to be here as he. She was Clarissa's friend, albeit a very recent one. And if he didn't like it, he could just leave.

"Mama," Clarissa broke in, "there are others I need to introduce." She turned to Brilliana. "This is Mrs. Trevor. She's a friend to both me *and* Niall."

As Niall stiffened, Brilliana groaned. Oh, she was going to give Clarissa a piece of her mind later!

Meanwhile, Lady Margrave swatted her son with her fan. "You sly-boots, I can't believe you didn't tell me you had already met Mrs. Trevor." She turned to eye Brilliana with blatant curiosity. "How lovely to meet you. I heard from my daughter that you're a widow?"

"I'm afraid so, ma'am. A rather recent one."

The dowager beamed at her. "But not *too* recent, since you're out of mourning."

"Yes. My husband died over a year ago."

Lady Margrave cast her son a covert glance. "How very . . . interesting."

When Niall rolled his eyes, Brilliana wanted to laugh. She might have, too, if she hadn't been so annoyed to see him.

His mother seemed oblivious to her son's irritation as she looked Brilliana over. "You seem very young to be a widow."

"So I'm told." At least half a dozen times a week. "But I'm sure you hear that nearly as often as I."

With a titter, the countess patted her gray-blond hair. "Well, people do tell me that I look young enough to be Clarissa's sister."

Lord Blakeborough gave a laugh that turned into a cough when Clarissa raised an eyebrow at him.

"There's certainly a family resemblance," Brilliana said diplomatically. In Niall as well as Clarissa, for he had his mother's eyes of warm hazel. Those same eyes were now examining her with the ruthlessness of a soldier assessing an enemy.

Was she his enemy? Not exactly. He was simply one man in a long line of them who'd betrayed her trust, starting with her father and ending with her husband, who'd lied to her about why he'd gone to London to gamble away their money.

All of them had abandoned her in one fashion or another, leaving her heartbroken and destitute. Never again would she rely on one of *them*. Niall had been a mistake, and these days she was trying to learn from those.

When Clarissa went on to introduce the other guests, Brilliana released a breath. Well, she'd survived that. Though she did have to wonder how Niall's father had ended up married to such a flibbertigibbet as Lady Margrave. He'd seemed a somber sort when she'd met with him.

Dinner was announced, and Brilliana couldn't help noticing that Niall pointedly ignored her as they went in.

Fine by her. Especially since she was seated next to Lord Fulkham, who was a most entertaining companion and proceeded to regale her throughout the meal with tales of his trips abroad.

As the dessert was served, he shifted the conversation to her. "So, how much longer will you be in London?"

"I'm not sure. But at least until Delia and Lord Knightford return from their honeymoon. Silas will want to see his aunt before we head off into the country."

"So the lad is here in London with you?"

"Yes, of course. My aunt was kind enough to hire a nursemaid for him."

"That's very generous for an aunt by marriage."

"It is indeed. She's been very good to me and Silas."

He glanced across to where Aunt Agatha was talking animatedly with an older gentleman who looked as if he'd rather be anywhere else. "I understand that Lady Pensworth has even provided a dowry for you."

Her breath caught in her throat. He was asking about her *dowry*? Surely Lord Fulkham wasn't interested in her like *that*. She dearly hoped not. He might be good-looking, with crystalline blue eyes and wavy raven hair, but she had no desire to marry again. Between Reynold and Niall, it was clear she had bad luck when it came to men.

Besides, there was something very calculated in the way he'd asked the question. She couldn't see him as a fortune hunter, but still, it was probably best to handle this delicately.

She smiled at him. "Don't tell me that you're playing matchmaker, too, sir. Bad enough that my aunt and Clarissa keep trying to find me a husband."

That seemed to startle him, for he eyed her askance. "How do you know I'm not asking for my own information? I am a bachelor, you know."

"Yes, but you're much too important a fellow to consider me for a wife. No doubt you have your eye on someone who can advance your political interests. I certainly cannot."

His gaze sharpened on her. "I see."

She had a funny feeling he saw more than he let on. It made her distinctly uncomfortable.

"But actually, what I meant was," he went on, "that your aunt has taken on a rather unusual task in providing you with a dowry. You have other family members who ought to be assuming that position." He searched her face. "Your father, for example."

The breath went out of her. Dropping her gaze to her custard, she murmured, "My father and I are not . . . close."

She hadn't seen him since Mama's death over six years ago, and she hoped never to see him again, considering what he'd done to ruin her life.

So she was relieved when Clarissa rose and asked the ladies if they wished to retire to the drawing room. As she followed the other ladies out, she wondered why he was prying into her personal affairs. If he wasn't interested in courting her, it made no sense.

Then Mrs. Vyse approached her on their way to the drawing room. "I wonder if you'd take a turn with me in the garden? I find it a bit stuffy in here. Don't you?"

That put Brilliana on her guard. First Lord Fulkham, then his sister-in-law. What on earth was going on? Had the woman been sent to assess Brilliana's interest in him?

Whatever the case, perhaps it was time to get to the bottom of it, so she would know how to act.

Brilliana smiled. "Why, certainly, Mrs. Vyse. That sounds wonderful."

Two

Once the ladies were gone, Niall relaxed. He'd spent the past hour and a half trying not to stare at Bree, pay attention to what she said, or listen in on her conversation with Fulkham. It was damned well giving him a headache.

Marriage and bearing a child should have dampened her beauty and ruined her figure. Instead, she was not only as lovely as ever, but she'd somehow gained more confidence, a very attractive quality in a woman who had once been rather shy and cautious. Or had seemed to be so, anyway.

And what the blazes did Fulkham mean by making her laugh and smile and look utterly engrossed? Was the man hunting a wife?

Possibly. Fulkham was around Niall's age, and he needed a wife to help him achieve his political aims. No one trusted a bachelor in politics. If a man couldn't manage a woman, how could he manage a country?

Fulkham approached to offer Niall a glass. "Port, old boy?"

"Thanks." Niall took it and downed some, eager for anything that might blot Bree from his brain. If that were possible.

"I need to speak with you privately," Fulkham said, lowering his voice. "It's a matter of great importance."

Niall snorted. Fulkham thought *everything* was a matter of great importance. That probably came of his being a spymaster, diplomat, and right-hand man to a cabinet minister. And Niall should know, having served as a spy for him during his exile.

Fulkham gestured to the door leading into the hall. "Your brother-in-law said we may use his library for this discussion. So if you'd be so kind . . ."

"Of course." Niall could hardly refuse, since Fulkham was largely responsible for obtaining Niall's pardon from His Majesty, William IV, the new ruler of England.

Fortunately, Edwin kept his library well stocked with good French brandy, so as soon as they entered, Niall ditched his port to pour himself a healthy portion of spirits. He suspected that port wouldn't prove strong enough for whatever the undersecretary wanted to say.

But Fulkham didn't get to the point right away. He strolled over to scan Edwin's bookshelves and asked, "Are you settling in at Margrave Manor?"

Small talk? That wasn't like Fulkham.

Niall took a long pull on the brandy. "Yes. Why?"

"Blakeborough said you were pleased with how well your cousin managed your estate in your absence."

"Not so much pleased as relieved. Warren isn't the sort of man one expects to be good at such matters, but he is conscientious, thank God. As I'm sure you know, running an estate from afar through managers would have been tricky."

"Especially when you were otherwise occupied—with avoiding that French ambassador's first secretary Durand in his insane quest to avenge Whiting, and with doing certain . . . tasks for your country."

Niall stilled. "I hope you're not thinking of asking me to continue my work for the foreign office now that I've come home. I had a bellyful of deception and blood and betrayal after Portugal."

A pained expression crossed Fulkham's face. "I do regret that you had to witness those reprisals against our liberal allies in Porto."

"Reprisals!" Niall snorted. "They were mass assassinations." And sometimes he still couldn't put the memories from his mind.

"At least you got *our* people away. If the Miguelists had succeeded in killing them, England might have been forced to go to war. There would have been more bloodshed."

"Still, some of those soldiers were my friends." And no, he couldn't have changed anything— they'd *chosen* to take their stand against the absolutists. But images of a garrison full of slaughtered Portuguese soldiers still haunted his sleep.

"That bastard Miguel. You should have seen him when he came to England only a few months before that. He was all smooth words and expert manners. Even Wellington had no idea that—"

"He and his dear queen mother had such a taste for blood?" Niall swallowed some brandy, relishing the burn. "The human capacity for deception never ceases to amaze me." He cast Fulkham a hard look. "Which is why I'm done with all that."

Before Fulkham could answer, the door to the library opened. Mrs. Vyse and Bree entered, throwing Niall entirely off guard.

He wasn't the only one—Bree gave a start when she saw him. She cast a quick glance at Fulkham. "Oh . . . please forgive us. Mrs. Vyse wanted to show me a novel that Clarissa owns, but we can come back later."

"Nonsense," Fulkham said, surprising Niall. "Please take a seat, Mrs. Trevor. There's something I need to discuss with you. And with Margrave."

Niall froze. Him and Bree? What was Fulkham up to?

When Bree hesitated, Fulkham said in a voice

that brooked no refusal, "I'm afraid, Mrs. Trevor, that I must insist you join us."

Bree blinked at the command, but sat down warily on the edge of a chair.

Fulkham smiled at Mrs. Vyse. "Thank you for aiding my little subterfuge, my dear. It's imperative that no one but our host and hostess realize that we're having this talk. You'll improvise to make sure they don't, won't you?"

"Of course." Mrs. Vyse's eyes twinkled. "I learned from the best." Then she left, shutting the door behind her.

Damnation. Fulkham had set this up on purpose. "What is this about, Fulkham? And since when does Mrs. Vyse do your bidding?"

"Since before she married my late brother. But that's neither here nor there." He gestured to a chair. "Why don't you take a seat as well?"

"I prefer to stand. Now tell me what the blazes is going on. Why are we meeting at a dinner party? And why all the 'subterfuge,' as you put it, when you could simply have invited us to your office?"

"Actually, I couldn't have." Fulkham gazed sternly at Bree. "No one—and I mean *no one*— must know that we three are acquainted in anything but a social capacity."

"Why is that?" Bree asked, surprising Niall with the forthright question. She'd always been quiet, unwilling to cause trouble.

Her marriage seemed to have changed her. Or perhaps she'd always been this way, and he just hadn't seen it in the midst of his obsession with her.

"Because I require your assistance in a sensitive matter that cannot become known beyond this room." Fulkham set down his port. "Not yet, anyway."

"Why us?" Niall asked.

"For one thing, it has come to my attention that you two were well acquainted before you left England."

Bree glanced at Niall in alarm.

"Don't look at me," he snapped. "I didn't tell him."

She scowled. "No, but you just confirmed it with your answer."

The snippy reply made Fulkham chuckle. "I already had it confirmed, Mrs. Trevor. I found your maid from seven years ago, and she readily admitted that you and Margrave had a . . . er . . . friendship."

"Christ," Niall muttered.

"Besides," Fulkham went on, "several people saw the two of you react dramatically to each other a few weeks ago. So it's no great secret."

She was blushing furiously now, reminding Niall painfully of the old Bree. The one who'd crushed his heart under her pretty little heel.

"Fine," Niall clipped out. "We knew each other. What of it?"

Fulkham stared at Bree. "I'm afraid this has to do with Mrs. Trevor's father, Sir Oswald Payne."

With a frown, Bree rose. "Then it doesn't concern *me*. As I told you earlier, I'm not remotely close to my father. I haven't seen him in years, not since my mother's funeral."

Niall started. Her mother had been dead for "years"? That shook him a little, given Father's skepticism concerning her sickly mother. How many years had it been? He would have to find out.

"I realize that you and your father aren't speaking," Fulkham said. "Unfortunately, he's landed himself in a bit of trouble recently."

"Doesn't he always?" she said bitterly.

"Ah, but this time he's facing the possibility of something worse than debtors' prison." Fulkham's voice hardened. "You see, several weeks ago, counterfeit twenty- and fifty-pound banknotes started showing up at various merchants. It took some effort, given how widely notes are generally disseminated, but the Home Office eventually traced a couple back to your father, who'd used them to pay off creditors."

As Niall gave a low whistle, a dangerous glitter appeared in Bree's eyes. "Then arrest him. I washed my hands of him long ago."

"Good God, that's cold-blooded," Niall said. "I know your father's gambling was problematic, but surely—"

"You know nothing about my father, sir," she said hotly. "If you did, you wouldn't be shocked by the possibility of his behaving criminally."

Fulkham narrowed his gaze on her. "Do you

realize that the punishment for counterfeiting is death?"

Bree sucked in a sharp breath. Clearly, she had *not* realized it.

"So you see, my dear," Fulkham continued, "if we simply arrest him, he will hang. Then you—and your young son—will once more be embroiled in a scandal, but one far worse than that caused by your husband's death last year. I don't think that's what you want."

When Bree paled and sank into her chair, Niall felt a sudden perverse urge to protect her. "That sounds distinctly like a threat, Fulkham."

"Not a threat," the man said calmly. "I'm merely stating the facts so that Mrs. Trevor knows exactly what the situation is." He steadied his gaze on her. "But if you will help me with this matter, I can keep your father from the noose even if he's guilty."

"If?" Niall stared him down. "You just said he was."

"No. I said that we traced the notes to him. The problem is, we don't know if he merely passed them on unwittingly from someone else or if he created them."

When Bree snorted, Fulkham said, "What?"

"Papa isn't talented enough to create forgeries. He could certainly pass them on, but the kind of ability required to make believable copies of a banknote?" She shook her head. "That's beyond him."

"If you say so," Fulkham said. "But he could hire talented artists to do it, which is practically the same thing, if he's paying them and overseeing the operation. That's why we need to find out where the notes came from, how many are out there, and who is ultimately behind the counterfeiting."

Fulkham downed the remainder of his port. "If we arrest Sir Oswald and he's culpable, he'll never tell us anything. And if he's not culpable, we'll alert the real criminals, who will simply pick up and flee, or move their operation elsewhere. We need to know more before we make any arrests."

Bree blinked at him. "I really don't see how I can help you with that."

"No doubt he wants you to spy on your father," Niall drawled, familiar with Fulkham's tactics. He turned to the spymaster. "Just send in one of your many lackeys to do the spying."

"You know that won't work. He's a private citizen. He's not looking to hire staff, his club of card-playing friends hasn't added anyone to their ranks in a few years, and he moves little in society beyond them. Besides, if he's behind this, he's not going to reveal it to some stranger with no connection to him." Fulkham toyed with his empty glass. "Indeed, that's where you and Mrs. Trevor come in."

"I don't understand," Bree said.

Ah, but Niall did. Unfortunately. As he steadied a hard look on Fulkham, something like guilt seemed to flash over the man's face, but it was gone so fast, Niall was sure he'd imagined it.

"It's simple, really." Fulkham set down his glass. "I want you and Margrave to pretend to be engaged, so he can get close enough to your father to find out what Sir Oswald and his friends are up to."

"No," Niall said tersely. "Absolutely not."

Fulkham arched an eyebrow at him. "I expected a protest from Mrs. Trevor, but not you. After all, you owe me a great deal."

God rot the man. It was true: Everything Niall had gone through on Fulkham's account still didn't compare to what Fulkham had done for *him*. And he always paid his debts.

Bree shot Niall a quizzical glance. "What do you owe him?"

"Fulkham is largely responsible for arranging my pardon."

Fulkham was also the man who'd made sure that Edwin wasn't prosecuted for killing Durand, after Durand attempted to abduct Clarissa. To get to Niall. Who'd killed Durand's cousin, Whiting.

Thanks to Fulkham, neither he nor Edwin was hanging from a gibbet right now. And Clarissa's secret was still safe.

God, this was a tangled web, and Fulkham was tangled up in all of it.

"I realize that I owe you my entire future," Niall told the arrogant spymaster, "but surely you can find another way for me to repay you for your time and effort on my behalf."

Bree jumped up to glare at Fulkham. "And *I* don't owe you anything."

"Except your father's life," Fulkham said.

The remark wilted her like a cravat in a Turkish bath. She turned to Niall. "Is he . . . telling the truth? Would Papa hang?"

God, seeing her so torn—and turning to *him* for comfort—struck him hard. "Without your father's being proved innocent or having someone like our 'friend' here intervene, I'm afraid he would. The laws in that respect are still harsh. Counterfeiting is considered treason, believe it or not."

"But judges take the word of the government into account," Fulkham said. "Even if your father is guilty, I can push to have him charged with fraud instead, which would get him fourteen years' transportation rather than hanging. *If* I so choose to persuade the magistrate on your father's behalf."

"You're a cold one, Fulkham," Niall snapped.

"In service to my country, I'll be as cold as it takes."

Niall knew that from personal experience. "I don't understand why *you're* the one handling this. You're not in the Home Office."

"But I have a connection to the two of you."

"In other words, the Home Office knew that you alone could blackmail us both," Niall said cuttingly.

"You could put it like that, I suppose." Fulkham went over to pour a glass of brandy, then brought it to Bree, whose face was the color of ash. "Here, Mrs. Trevor. I think you need a bit of this."

"Ladies don't—"

"Drink it," Niall ordered. For once, he agreed with Fulkham. She looked as if she might faint at any moment.

She took a sip, coughed, then took another. At least that put a little color back into her cheeks.

Fulkham turned to Niall. "You know, old boy, you're the only one who can pull this off—the only one who knows her well enough to make it work. And if you do this one thing for me, we'll consider everything else even. I won't ask anything like this of you again."

Deuce take the bastard. Fulkham knew exactly how to tempt him.

And in truth, this scheme was nothing compared to what he'd done and seen in Porto. He wouldn't even be balking if not for the fact that it was Bree he'd have to spend time with.

But perhaps that was actually a good reason to accept. If he got to know her for the scheming chit she really was and not the sweet girl he'd foolishly invented and fallen in love with, he might finally be able to purge her from his thoughts. Nothing like a dose of reality to banish a dream that wouldn't die.

"Very well," Niall said. "I'll do it. As long as you swear this is the last time."

Relief crossed Fulkham's face. "You have my word."

"Good." Now that Niall had agreed to the scheme, he'd best get the details of the plan straight. "So, what you want is for Brilliana to introduce me to her father as her fiancé, and me to insinuate myself into his circles."

"Exactly."

"What if he won't see me?" Bree asked.

Fulkham snorted. "Has he tried to call on you since you've been in London?"

She tipped up her chin. "A few times, yes. I refused to admit him."

"Why?" Niall asked, still shocked by the depth of her bitterness toward the man.

A veil came down over her features. "Because his only reason to see me was undoubtedly to elicit money from me or my aunt. I refused to submit her to that, and I personally didn't have it to give him, anyway."

Niall had a sneaking suspicion there was more to the story than she was letting on. The man was her *father*, for God's sake.

"I'm sure Sir Oswald has another reason for trying to see you." Obviously Fulkham had had the same thought as Niall. The baron regarded her with a steady glance. "He probably wants to meet his grandson."

"That's precisely why I didn't want them to meet. Because my father would try to use him, too, if he could." Panic flashed in her eyes. "Oh no,

and now you want me to . . . to let Papa back into
my life? How can I allow Silas to be around his
grandfather, knowing that the man is a criminal?"

"*Might* be a criminal," Fulkham corrected her.
"We're not sure yet. Besides, if the boy is only
sixteen months old, he won't remember him
later."

Bree rose to wander the room, clearly agitated.
"There are other issues, too. My father isn't stupid. He's likely to find it suspicious that after
turning him away repeatedly, I'm suddenly interested in renewing the connection."

"That's where Margrave comes in." The undersecretary turned to Niall. "Say whatever you
must to put Sir Oswald at ease. Tell him you
insisted upon meeting her father, that you persuaded her to mend fences, that you want his
approval. I don't think it will be hard to convince
him. I'm sure he'll find it understandable that his
daughter's impending marriage would alter how
she regards her father."

"Then he doesn't know his daughter very
well," she said.

Niall stifled a laugh. That was one way Bree
hadn't changed. She was still stubborn. Whatever
had caused the rift between her and her father
wouldn't easily be forgiven or forgotten. It must
really stick in her craw to have to be part of this.

He could understand that. "So, we meet with
Sir Oswald. Then what? A public announcement
of our betrothal?"

"You two can figure that out as you go along. If Sir Oswald presses for such a thing—or seems suspicious that the engagement isn't genuine—then do it. If not, feel free to keep it private as long as you can." Fulkham glanced at Bree, and his expression softened. "I doubt Mrs. Trevor will want the scandal that goes with a broken engagement if she can avoid it."

Bree lifted her chin. "Being known as a jilt will hardly affect me, since I've no desire to marry again."

That surprised Niall. "You expect us to believe that a woman of your youth and beauty, with a young son who needs a father, would choose to remain alone the rest of her life?"

She crossed her arms over her chest. "I have no reason to remarry and, quite frankly, see no point in it."

How could that be?

He scowled. Unless she was still so in love with her late husband that she believed no one could ever take his place in her heart.

The thought tightened a vise about his chest . . . until the cynical part of him reasserted itself. Her sort didn't fall in love. They were too busy seeing what they could get. Which reminded him . . . "If you're so determined not to marry, why is your aunt providing you with a dowry?"

"I don't know," Bree snapped. "Why don't you ask her? It wasn't *my* idea, I assure you. I'm not in your situation, sir. I don't need a wife to bear my heir. In fact, you might suffer more from the scandal of a jilting than I would. So it's really *your* decision how to handle our faux betrothal."

"Trust me, Mrs. Trevor," Niall said coldly, "a broken engagement would prompt few women to turn down a man of my consequence. Especially when I'm no longer headed for exile and a lifetime of hiding."

She blinked at him as if she didn't understand his veiled meaning.

The hell she didn't. She could stare at him with that innocent, wide-eyed look all she wanted. He'd long ago realized that she was out for whatever she could get, and had thrown him over once she realized he was never going to provide her with the exalted life she'd apparently craved.

Well, he hoped she wasn't secretly thinking to get it from him now—in marriage or otherwise. His time abroad had taught him that people could be incredibly deceitful when they were pursuing money and power. So if she was playing a deeper game, then she was out of luck. Because he was too wise to fall for that now, no matter how much she tempted him.

Three

Brilliana tried to decipher the undercurrents between the two men. She felt trapped, just when her life was beginning to even out. How dared Lord Fulkham upset everything again?

She needed her sister-in-law's advice, but Delia wouldn't be back from her honeymoon in Italy for a few weeks.

Brilliana didn't want Papa to hang, no matter how much she resented how he'd blackmailed her into marrying Reynold. But neither did she want to be forced to spend days, maybe weeks, in Niall's company. Especially when he acted as if *she* were the one who'd abandoned *him*.

She hadn't fought a duel over some light-skirt. *She* hadn't run off to the Continent and lied about bringing out the person she allegedly loved to join him. And *she* hadn't waltzed back into England as if she'd done nothing wrong.

How unfathomable that he expected her

to do this with him! Lord Fulkham, she could understand—he was with the government and thought that one's country should take precedence over everything. She might agree with him, too, if it didn't involve Niall.

Curse the man for agreeing to this scheme. So what if the undersecretary had finagled him a pardon? It wasn't as if Lord Fulkham could withdraw it now. And surely there were other ways Niall could repay the political favor. Fulkham wasn't blackmailing *him*, just her. Niall didn't have to do this, especially since Fulkham seemed to be his friend.

A nasty suspicion took hold of her. Could this be some elaborate scheme between the two men to . . . to . . .

To what? Punish her for not going away with Niall years ago? Get her into Niall's bed now that she was a widow?

That last seemed unlikely, but given what she'd learned after he'd left England, she wouldn't put it past him. And if Niall *were* up to something unsavory . . .

"Lord Fulkham, couldn't I just handle this on my own?" she asked. "There's no need to inconvenience Lord Margrave. I could tell Papa that I want Silas to know his grandfather, and that would be enough to convince him that I am genuinely interested in reestablishing our . . . relationship."

"And then what?" the undersecretary said. "Your father isn't going to tell *you* about his illegal activities. Or involve you with them. But he *might* do that with Margrave, your soon-to-be husband. I need Margrave to become part of Sir Oswald's circle of card-playing friends—something you cannot do as a woman."

"But won't he be suspicious of Lord Margrave if he hears that you helped his lordship gain his pardon?"

"Our connection isn't known to anyone except Margrave's family and now you," Fulkham said. "Besides, Margrave will say that his years abroad have left him short of funds, and that's why he's interested in marrying a woman with an estate and a dowry, why he's eager to try his hand at the tables, et cetera. I've got various people ready to enhance Margrave's reckless character with tales about his desperate need for funds and his willingness to do anything to get them. They'll start the rumor mill running this evening at the clubs, and by morning, everyone will know the supposed truth about Lord Margrave."

"Thanks," Niall said dryly. "Just what I need to rejoin respectable society and find a wife—a reputation as a 'reckless character.'"

Brilliana ignored the shaft of pain that the words *find a wife* sent through her heart. Her foolish, foolish heart. "Don't worry. All your sins will be swept under the rug as usual, since you're a man of 'consequence' and all."

That seemed to spark his temper. "'*As usual*'? What in blazes is that supposed to mean?"

"You're the man who got pardoned for murder because you have friends in high places," she said.

"Now see here—" Niall began.

"Meanwhile," she went on bitterly, "once this is done, I'll be the woman who betrayed her father to the authorities. So I don't know what *you* have to complain about. When a man has a reckless reputation, it only makes him more attractive to women." Only look at how *she'd* behaved when Niall had started paying her attention. "But when a woman has one—"

"If you prefer," Fulkham said, "we'll make it seem as if you were unaware of what Margrave was up to."

"And you *did* say you have no interest in marrying." Niall's hard gaze bored into her. "So why do you care what people think of you?"

"I don't. I care what they think of my son."

Niall snorted. "The scandal over this will be long dead by the time he's old enough for it to matter."

It was so easy for him to say that. He was a *man*. "Really?" she said sweetly. "Having his grandfather branded a criminal for the rest of his life will affect him. Don't pretend that it won't."

"But that's true whether you help us or not," Fulkham put in. "Having his grandfather hanged will be worse. Is that what you'd prefer?"

"No, curse it! Of course not."

She really *was* trapped, especially now that the two men were joining forces against her. No way out—again. Only this time it wasn't debtors' prison she was trying to keep Papa out of. It was death. A vastly different matter entirely.

At least this time she didn't also have Mama to consider.

Still . . . "I don't understand why Lord Margrave has to be the man to do this," she said bluntly. "He and I don't get along particularly well, and Papa might notice that, despite all our attempts to pretend otherwise. Surely you have other lackeys, as Lord Margrave puts it, who would not provoke such strong feelings in me. Who could make the endeavor more convincing."

Fulkham laughed. "More *convincing*? The air fairly thrums when you two are in the same room. Granted, it may thrum with animosity, but no one could doubt that there is *something* between you."

A look of determination replaced his amusement. "Besides, Margrave's situation—as a man whose reputation is easy to manipulate at present—makes him most useful for my purposes. Not to mention that as members of St. George's Club, we'll be able to meet and discuss what he's found out without anyone thinking it odd. They'll assume we're just involved socially. Everything about his situation makes it ideal for my plans."

"But not for mine," she protested. "I'd planned to return to Camden Hall soon so that I could begin putting the estate to rights. Now I'll have to linger here for Lord knows how long, while you chase some elusive counterfeiter who may or may not be connected to my father."

"She has a point," Niall said. "I have an estate to manage myself, one that's been left to the care of others for far too long."

"Then take her with you from time to time," Fulkham said irritably. "It would do her good to watch you work." He met Brilliana's gaze. "You did say you wanted to learn more about estate management. I can't think of a better teacher than Margrave."

She glanced from him to Niall, whose expression was entirely unreadable. "Might I have a moment to confer with his lordship before I give you my decision?"

Fulkham looked over at Niall, who gave a tight nod. "Very well. But don't take too long. People will start wondering what has happened to us, and I can't have that."

As soon as Fulkham left, a painful silence descended between them. After a moment, she said, "There's really no way out of this for me, is there?"

"None that I can see," he said in that low rumble that did shivery things to her insides even after all these years.

Drat him. "I had no idea that Lord Fulkham could be such a beast," she grumbled.

"He's just doing his job."

"No, he's blackmailing *me* into doing his job."

"I could say the same thing. You don't hear me complaining."

"Because it's not *your* father who will hang if we fail."

He stepped toward her. "No, but I owe Fulkham an enormous debt that I feel honor-bound to repay. If this is the only way to manage that, then I will damned well do as he asks. And so will you, by God."

Lord, but she was tired of bullying men. First Papa, then Reynold, and now Niall and Lord Fulkham, all using her to get what they wanted.

She searched Niall's face. Was his feeling of indebtedness his only reason for taking this on? "So you didn't drum up this little scheme with Lord Fulkham just to get me in your clutches again."

"My *clutches*? That's not how I remember things. I remember asking you to *marry* me."

She wrapped her arms about her waist. "You asked me to run away with you. It's not the same. You asked me to *trust* that you would marry me eventually."

"And you doubted that I would?" he asked hoarsely. "Oh, God, is that why you didn't go with me?"

"I told you—I didn't go because of Mama. I had to stay with her."

"Right." The chill in his gaze unnerved her. "Yet that didn't stop you from marrying Trevor."

She had half a mind to tell him *why* she'd married Reynold—because Niall had shown his true colors by abandoning her.

But then he would know how hard she'd fallen for him back then, how easily he'd ensnared her. He would think he could ensnare her again. And that was *never* going to happen. Better to let him keep thinking that she'd married Reynold because she'd wanted to.

"Reynold wasn't asking me to travel to another continent."

"Without a wedding ring on your finger," he said snidely.

She tipped up her chin. "Exactly. Consider my position. You'd already balked at telling your family about me. So you can't blame me for worrying that you were just . . . well . . ."

"Taking you off to have my wicked way with you. So that's how you saw our last encounter—as my plotting a tawdry seduction." He uttered a mirthless laugh. "And now you think that Fulkham and I might have cooked up a counterfeiting scheme involving your father, in order to help me lure you into my bed? Is that what you're insinuating?"

When he put it that way, it sounded a bit ridiculous. "I . . . I suppose not."

"How do I know that *you* didn't cook up this scheme with Fulkham for your own nefarious purposes?"

She huffed out a breath. "Don't be absurd.

You're the one who's a friend of his. I barely know the man."

Eyes darkening, he stepped right up to her. "That's not how it appeared at dinner. The two of you were quite cozy, laughing and chatting like old friends. Or perhaps lovers?"

The accusation was so unfounded that it made her gasp. "How dare you?" She thrust her face up into his. "I am not that kind of woman, drat you!"

A muscle worked in his jaw. "Nor am I that kind of man." He bent so close that she could smell the brandy on his breath. "But trust me, if I wanted to lure you into my bed, I wouldn't have to resort to some ridiculous scheme to do it."

The sheer arrogance of that statement astonished her. "Really? You're that sure of your ability to 'lure' me?"

That seemed to catch him off guard. "Damnation, that's not what I me—"

"Well, sir, I may have been fool enough to believe all your sweet words and kisses years ago, but I know better now than to listen to a seducer's lies."

His eyes glittered. "They weren't lies, and you know it, Bree."

His nickname for her, the nearness of him, the fact that his eyes were the color of warm honey just now . . . all conspired to remind her of what they'd once been to each other.

She couldn't catch her breath. Or move. Or speak.

They stood locked in silence while his gaze played over her face, hard and hungry. His breathing quickened the way it used to when he was about to kiss her, and she actually braced herself for the touch of his lips to hers.

Then he seemed to catch himself. Muttering an oath, he whirled away.

Relief coursed through her. At least she wanted it to be relief, anyway.

"Fortunately for you," he bit out, "I have no desire to lure you into anything. Believe what you want about this scheme, but spending time with you would not have been my first choice for a way to repay Fulkham."

"So if we're both unhappy about that, how are we going to convince my father that we're in love?"

"We don't have to. We just have to convince him that we wish to marry. People marry for all sorts of reasons. We'll simply pick another one, Bree."

"Stop calling me that."

He leveled a hard glance on her. "Why?"

Because it's too much like before. Because it brings back memories. Because it makes me forget who you really are.

She met his gaze steadily. "My father is unaware of our past . . . friendship, remember? If you call me Bree, he'll find it odd that you have a pet name for me when we can't have known each other long. I'm sure he's heard the news about your recent return to England. Apparently, it was in all the papers."

She only wished she'd seen it, but at the time, she'd been so busy dealing with Delia and Silas and Aunt Agatha that she'd missed that particular article.

"Then I won't use the nickname around *him*." He smirked at her. "Bree."

"Oh, you are such a . . . a rogue."

That wiped the smirk from his face. "Well, I *am* supposed to be playing a reckless fellow who needs money." His eyes narrowed. "Actually, that would work. I could be marrying you for your dowry."

She stiffened. "My father may be unreliable and untrustworthy, but he's not so awful that he'd want to see me wed to a fortune hunter." Especially if the association was of no benefit to *him*.

"Fine." He scrubbed a hand over his face. "You already think me a rogue, so how about if I want to marry you simply to have a beautiful wife in my bed? And what if you're willing to go along because you want to be a countess, not to mention the mother of the next Earl of Margrave? That sort of transaction is fairly typical in our circles."

She eyed him warily. "Is it believable, though? Why should you marry a beautiful woman of no consequence, when you can satisfy your desires with any available light-skirt?"

He shrugged. "Plenty of women snag lords based on appearance alone. Look at the Gunning sisters. Their father was a nobody, and their mother little more. One of them married a duke and the other an earl. For a man, it's rather like acquiring a fine piece of art to show off to one's friends."

"How flattering," she muttered. "I get to be the Rembrandt you flash around."

"More like the Botticelli." His gaze dipped down to her breasts, and there was no mistaking the glint of desire there before he jerked it back up. "*The Birth of Venus* comes to mind."

Oh, Lord. Wasn't that the painting of Venus rising naked from the sea on a shell? Scoundrel. And he'd said that this wasn't about trying to seduce her.

Shaking off a frisson of awareness, she glared at him. "That makes it so much more palatable." Reynold had essentially married her for her looks, and she'd liked it no better with him.

A chuckle escaped him. "I'm not saying that *I* feel like you're a work of art to show off. Just that plenty of other men feel that way. And I can *pretend* to feel that way."

"Yes, but will Papa believe that you'd want me just for my appearance? That's the question."

He scoured her with a heated look that burned wherever it touched. "Trust me, any man with eyes would believe it."

Before she could react to that shockingly intimate glance, he turned and began to pace. "And it would work for our scheme in other respects. A man pursuing beauty will pay anything to gain it. That gives me a reason for needing quick funds—so I can buy you whatever pretty thing you want, including a proper wedding." He halted in front of her. "I daresay you could make *that* role believable. Then you won't have to pretend to be in love with me."

The edge in his voice gave her pause. He was hinting at something insulting—she felt sure of it. But what?

Or perhaps she was just so annoyed with him in general that she saw insults wherever she looked.

"I guess that would work," she said. "I'd certainly rather play a grasping female than one who's mooning over you." *As I so foolishly did before.* "Though Papa might not believe I could be so mercenary."

"Why not?" he said evenly. "He's mercenary, so surely he expects his daughter to follow in his tracks. Besides, people change. He hasn't seen you in years, so he doesn't know *whom* you've become."

That was certainly true.

"And you do have a son to consider, who needs a father. That's another reason for you to wed."

She arched an eyebrow at him. "Yes, but I'd be a fool to marry a reckless character like you and risk my son's future inheritance, wouldn't I?"

A self-deprecating smile tightened his features. "Ah, but I have a title. Some women are fools for titles."

"True." That was difficult for her to fathom. She'd never cared much about such things. "Very well. We'll do it your way. I'll play a dimwitted upstart eager to rise in the world, and you'll play the licentious lecher who wants me for my body. And we'll do it to capture my dastardly father in an act of 'treason.'" She gave a shaky laugh. "It sounds like something out of a gothic novel."

"With any luck it will end like a novel, as well, with the virtuous heroine prevailing over godlessness. And your role needn't include being dimwitted. Now, *that* I would find hard to believe."

The compliment startled her, especially since it held the same edge as before, making her wonder if it really was a compliment. "Thank you. I think." She wanted to say that she couldn't see him as a licentious lecher, either, but the words stuck in her throat.

Although that reminded her of something she'd better settle before they launched into this. "Yours *will* be just a role, I hope. No need to . . . er . . . behave lecherously to play it."

"What? But I was looking forward to that part."

"Niall—"

"Relax, Bree," he said acidly. "I won't assault your precious virtue. I'll have my hands full just trying to keep up with your father's machinations." As she let out a breath, he added, "And speaking of that, we should arrange a visit to him as soon as possible. Assuming that you've decided to do this."

"As everyone keeps pointing out, I don't have a choice." She sighed. "But I do have one other question. How do you wish to handle announcing the engagement? Do we tell only Papa and hide it from anyone else, the way Lord Fulkham said we might? Or do we leap into it wholeheartedly and deal with the consequences later?"

"I prefer to leap in wholeheartedly, myself."

"Why does that not surprise me?" she said. The man had always leapt into everything— meeting her, courting her . . . leaving her.

"Hear me out. It will be hard enough to manage the subterfuge involving the counterfeiting. If we have to keep track of who knows what about the engagement, too, we'll forget ourselves and muddle everything."

He flashed her a rueful smile. "Besides, we'd never keep it from my mother. Don't let her flighty behavior fool you—she can sniff out a secret at ten paces, especially one of that sort. As for your aunt—"

"Oh no, my *aunt*!" Her stomach knotted. "Goodness gracious, I forgot all about her. How am I supposed to lie to her after everything she's done for me and Silas?"

"Did you ever tell her about our previous association?"

"No." She thought a moment. "But Delia and Clarissa told her about our encounter two weeks ago at Stoke Towers."

"Then it shouldn't surprise her that we know each other well enough to get engaged."

She bit her lip. "Still, she'll hate me when she finds out our betrothal was merely a ruse."

"No need for her to find out at all. Once the counterfeiters are routed, you can pretend to be appalled that I used you as a pawn in my spying, and then you can break off the engagement. She'll probably applaud you for jilting me."

"I doubt it. She'll probably applaud *you* for turning Papa in. She doesn't like him, because of what he—" She halted, before she could reveal too much of her mortifying past. "Besides, in the meantime, I'll have to make her think I'm eager to marry you, and I'm awful at playing roles. Unlike Delia, I can't pretend to be something I'm not."

When he snorted, she stared at him. "What do you mean by that?"

He turned instantly wary. "By what?"

"Your snort! It sounded as if you didn't believe me. When have you seen me pretend anything?"

"During those months we were secretly courting, for one thing." His expression turned curiously wary. "You had no trouble pretending not to know me when we were in public."

She swallowed. "That was different. We hardly saw each other in public, since I wasn't yet out. But every time I told some tale to Mama so I could sneak out and meet you, I felt horribly guilty. Thank heaven she was too sick to notice how bad a liar I am."

He snorted again.

"Why do you keep *doing* that?"

"Doesn't matter. Look, we've got to go into this full force. Hell, we should announce it here, tonight. Clarissa will be ecstatic, and Mother—"

"*Clarissa*, oh, heavens! She'll hate me after this, too!"

"No, she won't," he said firmly. "I'll smooth it all over, I swear."

"Niall—"

"Just think of your lad, all right? You're doing this for him. Not Fulkham, not your country, not even your father. You're doing it to save your *son's* future. That's all that matters. The rest will fall into place."

"But what do I say if Clarissa wants to know details—how we fell in love, *when* we fell in love?"

"Tell her what we're telling Sir Oswald. This is a sensible arrangement—a way of giving your son a father, that's all. Clarissa will understand that."

"I'm not so sure. Clarissa is something of a romantic."

"But she knows that you're not, doesn't she?"

Brilliana caught herself before she could protest his assumption and reveal exactly how susceptible she still was to him, how much her heart had bled when he'd left. If he knew, he'd take advantage of it to get her into his bed. "Yes, she does."

He nodded, as if that confirmed something. "You needn't give her the nonsense about my checkered past and your mercenary desires. Just tell her—and your aunt, if you like—the part about how we're making a practical arrangement. They won't find that odd for a bachelor needing an heir and a widow needing a father for her son. Then, when everything falls apart, you won't feel guilty for deceiving them, and they won't worry about your broken heart."

"Right." *She* would be the only one worrying about her broken heart.

No, curse it! She would *not* lose her heart to him again. It was time she accepted that the man she'd loved had never existed. It was time she took control of her own happiness. Once this was done, she would purge Niall from her system, retire to Camden Hall, and live out her days there with Silas.

"Can you manage that?" he asked.

Perhaps, if she approached it the way he suggested. In a way it was the truth. This *was* a practical arrangement, to further Silas's future. Only the marriage part was a lie.

"I believe so, yes." She rubbed her arms. "I'll have to, won't I?"

He eyed her closely. "Don't think of it that way, or your resentment will show. Think of it as an adventure. Your first effort at being a female spy. If you really mean to bury yourself in the country after this, then here's your chance to have a bit of fun." A trace of irony threaded his voice. "To flit about town on an earl's arm and get invited to all the best parties."

"Where I have to pretend to be something I'm not," she said glumly.

"You'll get used to it." He came toward her. "Tomorrow I'll come fetch you at your aunt's at two, and we'll go pay our first call on your father, if that's all right with you."

"The sooner the better, as far as I'm concerned. I just want to be done with this as quickly as possible."

The door to the library opened, and Lord Fulkham stepped in. "Have you made a decision, Mrs. Trevor?"

Niall glanced at her expectantly.

"Yes. I'll go along with your scheme."

"For as long as it takes to catch my counterfeiter?"

She nodded.

Niall stepped forward. "We want to announce it tonight, while everyone is here. We both feel that making one grand announcement and having everyone know would be less demanding than juggling which people know what."

"I see." Lord Fulkham strode over to pour himself a glass of brandy, then stood there sipping it. "That actually might work better in convincing Sir Oswald, as well." He stared at her. "Your father will hear the gossip about your betrothal, and just as he's getting his feelings hurt that you haven't involved him, you'll show up to introduce him to Niall. He'll be so pleased to have you seeking him out that he might not notice the strangeness of it."

"You attribute an enormous amount of familial affection to my father," she said dryly. "I daresay he won't care one way or the other."

"You'd better hope he does," Lord Fulkham said, "or this scheme will be for naught."

"One more thing," Niall said. "I assume you've already looked into her father's compatriots to the extent that you can without being obvious. So I'll need a report of everything you know, whom you suspect, et cetera."

"Of course. I'll have that sent over first thing in the morning, along with samples of the counterfeit notes for you to examine and instructions on what to look for. You'll need to be able to recognize the flawed ones when you see them." He held up his glass. "But for tonight, let me be the first to congratulate you two on your engagement."

When she couldn't stifle a snort, Niall said, "Oh, stubble it, Fulkham." He offered her his arm. "Come, Bree. Let's show this arrogant arse what we're made of, shall we?"

As she took his arm, determination coursed through her. She *would* show Lord Fulkham what she was made of, him and her father and everyone else. She would weather this as she'd weathered her arranged marriage to Reynold, and the awful things that had come afterward. She would do it for Silas, and only Silas.

Then, when it was done, she would retire to Camden Hall, hopefully with more knowledge about estate management than she'd had before. And with any luck, she wouldn't have to deal with society sorts or Niall or her dratted father ever again.

Four

By the time Niall left the library with Bree, the gentlemen were coming down the hall to join the ladies in the drawing room.

He stared at her, a lump catching in his throat. God, she was beautiful in that forest-green dinner gown, which skimmed her breasts with loving care and left far too much of the rest of her to the imagination. He would love to see what lay beneath the froth of petticoats that women wore these days. He had no doubt she would be a Botticelli indeed.

Well, except for her prudery and her absurd worries that he might be plotting to get her into his bed, that he might have plotted to get her there years ago. That angered him. The fact that she would even believe—

Don't think about that right now, man. You're supposed to be happily anticipating announcing your engagement, remember?

Right. To a woman who looked as if.someone had just stolen her joy. How annoying. Years ago she'd refused to marry him, and now that she had her chance to get her hooks in him again, she balked?

That made no sense. And was rather insulting. He'd make any woman a good husband, blast it. Not that he wanted to be one to her, but still, she ought to be running after him like the other females in society.

Unless she'd truly loved Trevor.

The very thought of it was like an itch under his skin that he couldn't scratch. He hadn't been able to make her love him enough to leave her family behind for him, but Trevor had succeeded?

Although her point about her mother's being unable to go abroad had been valid, he supposed. Still, he found it hard to believe that her mother had been her only sticking point. If so, Bree would have waited for him until her mother died. Then she would have sent word.

But she hadn't even waited a full year before marrying some other fellow. Deuced bastard. If anything showed that she hadn't truly loved *him*, that did.

Well, this would be over soon enough.

He halted at the threshold of the drawing room to gaze down into her grim face. "Are you ready for this?"

"No. But waiting won't make me any more ready."

"You might want to smile. You're announcing your impending wedding, but you look like you're going to your execution." He forced a teasing note into his voice. "You may not be aware of this, but I *am* considered eminently eligible."

That softened her features. "And modest, too."

"Why should I be modest?" he quipped. "I'm an earl, for God's sake. We have and deserve everything, don't you know?" When that actually got a smile from her, he murmured, "It will work out in the end, Bree. I swear."

"It didn't work out last time."

"That's because we actually planned to marry. It's much easier to manage imaginary engagements. You can dissolve those at a moment's notice with little difficulty."

He was rewarded by her throaty chuckle.

But when he started to enter, she halted and said, "Hold on." She reached up to straighten his cravat and smooth a lock of his hair. "That's better. *Now* we're ready."

The wifely gesture made his pulse stutter. Damn her. Every time he thought he had her figured out, she did something so . . . so bloody endearing that he wanted to toss his opinions of her out the window.

Careful, man. She's not the woman you thought you knew.

He'd simply have to keep reminding himself of that.

When they entered together with her hand

on his arm, they drew furtive looks of curiosity. Niall debated whether to consult with Clarissa about the announcement or ask Edwin's permission. But that would require too much explanation. Best to let the cat out of the bag without swinging it around first.

The footmen were serving wine, so he snagged a glass and tapped it to gain everyone's attention.

Then he took Bree's hand in his. "Forgive me, sister," he said, with a nod at Clarissa. "Although I don't want to take over your dinner, I do have something to announce, and I figured I'd take care of it while many of our friends are together."

The room fell so silent that he could hear the crackling of the fire in the hearth. "Some of you may have noticed that Mrs. Trevor and I have been absent from the party for a while. Well, there was a reason for that. I wanted a private moment with her so I could ask her to be my wife. And fortunately she has made me the happiest of men by consenting."

For a second, he thought he'd blundered in where he shouldn't have. No one spoke, no one moved. Everyone gaped at them.

Then Mother broke the silence. "Oh, my dears! How *wonderful!*"

That opened the floodgates. Edwin congratulated him with a hearty clap on the shoulder. Clarissa exclaimed that she'd always *known* they belonged together.

And the rest of the women crowded around Bree to ask her precisely the sort of things he knew she'd been fretting over: When had it happened? How had they known they were in love? When was the wedding?

To Bree's credit, she fielded the questions much better than she'd implied she would. So much for her inability to "pretend," which he'd thought was nonsense in the first place. She'd pretended to be madly in love with him years ago—this should be easy.

Suddenly Niall caught sight of Lady Pensworth in the corner, surveying the scene with a wary eye. Uh-oh. At least one person in the room did not look happy about this.

Leaving Bree to the ladies, he strolled over to her aunt. "Forgive me, Lady Pensworth. I realize I should have consulted with you first, and I do intend to go through solicitors and draw up settlements and such." He glanced back at Bree with what he hoped was an expression of adoration. "But I've waited seven years for this. I didn't want to wait another week more."

She eyed him closely. "Delia mentioned that the two of you knew each other previously. In Bath, was it?"

"Yes, when I accompanied Mother on her trip to take the waters. Lady Payne was there to take the waters as well, and Bree and I happened to meet in the park one day. She wasn't yet out, so

we only saw each other outside the usual ave-
nues. But we were very . . . close."

"Yet until you showed up a few weeks ago,
she's never so much as mentioned your name."

Of course not. The blasted female hadn't
thought one whit about him once he'd left.

He forced a smile. "She's hardly going to talk
about her former suitor with the aunt of her husband, especially when said former suitor is off in
another country where she's unlikely to see him
again."

"Due to that pesky little incident with the
duel, you mean." Lady Pensworth eyed him over
the top of her spectacles.

He stiffened. "Yes."

"And what was the reason for the duel?"

He kept smiling and told himself that this was
practice for what would probably be a worse
interrogation by Bree's father tomorrow. "All parties involved in the duel agreed not to divulge
the reasons."

"The other party is dead. I hardly think he'll
object."

"No, but I do. Perhaps we could have this discussion at another time, in a more private setting?" Where he could handle the old harpy
without everyone looking on.

She dipped her head. "If you wish. Though I
am not the one who chose to eschew the usual
formalities by announcing the betrothal willy-
nilly without consulting her relations."

"Your nephew's widow isn't some blushing innocent," he said in a steely voice. "And she can do as she pleases."

"Fortunately, so can I." When he glowered at her, she added, "Very well, we'll continue this discussion at a later time. But I really only have one other question of significance. Do you love her?"

Oh, God. It had been one thing to advise Bree how to mislead her relations, but it was quite another to be faced with lying to them himself. The sort of spying he'd done for Fulkham hadn't prepared him for anything this personal.

Keep to the plan. A practical arrangement, remember? "I respect her. I enjoy her company." He met Lady Pensworth's gaze boldly. "And I need a wife to bear my heir. She will do nicely, I think."

There. He'd established the ruse without having to spout lies about love and rapture.

Lady Pensworth sipped her wine. "I do hope you've informed *her* of those cold-blooded reasons for marrying her."

"Of course. And she has her own 'cold-blooded' reasons—she wants a father for her son and someone to help her with Camden Hall."

"She does, does she? Odd that she hasn't mentioned that wish to *me*."

"Forgive me, Lady Pensworth, but there are things a woman will tell her fiancé that she won't tell a relation."

Lady Pensworth's eyes narrowed on him. "Even a fiancé who hasn't bothered to visit her or court her in the month he's been back in England?"

God rot it, the woman was suspicious. But there wasn't a thing he could do about it. "Other than your concern about Bree's feelings, have you any other objections?"

She blinked. "Bree?"

"Sorry. Brilliana. Bree is the nickname I had for her, and now I can't break myself of the habit of using it."

"You gave her a nickname, eh? Interesting." She seemed to regard him in a new light. "So, you're marrying her to gain your heir, then."

"And because we suit each other. It *is* a good match."

"Just not a particularly romantic one."

"I'm not particularly romantic," he shot back.

"Yes, but *she* is."

He couldn't resist a cynical smile. "Are you sure about that?"

"I know Brilliana quite well," she said frostily. "And I would hate to see—"

"There you are." Bree took him by the arm. "Your mother and sister want us to lead out the dancing."

"There's dancing?" he said, startled.

"Surely you know your sister well enough to realize that any event she hosts must involve dancing of *some* kind. And now that you and I have made our announcement, she thinks it only right that there be more of a celebration. Which calls for dancing."

He glanced back to see servants moving chairs out of the way and a young lady taking a seat behind the pianoforte. "Ah, that makes sense."

His stomach knotted. This would be his first time dancing with Bree. In Bath they'd been unable to meet at social affairs, so no balls or assemblies.

Bad enough he would have to squire her around for weeks. Now he'd have the added torture of holding her in his arms, breathing in her scent, watching her lush curves undulate in a decided echo of the act of love itself.

Damn Fulkham to hell.

He turned toward Bree, but Lady Pensworth stayed him with a hand on his arm. Apparently the inquisition wasn't over.

She fixed Bree with a questioning look. "Lord Margrave has just been telling me about your reasons for marrying. It all sounds very—"

"Practical?" Brilliana said lightly. "I know." She leaned toward her aunt. "Don't tell his mother and sister, but his lordship and I aren't romantic sorts. He needs a wife, and I thought it was time I found a suitor who can be a father to Silas. It's important for my son to have a man to look up to. I'm sure you agree."

Niall met her aunt's gaze evenly, trying hard not to gloat. Bree couldn't have answered any better if he'd crafted her answer himself.

"Besides," Bree went on with a suspicious gleam in her eye, "Niall isn't eager to weather the marriage mart when he already knows me so well. It's most trying for a man his age."

A man his— What the blazes? He was only thirty, for God's sake!

A faint smile crossed her aunt's face. "Yes, I can see how it would be taxing."

Oh, he was *not* going to let this stand. "Almost as taxing as running an estate alone will be for Bree. Being a woman, she recognizes that she needs a man to take such matters in hand."

When Bree glared at him, he smirked at her. He was congratulating himself for getting his own back when Lady Pensworth said in a voice like ice, "Not all women need a man to 'take such matters in hand.' I've run my brother's estate for years, since he can't be bothered. So far, I've had no complaints from his tenants."

Damnation. He'd overplayed his hand.

"Thank you, Aunt Agatha, for clarifying that," Bree said, then tugged on Niall's arm. "They're calling for us. We'd better go."

"Yes, of course." Grateful for the reprieve, he let her pull him away. Hard to believe he was actually looking forward to the part of this mission that involved cornering criminals and risking life and limb.

Because Lady Pensworth would give any criminal a run for his money.

As they headed off to where dancers were

assembling, Bree started laughing. "I wish you could see your face. Aunt Agatha certainly took *you* down a peg."

"I am *not* avoiding the marriage mart, blast it. Why would you say that?"

"To further our ruse." Her face was the very picture of innocence. "Wasn't that what you directed me to do?"

"I didn't tell you to make me sound like I'm in my dotage."

"No." Her eyes twinkled at him. "I came up with that all on my own."

"For someone who feared she'd have trouble pretending," he grumbled, "you're doing exceedingly well."

"I merely decided to take your advice to treat this as an adventure and enjoy myself."

They halted in the middle of the room, with every eye upon them. "And your idea of an adventure is to mock me publicly?"

The music struck up then. A waltz.

"Was I mocking you?" she said as he took her in the proper hold. "I thought I was merely stating a fact. You *are* a bachelor of a certain age."

He tugged her far too close for propriety, and two spots of color appeared on her cheeks, which pleased him inordinately. "Don't press your luck, sweeting." Then he began to dance.

Bree followed his lead like a woman born to waltz. She was all fluid grace and perfect symmetry, her body sweeping through the room as if borne by the music itself. It made him ache to whisk her right out onto a balcony somewhere and kiss her senseless.

But he'd promised not to "lure" her anywhere, so he would control himself. Although the longer her hand clung to his, the more he wanted to have her hand somewhere else . . . in his hair, against his bare chest . . . curving around his hardening cock.

He swore under his breath. How did this woman make him forget himself so easily?

Because when she was smiling as she was just now, with her face lit up like a sun-drenched meadow, she was so appealing that he forgot she'd once been a mercenary in skirts, coveting his title like the other debutantes. That when marrying him had meant exile and uncertainty, she'd married another man without so much as a letter to him.

"What did my aunt say?" she asked. "I tried to get over there quickly, but everyone had a million questions."

"And what did you tell them?"

She arched one eyebrow. "You first."

"Your aunt wanted to know the usual—how we met, what I felt for you, that sort of thing. I gave her exactly the answers that we agreed upon. Then you gave her nearly the same answers—thank you, by the way—so with any luck, she'll be satisfied."

"I doubt it." She glanced at her aunt. "She's scowling at us."

"Not at us. At *me*. I don't think she approves, despite my explanation about our arrangement. She says you're too romantic to marry for practical reasons." He eyed her closely. "Is that true?"

She looked away. "I suppose it was true once. But life has taught me that romance is foolish."

"Was it really *life* that taught you that? Or your marriage? What happened—was it not a love match?" He couldn't keep the snide tone from his voice.

And judging from the way she tipped up her chin, she made note of it. "Why would you assume that?"

"Because you now think romance is foolish."

"It has nothing to do with . . . I don't think . . ." She scowled at him. "I don't want to talk about my marriage with *you*, that's all. It's private."

Only with an effort did Niall hide his chagrin. It shouldn't bother him that she wouldn't tell him the details. What did it matter if she'd married Trevor for love? Or if she didn't want to talk about why the marriage had soured? *If* it had soured.

He was past all that with her, damn it.

Yet he couldn't stop himself from prodding, especially when something awful occurred to him. "He wasn't cruel, was he?"

"Don't be absurd," she said, so dismissively that he had to believe her. "Reynold and I got along perfectly well. He never raised his hand— or voice—to me. He was a good man."

The kind of man she could fall in love with? "Is that why you don't wish to marry again? Because you were madly in love with him and no other man compares? Or did he make you skeptical about marriage by proving to be a disappointment?"

"Why do you care?"

A good question, yet he couldn't stop. "I don't understand why you're no longer interested in spending your life with a man you love. That's what most women prefer."

"And you know exactly what most women prefer, being a man." She stared hard at him. "For your information, even if one marries the man one loves, a lifetime with him is not guaranteed. I'm a widow at twenty-four—hardly a ringing endorsement for the longevity of marriages. And given the usual man's tendency to wander—"

"Ah, so Trevor was a philanderer."

"I didn't say that!"

"You didn't have to. *Something* made you cynical about marriage. And that's a common enough reason."

"I'm not cynical about marriage, and my husband was never a philanderer. We were perfectly content until he found out about—" She glared at him. "I told you I didn't wish to discuss it. Besides, I wasn't thinking of him. I was thinking of you."

"Me!" The comment put him on his guard. He swept her into a turn. "I'll admit I was a bit of a rogue. But only until I met you."

She flashed him an arch smile. "Of course."

"You don't believe me?"

A veil came down over her face. "It doesn't matter what I believe. That was all long ago, and we're different people now."

He would have probed further, but the waltz ended then, and they weren't allowed to dance the next set together. With a certain glee, his friends all lined up to demand dances of her. And Clarissa insisted that *he* stand up with all of hers.

God rot them for conspiring against him in the usual fashion of friends teasing a new couple. He wondered what they'd think if they knew the truth.

And what *was* the truth? She'd certainly been evasive about that. He still didn't know why she'd married that damned Trevor. Why she'd never bothered to tell him of it personally.

Thankfully, the evening didn't go on much longer for him. Clarissa drew him aside to ask that he take home their mother, who was tiring.

He suppressed his snort. Tiring, right. That was Mother Code for *I'm bored.* Her bad hip kept her from dancing, and she never liked being left out.

Clarissa brought him over to the corner where Mother sat complaining—to Bree. Damnation. No telling what nonsense she was blathering. He only hoped she wasn't reinforcing Bree's impression of him as some sort of feckless scoundrel who'd abandoned his mother in her time of need.

He walked up to them. "Mother, Clarissa tells me you're ready to leave. I told her I'd accompany you."

As he helped his mother rise, Bree rose, too. "Will you be coming back?" she asked.

"Not tonight," Mother answered for him. "You'll have him to yourself very soon, my dear, but I've scarcely seen him since his return to England, and I do have a great deal to discuss with him."

That was Mother Code for *He was mine first, and don't you forget it.* Fortunately for Bree, she didn't care.

God, that depressed him.

"Good night, then," Bree said.

He nodded. "I'll see you in the morning."

Clarissa nudged him. "For heaven's sake, you just got engaged. You should at least kiss her good night."

The look of alarm on Bree's face was unmistakable. Good God, she really *wasn't* good at pretending. Before anyone could notice that, he stepped close and pressed his mouth to hers.

It was the briefest of kisses, but as he drew back and she stared up at him with wide, guileless eyes, for an instant he was back in Green Park, trying to coax the woman he loved into loving him in return.

And just as it had back then, his heart hammered in his chest and his blood ran wild. She looked sweet and beautiful and everything a man could desire. He wanted to throw caution to the winds and drag her back into his arms for the kind of kiss he *used* to give her.

Fortunately, his good sense prevailed. As she'd said, they were different people now. These days he was more conscious of his rank and wealth, and she was more guarded with men. Not to mention that they were both aware that this was just a ruse. Nothing else.

Or so he tried to tell himself, as he bowed to her and then left with Mother.

But as they headed for the door, he couldn't help noticing that Lady Pensworth was looking upon him decidedly more kindly than before.

Five

What a beautiful afternoon to be outside in the garden! Brilliana was grateful for the reprieve from London's usual damp, dreary weather. Aunt Agatha watched Silas play and babble, both of them unaware of the tumult in Brilliana's breast as she sketched her handsome lad.

He was utterly content. The poor dear didn't know or care that he was fatherless. Or the reason for it—because his papa's jealousy of Niall had been so intense that he'd . . .

No, she wouldn't think about that. It hadn't been her fault. She hadn't even known that Reynold knew of her former love until it was too late. She certainly hadn't known what he intended to do about it. If she had, she would have put a swift end to it.

But would he have listened to her? Reynold had treated her like—how had Niall put it?— "a fine piece of art to show off to one's friends."

Exactly the way Niall proposed to treat her, like Botticelli's Venus.

Remembering the hot glance he'd given her, she shivered—as she'd never shivered with her husband. Oh, that was wicked of her. She should have loved Reynold. She'd certainly tried hard enough.

But Niall had ruined that for her. And he would be here any minute to muck up her life some more.

Determined not to dwell on that, Brilliana glanced at her sweet boy and traced the line of his jaw on her sketch. Silas would make a perfect Cupid for her latest design. She knew it was futile to hope, but she couldn't give up her dream of designing for Wedgwood. The famous porcelain company had hired other women to work for it. Why not her? Granted, she'd sent them ten designs already and hadn't heard a word, but she would send them fifty more if that was what it took to get them to notice her.

Silas started fussing over his jack-in-the-box, which Lord Blakeborough had made for him and which the boy simply could not stop mangling. The clown leapt out on a rather long spring, so Silas had some trouble stuffing it back in the box after it jumped out.

"Jack, Jack, Jack," he chanted.

With a smile, Brilliana held out her hand. "Bring it here, my sweet. Mama will fix Jack."

When Silas merely pouted at her, Aunt Agatha

shook her head. "The lad is no fool. He knows that not everything can be fixed."

"He's just naturally suspicious," Brilliana said. "As is his mama."

Her aunt cast her a sharp glance. "You didn't seem very suspicious last night. You accepted Lord Margrave's marriage proposal rather readily."

Avoiding her aunt's gaze, she bent her head over her sketch. "I should think you'd approve of my choice. The earl is quite a catch."

"Is he? The gossips aren't so sure. I spoke to a few friends today. It seems that the town is already abuzz about how he needs funds for his estate."

Fulkham's lackeys had done their work swiftly. "The gossips like to stir up trouble for no reason but their own entertainment."

"Have you never heard that where there's smoke there's fire?"

"There is no fire here, trust me." The last thing she and Niall needed was her aunt interfering in Lord Fulkham's scheme.

"No? That's not how it looked last night when he kissed you."

Uh-oh. Brilliana fought a blush, praying that last night she'd covered her reaction to his kiss well—her heart thundering, her pulse leaping, her very skin aflame at the touch of his lips to hers. "I don't know what you mean."

"Don't play the fool with me, young lady. When Delia told me that you and his lordship had been acquainted before, I'd assumed that your association was casual at best. Clearly, I was wrong. There was definitely smoke in that ball-room last night when he bid you farewell."

"You imagined that. He was merely giving me the courtesy of any fiancé."

"Was he?" Concern showed in Aunt Agatha's face. "Be careful, dear. Margrave is the sort to break a woman's heart."

"My heart would have to be engaged for that to happen."

"And it isn't?" her aunt said skeptically. "You truly are marrying him just for practical reasons?"

Brilliana forced a bland smile. "I think I've proved that one can have a perfectly content marriage without involving one's heart."

"Really? I would say you've proved the opposite."

The astute comment made her grimace. Had the strain in her marriage been so obvious? "I can't imagine what you're talking about."

"We both know that you weren't entirely happy with Reynold. And given how the marriage came about, I don't blame you. I think your father ought to be shot, quite frankly, for putting you in such a position."

"You . . . knew about that?"

"Of course. There's not much that goes on in this family that I don't know. I only found out after it happened, or I might have tried to step in, but by the time I learned of it, it was done and settled, and you were married."

She flashed Brilliana a wan smile. "Still, I'd rather hoped you two were finding your way to contentment despite your rocky beginning, especially after the child was born. But then Reynold . . ." She sighed. "The thing is, I understand how you felt. Which is all the more reason I don't want to see you make such a mistake again. Especially since this time your heart would be engaged."

"My heart is *not* engaged with Lord Margrave, I assure you." Perhaps if she said it enough, she'd believe it.

"Does he know why you ended up married to Reynold in the first place?"

"No, indeed, and I prefer not to tell him. It's mortifying, to say the least. And none of his concern."

"He might think otherwise."

"I don't care." She had her pride, after all. If she told him Papa had essentially forced her into marrying Reynold, that she *hadn't* chosen her husband out of some deep love, Niall would realize that *he'd* been her only love. He'd guess just how vulnerable she was to him now.

What's more, he would probably mock her for not running away with him when she had the chance. And if she told him it was to save her mother, he would mock her even more. He'd thought her concern for Mama inconsequential. He would deem her a fool.

It was better for him to go on assuming she'd

been in love with her husband. Safer. After all, Niall's own protestations of love had been lies. So why should she let him know that hers had been genuine?

"Please don't tell him," she said. "I will reveal it myself in my own good time." Or rather, she wouldn't worry about it, since this situation was temporary.

Just then, a footman stepped out to announce that Lord Margrave had come to call on the ladies. Brilliana could have wept with relief at the reprieve.

"Speak of the devil," Aunt Agatha muttered, then told the servant, "Send him out here, if you please."

As the footman left, the nurse whom Aunt Agatha had hired for Silas came outside. "Shall I take the babe back to the nursery, madam?"

"No, indeed. It's time my fiancé met him." Brilliana set aside her sketchbook and waggled her fingers at Silas. "Come to Mama, sweeting, and let me fix Jack. You'll break him if you keep shoving the lid down without having all the clown inside."

He scowled and continued to struggle with the toy.

For some reason, that tickled his stern great-aunt so much that she laughed. "That boy is as stubborn and proud as his father, even at this young age."

"True." It had been Reynold's pride that had

sent him rushing to root out the man she'd loved. And it had been his failure that had sent him—

Lord, she must stop thinking of that! It wasn't her fault. It wasn't! And she certainly wasn't going to let Silas grow up to be like him.

"Silas, you come here right now and bring Jack to me!" He hesitated, but clearly recognized the peremptory note in her voice. Sullenly, he toddled over to her, dragging the clown by its already ragged head. She shoved the clown back in and pushed the lid shut, then, before he could grab it and run off, picked him up and set him on her knee.

"You see? There's nothing wrong with needing help." Lord knew that if his father had ever asked for her help in anything, she would gladly have given it. "You tried hard—that's all that matters." She lavished kisses on him as he struggled to get down and run off with his toy.

Then a voice sounded from the doorway out to the garden. "Such a foolish lad to be fighting so. A man would give much to be in his position."

Brilliana's heart faltered.

She looked over to where Niall stood leaning against the doorframe, looking even more luscious than usual in riding boots and buckskin, with his hair fashionably tousled and his lips curved in a faint smile. His Pomona-green coat brought out the green in his hazel eyes, which held an unsettling hint of envy.

"What a very pretty compliment, coming from a man who's not a romantic," Aunt Agatha cut in.

"I suspect you would do very well on the marriage mart, Lord Margrave."

"I doubt that," Brilliana said as she set Silas back on the ground, where he immediately went to cranking the handle of the box. "Any clever woman would see right through that insincere remark. Everyone knows that men hate being fussed over just as much as little boys do."

With a brooding expression, Niall pushed away from the doorframe. "Not all men." The very air between them seemed to heat, and for a moment, it felt just like when she'd been courted by him with tender care.

Then the jack-in-the-box sprang open and Silas gave a little clap of delight, which thankfully drew Niall's attention from her. "So this is your son, is it?"

"Yes. This is Silas." She patted his head, though he was utterly engrossed in shoving the clown back in the box again. "Silas, this is Lord Margrave."

Niall nodded slightly, now every inch the unobtainable earl she'd grown accustomed to seeing of late. "A pleasure to meet you, Master Silas."

And, to her horror, Silas began to howl.

❦

Niall's heart sank. He didn't know much about children, but that did not sound good. He hadn't meant to frighten the child, for God's sake. Had he been frowning? It was possible. Seeing her with her babe had nearly undone him.

That could have been *his* child, if she hadn't chosen another man to marry. Perhaps, even, to love? God, the possibility of that cut him clean through.

"Silas, my sweet!" Bree picked up the lad again and dandled him on her knee. "Heavens, what is wrong?" She glanced at Niall apologetically. "He's rather shy of strangers, but this is not typical."

"No doubt he's heard of Margrave's reputation," Lady Pensworth quipped.

Niall scowled at her, but the old battle-ax merely smiled unrepentantly.

Then the boy thrust his hand at his mother. "Ow!" he said as tears rolled down his chubby cheeks. "Ow, *ow!*"

Bree took his hand and examined it. "Oh, dear, look at this. You pinched your thumb trying to put the lid down. That's why you mustn't be so rough shoving the clown in." She kissed the red mark. "There, there now. It will be all right. Nurse will fetch salve for it, and it will be fine in two shakes of a lamb's tail."

The nurse, who'd been standing discreetly to the side, said, "I'll be right back, ma'am," and hurried into the house.

This time when Bree cuddled the lad, he let her hold him, thrusting his thumb in his mouth and leaning into her embrace as she rocked him and murmured soothing words of consolation about how brave he was being.

Niall could hardly bear to watch the tender scene. The child was like any other, he supposed—with reddish curls and brown eyes that mirrored his mother's, not to mention a very handsome face—but it was her reaction to him that made Niall's heart twist. She was as affectionate to the lad as any man could want the mother of his children to be. It took him completely by surprise.

Granted, just because a woman was grasping in her choice of husbands didn't mean she would neglect her babes, but his own mother had packed him and Clarissa off to the nurse whenever she could. He only remembered seeing Mother in the evening, when she came to kiss them good night. Indeed, most aristocratic parents were rather distant to their children.

Clearly, Bree wasn't that sort. And the way she fussed over young Silas, who took it for granted with the self-centeredness of all babes, made Niall's gut knot. Once, he would have given anything to be in the lad's place.

He frowned. What absurdity. How could he be jealous of a mere child? She was doing what any other caring mother might do. Why, for all he knew, this was just a show put on for Niall's benefit.

A sigh escaped him. That was unlikely. She wasn't trying to impress him these days. She'd gained the life she wanted—that of an independent woman with her own estate—and she had no use for him anymore.

Not that he cared. He was immune to her machinations now. If she had any. Which he'd just decided she didn't.

Deuce take it, he couldn't wait to have this particular mission over.

Meanwhile, the lad had already begun to forget his injury, for he was squirming on his mother's knee. Bree looked up at Niall. "Would you like to hold him?"

"God, no," Niall said hastily. Too hastily, judging from the cloud that darkened her brow. "I don't know a thing about children. I wouldn't want to alarm him."

"Better get used to being around babes, my lord, if you mean to fill your nursery," Lady Pensworth said bluntly. "You're not getting any younger, and you'll need at least an heir and a spare."

A fetching pink suffused Bree's cheeks, making Niall's pulse jump. It was all too easy to imagine engaging in the very pleasurable activity of filling their nursery. Not that he would need any such excuse to bed her. Just the sight of her all rosy and soft made him crave her. And if she belonged to him . . .

Best not to think of that.

Avoiding his gaze, Bree set Silas down. "I'm sure his lordship will feel differently about his own children." She chucked the lad under the chin. "Why don't you go show Lord Margrave your jack-in-the-box?" She glanced up at Niall. "Your sister's husband made it for him."

"Ah, yes," Niall said, relieved to be on more solid ground in the conversation. "Edwin likes building that sort of thing."

Silas merely stood there, one hand on the hapless clown and his other thrusting his thumb into his mouth as he eyed Niall with rank suspicion. Why did Niall get the feeling that the lad regarded him as the enemy?

Nonsense. What did Silas know about enemies? He was a baby.

But a damned cute one, who clearly had his mama wrapped around his finger. And that mama was going to be difficult to manage if she thought Niall disliked her child.

Stifling a sigh, he squatted to look the lad in the face. "Will you show it to me, then, Master Silas?"

Silas crept closer, then thrust his toy out, a trifle warily, as he kept his damaged thumb squarely in his mouth.

"It looks like grand fun. Can you make it work?"

His face brightening, the lad started shoving on the clown to get it in the box, then tried to close the lid before the clown was fully inside.

"Oh, dear," Bree said. "He keeps doing that." She rose from her chair. "Come here, my sweet, and let Mama do it."

That only made the child more determined to make it work—shoving hard on the lid as if that would solve the problem.

"Easy there, lad," Niall said. "You must be careful with it and be sure to get all the clown inside the box—and your fingers free—before you close the top." He opened the lid, then caught the boy's hand and carefully helped him shove the clown inside the box and press the lid down until it clicked into place.

Silas stared solemnly at him, then turned the crank until the clown leapt out, which sent the boy into gales of laughter. But before Niall could even revel in that laughter, the child started pushing on the lid with the same excitement as before, then fussing when he couldn't get it closed because part of the clown still stuck out.

Lady Pensworth laughed. "I'm afraid the lad is a bit young to be learning that lesson, Lord Margrave. But it was a good try."

Feeling disgruntled, Niall rose. "As I said, I don't know much about children."

Then he caught sight of Bree's face. Her eyes were decidedly softer than before. "You'll learn," was all she said.

He nodded, though he prayed he wouldn't be spending enough time with them to learn. Because he could very easily grow attached to the little devil. The babe was much like Bree— obstinate and inquisitive and entirely too . . . cute.

Though *cute* wasn't really the word for Bree. She could never be anything but beautiful. Today she wore a cream-colored day dress dotted with red embroidered flowers. On anyone else it might have looked simple, but on her it looked like a garden, one that had the odd effect of making her hair glow redder than a setting sun, since she wore no cap to cover it.

What he wouldn't give to be able to take that luscious hair down, to see how far the curls fell, how sweetly they curved about her hips and her—

Damn it, he must stop thinking about such things. This was neither the time nor the place. Not that there *was* a time or place for that. Not with her.

He grimaced. Sadly, that argument became less convincing by the moment.

Lady Pensworth was giving him quite the dark look over the top of her spectacles, and he quickly changed his train of thought.

"I don't mean to rush you, Bree, but perhaps we should depart. No telling how early your father leaves to go out for the evening, and we wouldn't want to miss him."

As Bree groaned, Lady Pensworth straightened. "You're paying a call on *Sir Oswald?* Whatever for?"

Uh-oh. It looked as if he had stepped awry. "To tell him of the engagement and ask his blessing on the marriage, of course."

"But—"

"You're right, we should leave at once," Bree said hastily. She turned to the nurse, who'd just returned with the salve. "Why don't you take Silas up now? It's time for his nap."

"Certainly, madam," the nurse said and picked up the boy.

Lady Pensworth sat with pursed lips while Bree gave Silas a tender kiss and sent him off with his nurse, but as soon as the child was gone, the baroness said to Bree, "I cannot believe you are even giving Sir Oswald the time of day."

Niall narrowed his gaze on the woman. "Why shouldn't she? He *is* her father, after all."

"And a very poor one, too. If you only knew what that man did to—"

"There's no time for such a dreary tale right now, Aunt Agatha," Brilliana said smoothly. "His lordship is right—we need to go."

"We have a few minutes yet," he said. "And I confess I'm curious about why you and your father don't get along."

"While I prefer not to discuss it," she countered with a quelling glance for her aunt. "I should hope you'd both respect my wishes."

Lady Pensworth sniffed. "Very well. But don't stay too long; I don't trust that man one whit."

"Don't worry, Aunt. Neither do I." With that, Bree took Niall's arm and tugged him into the house. He let her, but only because he wanted to get her alone before pursuing the matter. He needed to know more about the estrangement, if only so he could plan his strategy for his mission.

So he waited patiently while she donned a cloak of brilliant scarlet and an enormous bonnet with flowers that matched those on her gown. He said naught to her while they climbed into his carriage and he ordered his coachman to drive on.

But once they'd set off, he broached the subject again. "Enough of this reticence about your father, Bree. If I'm to get to the bottom of this counterfeiting business, I need to know exactly what caused the rift between you two."

She stared him down. "Why? Our mission has nothing to do with any of that. Besides, it's in the past."

"Clearly not *that* much in the past if your aunt is still worried about it." When she merely turned to stare out the window, he remembered what she'd said about having not seen her father since her mother's funeral. "It wasn't related to your mother's death, was it? I hope he wasn't somehow responsible for that."

Her shocked glance put that supposition to rest. "Good heavens, my father might be a gambler, but he's no murderer."

"Ah. Then I assume it has something to do with his gambling."

Jerking her gaze from him, she let out a heavy sigh. "Of course. What else would it have to do with?"

"What did he do, ask your husband for funds to pay his gaming debts? Cause an estrangement there?" That would explain why she'd become cautious concerning marriage.

"Certainly not," was all she would say.

"Then perhaps your father gambled away your dowry," he pressed. "Is that why your aunt had to step in to give you one this time around?"

Her chin quavered. "Something like that."

Hmm. That made more sense. She'd hoped for a rich, titled husband, and her father had made that impossible. So she'd had to settle for Trevor, who'd had property but no title. Was that why she'd married so soon after Niall's exile? Because she'd feared that if she didn't snap up the first eligible man who offered, she'd never marry at all?

Assuming she hadn't married the man for love. Which Niall still wasn't sure about. By God, it gnawed at him that she had let *him* go so easily, only to take up with a fellow of half his consequence.

And he still couldn't understand why she hadn't just written to him, so he could send for her.

Unbidden, his father's words from long ago came to him: *What good would you be to her once the two of you are in hiding in Spain? She won't be able to lord it over her friends as a viscountess or show off her fine town house or prance about to balls on the arm of an earl's heir.*

Right. That was why.

"So Trevor married you for your beauty alone, since you had no dowry to give him," he said coldly. "And you married Trevor for what? Love? His property?"

She tensed up. "I told you, I don't wish to discuss my marriage with you."

"Why not?" Resentment welled up in him. "Afraid that I'll find out exactly how disappointing he ended up being?"

"He was a good husband," she bit out. "And he gave me my son. For that, I will always be grateful."

"Yet according to my cousin, he abandoned that son—and you—by gambling away all your funds, then drinking himself into oblivion and stumbling into the river, where he drowned. That's not what I'd call a good husband."

She gaped at him. "Warren told you that?"

"He mentioned it, yes."

"Don't you think it's rather like the pot calling the kettle black to accuse Reynold of abandoning me, when you abandoned me first?"

"That's not how I remember it, Bree," he said softly.

"Well, no matter how you remember it, that's how it happened."

His temper flared. "Admit it, you would have been better off with me, exile or no, than with a fool like that."

"Don't call my husband a fool," she hissed. "You don't know anything about him."

Her defense of the bastard really irked Niall. "I know that he didn't appreciate you, or he wouldn't have left you to raise your son alone." He leaned across the carriage. "I suspect that he didn't have your heart. That he didn't fire your blood or make you feel the things that *I* made you feel. That I *still* make you feel, blast it."

Panic flickered in her eyes before she shuttered her features and slid to the other end of the seat to escape him. "That's not true," she whispered.

It was, and the need to hear her admit it settled in his gut like a chunk of lead. Damnation, he'd keep pushing her until she admitted that she'd made a mistake. That she should have run off with *him*. That she regretted her choice. Only then would he be satisfied.

Throwing himself into the other seat, he dragged her into his arms. "The hell it isn't."

Then he caught her head in his hands and kissed her. Hard. Intimately. He pressed his tongue against her teeth to gain entry, the way he'd never dared to when they were courting. The way he knew she would like now that she was a widow, now that she'd experienced a man's bed.

The way he'd dreamed of kissing her for seven years.

When she froze, he feared he'd gone too far and put her even further on her guard. But as he slid his hands into her hair and ran his tongue over her trembling lips, she opened her mouth, and he exulted.

In this at least, she was his again. And he meant to make the most of it.

Six

Brilliana tried to resist Niall's kiss, but it was impossible. She'd dreamed of this for years, and now that his mouth was on hers, she realized her memory hadn't done it justice. Especially since they'd never kissed this way in their youth. How she wished they had! She'd never liked it when Reynold did it, but with Niall it was glorious. He plundered her mouth like a pirate at sea, commanding everything before him. His breath mingled with hers, his lips molded every line of hers, and his tongue . . .

Oh, it took and gave and played and drove, as if he meant to possess her again. Only this time, he meant to take both heart *and* body.

The thought of it made her so light-headed that she clung desperately to his arms. Just to steady herself. Not to pull him closer so *she* could possess *him*. No, indeed.

And what well-wrought arms he had, much

more so than she remembered. She wanted to stay in them forever, to keep kissing his warm mouth, smelling his sandalwood scent . . . feeling the flex of his muscles through his coat sleeves.

The urge was so strong that when he broke the kiss, she nearly moaned. Then he murmured her name in a tone that sounded as full of wonder as she felt, and tugged her right atop his lap.

Goodness gracious!

And the kissing began all over again, even fiercer and hotter than before, so hot she thought she might go up in smoke. So hot that she knew she *ought* to halt him. He was a rogue—she shouldn't encourage this. It meant naught to him but seduction.

But she couldn't bring herself to stop him. She wanted this taste of him too badly, this taste of their past together. This sweet, heady reminder that she was a woman with needs that he could satisfy, if she let him.

She couldn't, *mustn't*, let him. And yet . . .

"I can't believe I forgot this," he murmured against her lips. He settled her more firmly on his lap. "Do you feel what you do to me, sweeting?"

Oh yes. The bulge in his trousers made that perfectly clear. "Yes. But we can't. . . . I won't. . . ."

He took her mouth again like the ravisher he was. Only he didn't stop there this time. He covered one of her breasts with his hand, kneading and tempting and provoking her to madness.

And it felt so *good*, drat him. It had been over

a year since she'd been touched by a man; she'd forgotten how exquisite it could feel. Especially when the man touching her had once held her heart—

No! She mustn't let him do this to her again!

Wriggling out of his arms, she threw herself onto the other seat and fought to catch her breath.

"Bree . . ." he said in a low voice, leaning forward as if to reach for her again.

"Stop that!" She slid as far from him as the seat would allow. "You . . . you said you wouldn't try to take advantage of the situation." Oh, how she wished she didn't sound so desperate. "You promised!"

"I didn't promise any such thing," he ground out.

To be fair, that was true. Wrapping her arms about her waist, she drew into herself. "Not precisely that, but you said you wouldn't 'behave lecherously.'"

Anger flared in his face. "And that's how you saw what we just did. As a sordid attempt to 'lure' you into my bed."

She thrust up her chin. "Wasn't it?"

"If it was, then you weren't exactly opposed to it." He leveled a hard gaze on her. "It seemed to me that you were as eager for me just now as I was for you."

"You started it, though," she said inanely. Lord, she sounded like a child.

"And you continued it." A mocking smile crossed his lips. "You're a widow, Bree. You can do as you please, you know. Plenty of widows take lovers. If you want me—"

"I don't."

His eyes glittered at her. "You gave a very convincing performance otherwise, sweeting."

Well, she could hardly deny that. "I was . . . swept up in the moment. It's been some time since I . . ." When his smile broadened, she gritted her teeth. "It doesn't matter why I gave in. Temporarily. It won't happen again. It mustn't."

"I would dearly like to know why not," he drawled, laying his arm on the back of the seat with that supreme self-assurance she remembered so well.

She'd been captivated by it once. She wouldn't make that mistake twice. "Because I'm not fool enough to fall for your attentions again."

His gaze darkened. "You can tell yourself that all you like. But Fulkham wasn't lying when he said that 'the air fairly thrums' between us. Still, after all these years. And that kind of feeling doesn't just disappear because you think it foolish."

How she wanted him to be wrong. But the idea of taking him as a lover tantalized her.

Or it would have, if she hadn't known how it would eventually end, both in bed and out. The actual lovemaking always proved disappointing. "It doesn't matter what I feel. My plans for the future do not include you."

"Nor do mine include you," he said bluntly. Then he raked her with a hot glance that touched her mouth, her breasts . . . and lower, before meeting her eyes again. "That doesn't mean we can't thoroughly enjoy our situation while it lasts. We're both free to do that at present."

"*You're* free," she snapped. "Men always are. But I have a son and a reputation to uphold, for his sake as well as my own. And if you should happen to get me with child—"

He shrugged. "There are ways to avoid that."

"With which you're thoroughly familiar, I'm sure."

She'd expected her snippy remark to insult him. Instead, it only seemed to amuse him. "All I'm saying—"

"I know what you're saying, but—" The carriage shuddered to a halt, and she could have wept with relief. "We're here."

He glanced out, his lips tightening into a thin line. "So we are."

The footman quickly put down the step, opened the carriage door, and hurried up the town house steps to knock at her father's door.

Niall disembarked, then turned to help Brilliana climb out. But he didn't release her at once. Instead, he stood there with his hands gripping her waist as he stared down at her, looking for all the world like a real fiancé.

"We'll continue this discussion later," he said in a low, husky voice.

Her throat tightened. She really wished he wouldn't look at her like that. It did wicked things to her insides. "I shan't change my mind."

He chuckled. "You don't know how persuasive I can be."

Oh, but she did. That was the trouble. "Perhaps you've forgotten how stubborn *I* can be."

His amusement faded, replaced by a searing intensity she found far more unnerving. "Trust me, I remember only too well. But you are no longer a sweet young innocent and I am no longer a besotted young fool. I suspect we would do much better together these days."

She slipped from his arms and rushed up the steps ahead of him. She refused to let him win in this, even when she was painfully conscious of his steps echoing behind her, of his gaze on her back—and probably her backside, too. It felt as if she'd stepped back in time to when she was seventeen.

It only made matters worse that nothing about the Payne town house had changed. The same pot of nasturtiums sat at the far end of the porch, the front door held the same brass wolf-head knocker, and the fanlight iron still needed blackening. Memories flooded her, more bad than good. She had hoped never to return here.

So much for that.

Jenkins appeared in the doorway, the same genial old butler he'd always been, albeit a bit balder. And clearly curious about her appearance here with a gentleman of Niall's consequence.

"As I live and breathe, it's you!" he cried. "Your father will be so surprised to see you, Miss Bri . . . I mean, *Mrs.* Trevor."

She pasted a smile to her lips. "Good afternoon, Jenkins. I take it that Papa is home?"

"Oh yes." He cast a furtive look at Niall.

"If you would, please let him know that Lord Margrave and I have come to call."

"At once, madam." He glanced behind her. "And the . . . er . . . child? Isn't he with you?"

"I'm afraid not. I preferred to visit Papa without him first."

Jenkins looked disappointed, but then, he'd been with the family for years. No doubt he had a natural curiosity about her son.

She felt a quick stab of guilt at having not brought Silas along, but she still wasn't sure she *wanted* him to know his deceitful, betraying gambler of a grandfather. Who might just be a counterfeiter to boot.

As they waited to be announced, Niall glanced around at the worn rug, the walls in need of paint, and the fraying curtains. "For a man who might be involved in something criminal," he said in an undertone, "your father doesn't exactly live large."

"No. He's always too busy staying ahead of his creditors for that." With a jolt of pain, she stared at the space where her favorite cabinet used to stand. "And given that my entire collection of Wedgwood seems to have disappeared, I'll wager he's not doing very well with that." Her throat tightened. "I'm sure he got a pretty penny for it."

"I'm sorry, sweeting," Niall said in a low voice. "I know how much you admired Wedgwood's designs."

The fact that he remembered made her heart turn over. A pox on him for that. "Well, if my father is part of this conspiracy, I warrant it's only because he owes money everywhere."

The tap of a cane in the hall a few moments later was their only warning that someone approached. She was surprised to find it was Papa.

And when he came into the light, she saw that the cane wasn't the only thing new about him. His hair had gone fully gray. There were new wrinkles around his eyes and mouth and a droop to his chin. The belligerent, heedless fellow she remembered didn't seem quite so belligerent anymore. And when he clutched the cane with both hands, an odd alarm stabbed her chest.

"What happened to your leg?" she burst out.

"Not that you care, girl, but the gout plagues me from time to time."

"I'm sorry to hear that," she said, realizing that it was the truth.

In spite of everything he'd done and all he'd cost her, he was still her father, and seeing him looking so *old* for a man only in his fifties . . . It made her want to cry.

"If you are, I'm surprised. You denied me even

a glance at my grandson." His expression turned resentful. "So am I to assume that your presence here means you have finally acknowledged your duty to your family?"

The unfair words were such a slap in the face that they lessened her sympathy considerably. Belligerence still lurked inside him, after all. "I fulfilled that duty long ago, Papa," she said quietly, "and you know it."

Something flickered in his gaze. Regret? No, Papa never felt regret.

Niall cleared his throat, reminding her that she wasn't here alone, and she started. "Papa, may I introduce Niall Lindsey, the Earl of Margrave."

"Her fiancé," Niall added in a strangely protective tone as he took her hand and planted it firmly in the crook of his arm.

Papa scowled at her. "You have a fiancé, girl? And this is the first I'm hearing of it?"

She bristled. "For one thing, it just happened last night. And for another, it's not as if I'm some wide-eyed innocent who requires my father's permission to—"

"Forgive me for not speaking to you first, sir," Niall said in an ingratiating tone as he squeezed her hand. Hard. "I was simply so swept up in my plans and afraid of letting her get away that I blundered right in."

Well, wasn't he just the smoothest fellow ever? And judging from the slight softening in Papa's features, her father had fallen for it. She wasn't sure whether to admire Niall for his swift thinking, or find him even more suspicious a character.

"But I do mean to start this marriage off right," Niall added, making a point of caressing her hand, which perversely freed a cloud of butterflies in her belly. "That's why I wanted to make up for my blunder by coming to meet you at once."

The way he'd refused to do seven years ago, when he'd had the chance.

That memory scattered the butterflies. He'd toyed with her heart and then had gone on to live his life as he pleased. So no matter what plans he wanted to lure her into privately now, she would resist.

She caught Papa watching her. Dear Lord, she simply must get better at hiding her feelings. "Yes," she said, forcing a smile, "we wanted you to be aware of the engagement."

"And to be part of the wedding plans, of course," Niall said.

She bobbed her head. She'd forgotten that Papa had to be more intimately involved with them, if Niall was to uncover his secrets. Heavens, she wasn't good at all with this subterfuge.

But Papa brightened considerably. "Well then, that's excellent. Always knew she'd marry again. Too pretty not to."

Brilliana stifled a sigh. That had been the only part of her Papa had ever noticed—her looks and what they could bring him.

Niall cast her a surprisingly tender glance. "Too pretty for the likes of me, no doubt. But I shall endeavor to be worthy of her."

Even knowing that the words were merely part of his role, they made her heart flip over—drat the man. She really must do something about these ridiculous reactions to him.

"Worthy of her!" Papa snorted. "Don't be silly. You're an earl. You're more than worthy of her."

"For God's sake, Oswald," said a new voice from down the hall, "the man is trying to pay my niece a compliment. Don't ruin it."

She blinked. "Uncle Toby?"

"In the flesh," he said jovially as he approached.

Her uncle had aged, too, but unlike Papa he still seemed hale and hearty. His dark eyes still gleamed with ever-present humor, and his clothes were of the finest quality, as always.

He came up to envelop her in a hug, then held her out to survey her. "I thought I heard your voice down here. By thunder, but it *is* good to see you. You're looking well."

"As are you." She beamed at him. "And I'm pleased as punch to see you, too. It's been a long time."

Niall nudged her, and she quickly performed the introductions. "Lord Margrave, may I present Mr. Tobias Payne, my father's younger brother and my favorite uncle? Uncle Toby, this is Lord Margrave, my fiancé."

"Your fiancé?" he said with a firm shake of Niall's hand. "Then a lucky man indeed."

"I quite agree, sir," Niall remarked. "I'm afraid I was unaware that Sir Oswald had a brother."

"That's because I'm rarely around," Uncle Toby said. "I live in France."

"Exactly," Brilliana put in. "So what are you doing in London?"

"Bedeviling me, that's what," Papa muttered.

Uncle Toby merely raised an eyebrow at that. "I came a couple of weeks ago to meet with some tradesmen who use my export business. Foolishly, I agreed to stay with my grouch of an elder brother while I was here. I've begun to regret it, I assure you."

"Don't you have an appointment somewhere that's supposed to go well into the evening?" Papa grumbled.

"I do, but I still have a few minutes to visit with my niece."

Papa scowled at him. "So you'll change your plans for *her* but not for me. Even though I told you how badly we need a fourth for our game tonight."

Irritation flashed in Uncle Toby's eyes. "I told you, Oswald, I am not playing cards with that group of rapscallions you call friends. I don't trust half of them, and the other half are so deeply in debt that their vowels are worth practically nothing."

"That's not true," Papa said hotly. "Why, Quinn

Raines is the director of Raines Bank, a perfectly respectable fellow."

A banker? Who dealt with currency? Surely that was a clue to their culprit.

"I know him," Niall said. "He's a member of my club. Seems a decent enough chap."

"You see?" Papa told her uncle. "The earl himself approves of my friends."

Uncle Toby merely snorted.

"Well, I haven't met the others, I expect," Niall said, "but I'd be happy to do so. Since you need a fourth tonight anyway—"

"Of course!" Papa cried. "By all means, come and join us at the Star and Garter. We'll have a jolly time."

She had to admit she was impressed. Niall had made that seem so natural that no one would have thought anything of his offer, least of all her father.

Though her uncle was now frowning at Niall. "Are you much of a gambler then, sir?"

"Of course he is," Papa said dismissively. "He's in a club, ain't he?"

Niall glanced from her father to her uncle. "I enjoy the occasional game of whist as much as the next fellow."

That didn't seem to satisfy Uncle Toby. "So you did a lot of it while you were on the Continent, did you?"

Papa tapped his cane on the floor. "Do you mean to keep me standing on my bad leg all day, peppering my future son-in-law with questions, brother? I thought you were in a hurry to leave."

Her uncle flashed him a strained smile. "I tell you what—why don't you take your daughter's fiancé upstairs to the drawing room, and I'll send her along presently. That'll give her a chance to tell me about her young man, while you ask him all the pertinent questions of a prospective father-in-law."

Although he'd probably meant the words to instruct Papa in what he should do on his daughter's behalf, that apparently went right over Papa's head, for he broke into a smile. "Excellent idea. I can break out the brandy." He clapped Niall on the shoulder. "Let's celebrate, sir, and leave my dour brother to my daughter for the present."

That made her a trifle nervous, but Niall pressed her hand and released her, which she took to mean that he wanted time alone with Papa.

As soon as the two men had moved out of earshot, Uncle Toby bent close. "The Earl of Margrave, eh? It seems my little niece has come up in the world. Smitten by your beauty, I suppose."

Careful, now. Remember that anything you say will go straight to Papa.

She didn't even know if Uncle Toby was involved in the counterfeiting, although that seemed unlikely. Not only had he been a well-respected business owner for years, but he'd generally been the one to get Papa out of his scrapes, to loan him money and advise him to stop his gambling. She just couldn't see Uncle Toby being part of a counterfeiting ring.

Still, best to be cautious and keep playing her role. "His lordship does dote on me," she said lightly.

"*Just* you? Or you and your late husband's estate?"

His concern for her welfare touched her. Especially given that Papa didn't care one whit about it. "What do you mean?"

He surveyed her closely. "Don't take this the wrong way, but I hear Margrave is strapped for funds after his long exile." Worry tightened his lips into a thin line. "Take care, my dear. I wouldn't wish to see you hurt by taking up with a fellow with pockets to let, no matter his station. And a gambler to boot. Given your father's tendencies, well . . ."

"It's fine," she said, torn between the desire to reassure him and the need to further her and Niall's scheme. "Lord Margrave isn't so reckless as all that."

"Are you sure? I would hate to see your marriage end up the way it did last time. Your father says you weren't entirely happy with your former husband."

She cast him a sharp glance. "I'm surprised that Papa even told you about the . . . er . . . true state of affairs in my marriage."

Uncle Toby shrugged. "Oswald says that you avoid him because he's the one who introduced the two of you. And you blamed him when it didn't end well."

She suppressed a snort. *Introduced* them. Right. She studied her uncle's features, but he gave no sign that he knew the truth of that cursed transaction.

Then again, how could he? Aside from the fact that he'd lived in France for years, her father would never have told him. Papa had always resented his successful younger brother, who had more character in his little finger than Papa had in his entire body. Who looked down on Papa for his incessant gambling, and would never have countenanced how she'd become part of repaying Papa's debts.

She had half a mind to set him straight about how her marriage had come about, but if he happened to mention that to Niall, the scoundrel would become even more stubborn about trying to get her into his bed.

And no matter what Niall thought, she didn't need a lover. Especially one who made her heart flip over with a heated look. An intimate kiss. A blatant caress that made her feel so . . .

Oh, curse him to the devil. Why had he come back? He was ruining everything.

Meanwhile, her uncle was still watching her with great concern. "Have you not considered that you might be marrying a fortune hunter?"

Remember the plan. Niall wants you for your beauty; you want him for his title. "Of course I have, but honestly, it doesn't matter. Last time, I married for . . . er . . . affection, and that, as you pointed out, ended badly. This time, I'm marrying for more practical reasons. Granted, his lordship has few funds to commend him. But my first son by him will be an earl. I can't discount that."

Her uncle gaped at her. "When did you become such a cynic about love?"

Withering under his clear disapproval, she murmured, "I'm not marrying him *just* for the title, you know. Lord Margrave is attractive and engaging and, well . . ." She didn't have to fake a blush. "I could do worse."

"You could do better."

She sighed. "I'm a widow with a son. I have few enough good matrimonial prospects even with the dowry." Remembering the picture Lord Fulkham wanted painted of Niall, she added, "Besides, he's a clever fellow. He has big plans for the future for both of our estates. With my money and his resourcefulness, he will do whatever it takes to achieve them."

"Will he?" Uncle Toby looked troubled. "Then you must take care, niece. That sort of fellow can make a dangerous husband."

"I know. But Aunt Agatha will ensure that our marriage settlement protects me." *The way my father couldn't ensure it the first time.* "So for very little risk, I'm gaining an exciting husband who will make me a countess." She pasted a smile to her lips. "How could I not find that appealing?"

"Hmm." He glanced up the stairs. "Well, if you want *me* to look over the settlement, don't hesitate to ask. Even if your father thinks to do so, he's rather heedless about legal matters."

To say the least. "Thank you, Uncle." She stretched up to kiss him on the cheek. "It's much appreciated."

Fortunately, she wouldn't be needing his services. Because the one thing she and Niall would *never* be doing was getting married.

Seven

Niall had come here prepared for anything. Except this.

Sir Oswald was clearly in a bad way financially. Aside from the obvious signs of neglect in the town house, the man's study was the kind of wreck only achieved by a dearth of servants— dirty dishes piled on a corner of the desk, dust settled upon all the surfaces, and candle wax caked on every sconce. If Sir Oswald *was* a criminal, he wasn't very good at it.

And so far, rather than proffering the usual questions about Niall's prospects, the man was more intent upon making sure that Niall didn't expect him to pay for the wedding. His concern for his daughter's future was decidedly lacking, and Niall was biting his tongue half off trying not to comment on that.

It was even more difficult not to ask directly about the estrangement between father and daughter. No point in dredging that up while things were going well—Niall didn't wish to make the man wary of him.

But perhaps he could find out more about Bree's marriage from her father. Surely *that* was an innocuous subject.

"Forgive me, sir, but I'm curious about your daughter's previous husband."

Sir Oswald's dark gaze arrowed in on him, alarm flickering in its depths. "Why? What has Brilliana told you?"

That gave Niall pause. Until he remembered that Bree had hinted at her father having gambled away her dowry, substantially lowering her prospects. "She says she doesn't like to speak of her marriage." When Sir Oswald looked relieved, Niall narrowed his gaze on the man. "Was it not a good match?"

"It was a *brilliant* match!" her father blustered. "Reynold Trevor was a man of property, with substantial wealth. I oversaw the settlement myself. All the advantages were on *her* side. And he was mad for her, too."

"*Too?*" Pain crushed Niall's chest. "So she was mad for him as well?"

Sir Oswald paled, then glanced away. "I'm sure she was. What young woman wouldn't be? A handsome fellow in raptures over marrying her? It's every young girl's dream." It finally seemed to dawn on him that he was speaking to her present fiancé, for he forced a smile. "Not that Trevor was anything compared to *you*, my lord. I'm sure she is even more delighted over *this* match."

If so, she hid it well. In light of her behavior years ago, Niall found that odd. She should be using this situation to draw him in, get him in her snare again.

Unless she was playing a longer, more subtle game. "I know that *I* am delighted," he said smoothly, wondering how to press the man for more information about Trevor's relationship to Bree.

"Excellent, excellent." Calculation gleamed in the old fellow's eyes. "And speaking of my daughter's late husband and his property, I was wondering what you plan to do about Camden Hall. Obviously, you and Brilliana will live at Margrave Manor."

Camden Hall? What the blazes?

Before Niall could even think how to answer, a voice came from the doorway. "We haven't settled all those details yet, Papa. We only just became engaged."

As Bree entered, Niall couldn't help thinking again how lovely she was, how poised and perfect. Tamping down an irrational jealousy of the late Reynold Trevor, he rose, though he noted that her father didn't bother with such a courtesy.

Instead, Sir Oswald settled back against his chair like a man sure of controlling his domain. "Ah, there you are, daughter. I'm merely saying that something must be done about your late husband's estate."

"Not my *late husband's* estate," she said testily. "Silas's. And his lordship and I will deal with that as we see fit."

Though this engagement was all for show, Niall understood her outrage. But discussing it might give them more insight into Sir Oswald's current financial situation and future plans, which Niall needed if he was to pursue this investigation.

With a glance for Bree that he hoped she would read as *Let me take the lead*, Niall offered her his chair before facing her father. "Still, I'm sure we're both curious to know your thoughts concerning Camden Hall, sir."

Just as he'd hoped, her father puffed out his chest. "Since my own property in the country is presently being leased by a gentleman, I'd be happy to help manage my daughter's. It would be better for you to have a member of the family doing that than some stranger, like one of those hired estate managers."

As Bree bristled, Niall laid a restraining hand on her shoulder. "That's a very generous offer, sir." And no doubt the scoundrel had some idea of lining his pockets along the way.

Or was this the man's strategy for escaping London and the watchful eye of the authorities? Was he actually offering to *live* there?

Niall went to lean against one of the bookcases. "But I understand that you have a close-knit circle of friends here in town, and we wouldn't wish to deprive them of your company."

"Oh no, I wouldn't reside at Camden Hall," he said hastily. "I'd simply make occasional visits there to take care of affairs. As you say, I wouldn't want to leave my friends."

And his counterfeiting operation? "Are these the same two who will be at the card game tonight?"

"Oh, there are a few more in my circle. But there's a fashionable affair tonight, so we're short of players." He rolled his eyes. "You know these younger fellows. Can't keep up their fun without rich wives, so Pitford and Dunsleigh are going to the Duke of Lyons's ball to see what young ladies they might hunt up."

According to Fulkham, Lord Pitford was a notorious wastrel and Lord Dunsleigh was a pup with a dandy's love of extravagant cravat knots. The undersecretary didn't consider either of them serious contenders, but wasn't ruling out anyone.

Niall was rather surprised that the duke had invited the two fortune hunters. From what he'd heard, though, Lyons's annual ball was a large affair attended by an enormous crowd. Perhaps he and the duchess had needed more men to partner their female guests.

Which might be why . . . "I was invited to that

as well," Niall said. Mother had been over the moon about it.

"My aunt and I were also planning to attend," Bree put in.

Of course *they* were invited. Bree's dowry made her eminently eligible.

Sir Oswald eyed Niall with alarm. "But you ain't *going*, are you, Margrave? It'll be a tedious affair—nothing more than a marriage mart. And now that you're engaged, you have no need for such. Besides, you did say you'd be my partner at whist tonight."

"Whether I attend the ball depends very much on your lovely daughter. Considering that she and I are both invited—"

"Pish-posh, she can go with her aunt. From what I saw of Lady Pensworth at Brilliana's wedding, she's dragon enough to hold any untoward fellows at bay."

Niall couldn't believe that a man who'd been estranged from his daughter for years could be so dismissive of her desires once she'd finally deigned to visit him again. "Yes, well, I do enjoy dancing with my fiancée."

"But fashionable couples never attend the same affairs," her father complained.

"The newly betrothed ones generally do," Niall snapped, then caught himself. He was supposed to be insinuating himself into Sir Oswald's circles, not teaching the arse how to treat his daughter properly. "But if Bre . . . Brilliana doesn't mind . . ." He trailed off with a glance that he hoped she would interpret correctly.

"It's fine," she said swiftly. "My aunt and I can attend and make your excuses while you play cards with Papa." Then she went on in a tone that bore the perfect blend of concern and wariness typical of a woman marrying a fortune hunter, "But you won't lose *too* much, will you, my dear?"

Ah, very good. She was getting into the spirit of the thing. Best to make him seem reckless from the beginning.

"What makes you think I will lose?" he countered.

"Yes, Brilliana," her father said. "And what right have you to lecture your husband on his gambling?"

Given her sudden stiffening, that remark didn't go over well. "He's not my husband yet, Papa."

"But he will be. And when he is, you won't be dictating to him about his card-playing, I'll wager. For God's sake, girl, he's an earl. He can do as he pleases."

This was the most vulgar conversation Niall had ever participated in. He began to understand Brilliana's resentment toward the man. Did nothing shame him regarding his daughter? Clearly, her mother had been the one to teach her how to behave in polite society.

Despite the conflict with his aims for the

evening, Niall smiled warmly at her, if only to counter her father's dreadful behavior. "Truly, sweeting, if you would prefer that I *not* play—"

That flustered her. "Oh no, I did not mean to say . . . That is, of course you may . . . you *should* play cards with Papa if you wish."

"Good, then it's settled," her father said. "We start at ten o'clock at the Star and Garter."

That gave Niall the opening to go in another direction with the conversation. "So, if Pitford and Dunsleigh aren't going, who's playing tonight?"

Fulkham had given him a list of eight men associated with Sir Oswald.

"Well, aside from Quinn Raines, there's Sir Kenneth Whiting."

Niall's heart nearly stopped. "Of the Essex Whitings?" Fulkham hadn't mentioned that name.

Out of the corner of his eye, he saw Bree stiffen. In a flash, he remembered telling her years ago that Joseph Whiting was the man he'd killed in a duel.

But her father hadn't apparently heard about Niall's duel, for he merely said, "I believe he's from Suffolk, but I'm not sure. Pitford brought him in recently. He's the man's cousin, here from out of town."

Forcing himself to relax, Niall said, "Ah." Whiting was a common enough English surname. No reason to assume that Sir Kenneth was related to Clarissa's assailant.

Though the fellow's recent appearance explained why Fulkham hadn't known of him—unless Fulkham had deliberately not told Niall of the man because he feared Whiting's involvement would make Niall balk.

Niall frowned. It would be just like Fulkham to keep that to himself, the damned bastard. It also made Whiting a good choice for counterfeiter, depending on how recently he'd joined the group—because being connected to Joseph Whiting in itself might show him to be a villain.

He chose his next words carefully. "So, are Raines and Sir Kenneth as feckless as your brother made them sound?"

Sir Oswald waved his hand dismissively. "Pay my sourpuss of a brother no mind. He always disapproves of everyone in my orbit."

That was interesting. Especially since Toby Payne's sudden appearance in England seemed markedly suspicious. "Yes, a pity that your brother doesn't play. I confess myself curious about his export business, since I've just returned from the Continent myself. Does he export from France to England, or the other way around? And what exactly does he export?"

"Wines from France. And other foodstuffs." Sir Oswald leaned forward. "He brought me some excellent French cheeses for my kitchen."

Not exactly the kind of business that would provide much help to a counterfeiter. If the man was a dealer in engravings or ink or some such, that might be different. "Well then, surely his French cheeses make up for his disapproval of your gambling."

"I suppose. Though, truth is, my cook don't really know how to serve them properly. Keeps trying to put mustard on the Camembert." Sir Oswald glanced at his daughter. "Now that you've remembered what you owe your old papa, you could take my kitchen in hand, you know."

When a look of horror crossed her face, Niall stepped in. "I'm afraid she'll be far too busy taking *my* kitchen in hand, sir, to manage yours."

"I was only saying—"

"Trust me, my kitchen will take up a great deal of her time. Indeed, I expect that entertaining on the scale expected of a countess will tax her exceedingly."

That reminder of Niall's position seemed to quell any further suggestions on Sir Oswald's part that Bree should manage his household. Thank God. Niall wasn't sure she could maintain *that* level of deception with her father.

These visits would need to be strictly regulated so she could feel easy enough to be convincing. The hard work of investigation would take place at the gaming tables, anyway.

Just then, the clock chimed, reminding him that they'd likely overstayed their welcome—and the limits of Bree's patience.

He rose. "If I am to join you this evening, sir,

and Bree is to have time to dress for the ball, we should pay the rest of our calls."

Bree's relief was obvious as she stood. "Yes, Papa, you know how it is with a new betrothal. Everyone must be visited."

As her father pushed to a stand, Niall added, "There's no reason for you to show us out, sir. I would not wish to tax your leg any further."

Sir Oswald blinked. "That's right kind of you, Margrave. Right kind, indeed. It does plague me something fierce today."

With a nod, Niall offered his arm to Bree and they headed for the door. But they hadn't even reached it when Sir Oswald called out, "Brilliana!"

Stiffening a fraction, she turned to look back at him. "Yes, Papa?"

"You will bring your boy to see his old grandpapa, won't you?"

A welter of emotions briefly crossed her face before she masked them: fear, resentment, worry. "Of course. When we get the chance."

Niall began to understand her reluctance to expose her son to her father. "Brilliana will be quite busy in the coming weeks," he told Sir Oswald, "so it may not be that soon. There's much to be done to prepare for the wedding, you know."

An odd regret flashed over the older man's face before he stiffened. "Wouldn't want to inconvenience my own daughter," he grumbled.

She stared at him with a certain wistfulness. "I'll see what I can do about bringing him by soon, Papa."

Before Sir Oswald could make some retort to her noncommittal remark, Niall said, "Now, we really must be going, sir. All those calls, you know."

And without waiting for an answer from the old bastard, he led her out into the hall. As they headed down the stairs, she murmured, "Are we really paying other calls after this?"

He lowered his voice. "Not unless you have someone in particular whom you wish to visit. Before I go to the Star and Garter, I need to stop by the club and find out more about your father's compatriots." Particularly Whiting. And Niall wanted to ask Fulkham about the uncle, as well.

When relief crossed her face, he couldn't resist raking her with a slow, heated look. "Besides, we're not finished with our discussion. And I mean to continue it on our way back to your aunt's." Because if she thought he was going to drop their argument from earlier, she'd lost her mind.

Their kisses and caresses had ignited him, and no matter how he warned himself not to fall into the trap of desiring her again, he couldn't help himself. He had to find out why she did this to him.

"There's nothing more to discuss," she said dismissively.

The hell there wasn't. They hadn't quite reached the landing and were blocked from sight both from below and above, so he took advantage of that to halt her for a kiss, a long, deep one that roused his blood, especially when she instantly responded. With his arm about her slender waist, he pressed her into him and took his time enjoying her mouth, his heart hammering all the while.

She tasted like mint leaves and tea, as refreshing as a crisp spring day. He could stand here kissing her forever. He slid his hand down her back to smooth over her bottom and she jerked away, her eyes alight with temper.

But a pretty pink blush spread from her cheeks all the way down her neck. He wondered if it went lower. He meant to find out, and soon. He wanted to learn why a widow who'd borne a child, a woman he'd been sure was calculating and grasping, could blush so believably.

So enticingly. "Nothing to discuss, eh? I can think of a few things."

"Like why your mind is always in the gutter, sir?" she snapped.

"And why you don't seem to mind it much." When she blinked and drew a breath to give him a set-down, he drawled, "Careful, now, sweeting. You don't want your father or the servants speculating about why you're so cross with your new fiancé."

"Then don't give them anything to speculate

about." With a sniff, she hurried down the stairs ahead of him. "Or you will become my *former* fiancé in short order."

He laughed. He liked this new version of Bree, the impudent one with a spine. It aroused him. Especially when her hand glided along the banister ahead of him with such delicacy that he couldn't help imagining it on his chest, his belly . . . his cock.

Deuce take it. He'd better get control of himself or that cursed cock would give him away to the servants downstairs.

So he hurried down to take her by the arm and slow her descent. "Relax, sweeting," he murmured. "It's not a race."

They had another whole flight to traverse, during which he could attempt to get his raging urges under command. By the time they reached the foyer, it was as if they'd never kissed at all.

Outwardly, anyway.

They approached the door, and Jenkins, who was apparently one of Sir Oswald's few remaining servants, appeared from the shadows to open it. He smiled at Bree. "I understand that congratulations are in order, miss . . . I mean, madam."

She smiled warmly at Jenkins. "Listening at doors again, are you?"

The old servant chuckled. "If a body doesn't do that around here, he won't know what's going on until the rug is pulled out from under him, I swear."

Her amusement faded. "I understand completely." She cast a furtive glance back up the stairs. "Papa isn't . . . too badly on the rocks these days, is he?"

The butler shrugged. "Still paying me and Cook and a couple of maids to stay on. But his brother isn't far wrong—most of his friends are rapscallions, and they'll bleed him dry if they can."

That piqued Niall's interest. What if someone else had used her father's gambling debts to force the man into putting the counterfeits into circulation? Then Sir Oswald would be more a victim of blackmail than a perpetrator of the crime. It was certainly something to consider.

"Thank you, Jenkins," Bree said, and pressed the elderly man's hand. "I promise to bring my boy Silas when next I visit."

The servant's face lit up. "It would be an honor to meet the young master."

She gave him a wry laugh. "He's sixteen months old. You may not think it quite such an honor when he's running and laughing in the foyer."

Jenkins turned serious. "This house could do with some running and laughing. There's been far too little of it since you and the mistress left."

She'd taken her mother away? Before the woman's death? She *had* said that she would go with him if she could take her mother, but . . .

Niall ignored his twinge of unease. Perhaps the

servant hadn't meant that the two women had left the household at the same time.

Jenkins shot Niall a furtive glance. "You will be married here, won't you?"

When she blanched at that reminder that this whole thing was a farce, Niall said, "We haven't yet decided where to have the ceremony, but we're considering my church in Mayfair."

The old servant bobbed his head. "Of course, my lord. I wasn't thinking. A man of your consequence would certainly wish something more impressive than a run-down town house."

"Thank you for understanding," Bree said, with an odd catch in her voice. "And now we really must go, mustn't we, my dear?"

"Yes," Niall said, and led her out.

She was quiet as they walked down the steps. Too quiet, as if a heavy weight was crushing the breath from her. Though he'd hoped to kiss her again once they were inside the carriage, her demeanor held him back. He watched and waited, hoping she would tell him what was bothering her.

As the coach pulled away, she gazed out the window at the town house. "I hate lying to them."

Ah. "I can understand that."

"Papa is one thing. At worst, he's part of a criminal enterprise, and at best, he's some criminal's dupe. But Aunt Agatha and Jenkins and even Uncle Toby . . ." She shook her head. "They don't deserve to be swept up in this . . . scheme."

This was probably not the time to mention that her uncle was as much a suspect as the others. For that matter, so was Jenkins. Anyone close to her father could have changed out those notes for the counterfeits.

"Uncle Toby has always been so good to Papa in the past," she went on. "If not for him, Papa would have ended up in debtors' prison a hundred times."

"How so?"

She shrugged. "Uncle Toby would speak to Papa's creditors, get extensions, loan him funds if need be. Of course, that was when my uncle was still living in London. After he left, he couldn't do those sorts of things for Papa anymore."

"Perhaps that's why he moved," he said wryly.

She sighed. "As you may have noticed, Papa can be a trial to those closest to him."

To say the least.

They rode a moment in silence before she swung an earnest gaze to him. "Which is precisely why I should thank you."

"For what?"

"For making this easier. For managing it all so deftly." Absently, she smoothed her immaculate skirts. "For nipping in the bud Papa's attempts to draw me back into his household."

"I wasn't doing it for you," he lied. "It's just part of the game—finding out his secrets. Determining whether he's guilty. Accomplishing our mission."

"You do it very impressively. I would never have guessed you weren't genuinely interested in pleasing Papa and playing cards with his scurrilous friends." Her face clouded over. "I'm afraid I wasn't nearly as adept at it. I hope I didn't ruin things."

"Not one bit. And of course you weren't as adept. You're a novice at this, while I am not."

She cocked her head. "What do you mean?"

He hesitated, but couldn't see any reason not to tell her. This was his last mission. He was back in England, where his efforts for his country would be lauded, not despised, if they were ever discovered. And if knowing something of his past made her feel more secure, more convinced that she was in good hands with him, it could only help their scheme.

"Has it not occurred to you to wonder about my friendship with Fulkham?" he said. "And why he was so sure I would agree to help him?"

"You said it was because he got you that pardon."

"Yes, but they don't just hand out pardons willy-nilly, even for men like me. Fulkham was able to argue that I deserved one because, among other things, I spent most of my exile feeding him information I gleaned while moving among the aristocracy of Spain and Portugal."

She gaped at him. "Wh-what are you saying?"

"I'm saying, sweeting, that for the past seven years, I've been serving as a spy. Off and on."

The expression on her face made it quite clear that she found the very idea preposterous. "I don't understand."

Her obstinate refusal to accept what he was telling her annoyed him. Did she really think him so feckless? "I'm not sure how I can put it any plainer."

"A . . . a spy. For England?"

"Of course for—" He muttered an oath. "I just told you I was feeding information to Fulkham. Who do you think *he* works for, for God's sake?"

"Yes, but why would he choose . . . Why, given your . . . well . . . reputation, would he think you would be good at . . . at such a thing?"

"He didn't. He took a chance on me since I was ideally situated and in something of a pickle, given that I couldn't return to England." When she merely stared at him with incredulity, he added irritably, "I first met him when he was posted in Spain. In the beginning he only knew me as Mr. Lindsey, but he eventually pieced together who I really was."

"An escaped murderer."

Although technically that was true, he hated that *she* saw him like that. Still. "Yes. He confronted me about it, and I was, as you might imagine, alarmed, but he said he was willing to keep my secret from the authorities in England if I would . . . keep my ear to the ground and send him information from time to time."

"What kind of information? I mean, what could you possibly—"

"I was still a viscount, you know. And after Father died, I was a newly minted earl—except that I couldn't return to officially accept the title. It put me in a rather unique position. As an exiled lord, I was expected to be bitter, so I could move among foreign aristocrats more as one of them, than as a suspicious intruder. And it helped that I made a concerted attempt to improve my Spanish and Portuguese."

"So that's why you and Lord Fulkham are so . . . chummy."

"Exactly. Fulkham had just been promoted and was returning to England. He wanted someone he could trust to give him the sort of reports he needed. And he deduced that I would be good at that."

"Excellent deduction," she muttered, but she still looked as if she was trying to reconcile his admission with her own opinion of him.

"What did you *think* I was doing all that time?"

"I don't know." She flicked her hand dismissively. "The same things all men of your sort do on the Continent."

A slow burning began in his throat. "Men of my *sort*? What sort is that?"

"You know, wild-living gentlemen of rank and means. You . . . you gamble and drink and cavort with mistresses and—"

"Wait one moment," he cut in. "Why on earth would you think I'd had a mistress?"

"Come now, Niall," she said coldly. "Did you

really expect me not to find out the truth about the duel?" When he froze, she added, "Oh, of course you did. Men like you blithely do as you please, and the women in your lives are supposed to look the other way. Well, it was hard to do that when I learned that you and Mr. Whiting fought over a mistress whom you shared. So if you had one while you and I were courting, then—"

"What the blazes?" He leaned forward, outrage boiling up in his belly. "Why would you think we dueled over a mistress, much less one we shared?"

She tipped up her chin. "Because everyone said that you dueled over some woman."

His heart sank. The gossips had gotten that much right? He'd hoped that Father and Mrs. Whiting had succeeded in squelching any talk about it, but he should have known better.

He scrubbed one hand over his face. What a deuced muddle. He wanted to set her straight, but it wasn't his secret to tell. And he still wasn't sure if Bree could be trusted with such a story. If she couldn't, or if she used the knowledge to blackmail him into getting her out of this scheme with her father—

That would be disastrous. Clarissa was happily married now; she and Edwin damned well wouldn't want the word to get out that she'd been raped before they met, or that Niall had dueled with Whiting over it. That kind of gossip cut one off completely from society. No one ever blamed the man; they always blamed the woman.

Then again, Bree was Clarissa's friend. Would she ruin her friend's reputation that way?

He couldn't take the chance, not without speaking to Clarissa. And with Clarissa six months pregnant, that might not be wise either. Women who were breeding were notoriously delicate. If bringing up the rape sent her into a decline or cost her the child, he would never forgive himself.

"Judging from your silence," she said tightly, "I can only assume that the rumors about the duel were true."

That brought him up short. "Of course not. What kind of man did you take me for?"

"You did have a reputation as a rogue."

He gritted his teeth. "Yes, but that was before I met you." When she looked unconvinced, he added, "Did you really think I could have wooed you—bloody well asked you to marry me—while also keeping a mistress?"

She thrust out her chin. "Why not? Other men of rank do it all the time. And you *didn't* ask me to marry you—you asked me to run off with you."

"Blast it, you keep making a distinction that I never did! I fully intended to marry you the moment we could arrange it."

"So you say."

"Do you think I'm lying?" That sent anger

roaring up in him. "Oh, for God's— Did you even care one whit for me? Because I begin to think you didn't. Certainly not if you believed any gossip that tarred me as such a scoundrel."

The carriage halted in front of her aunt's house, but neither of them moved to get out when the footman opened the door. "Leave us," Niall barked, and waved the man away.

As soon as the footman shut the door and disappeared, she said, "You left me no choice. You wouldn't tell me the real reason you fought the duel."

The words hung in the carriage, blunt and truthful. And he simply couldn't answer her unspoken question. "Unfortunately, that situation hasn't changed. Several people would be affected if the truth ever got out."

Her gaze narrowed on him. "*Several?* What, was your mistress married? You're protecting her husband? Her family? *Whiting's* family?"

"I had no mistress!"

"But you two did fight over a woman."

"I . . ." He gritted his teeth. "I cannot even reveal that much." Because if he said he'd fought over a woman who was not his mistress, it wouldn't take her long to figure out that it was his sister.

Assuming she even believed him. The fact that she had listened to gossip about him instead of listening to her heart—if she even possessed such a thing—stuck in his craw.

And that made him lash out at her. "I suppose you want me to believe that your entire reason for going off to marry Trevor only a few months after my departure was because you listened to some scurrilous gossip that said I was bedding another woman while courting *you*."

Her face grew shuttered. "That was part of it, yes."

"Right." Throwing himself back against the squabs, he crossed his arms over his chest. "So it had nothing to do with the fact that I was no longer going to be able to provide you with all the things you craved—the fancy house, the fine gowns, the prestige of being the wife of an earl's heir."

She gaped at him. "I never cared about any of that!"

"Really? I recall hearing you talk with your maid about 'snagging' an earl's heir."

A flush spread over her cheeks. "That was not . . . I was not . . ." She swallowed. "It wasn't how it sounded."

Now he was *finally* getting at the truth. "Wasn't it? Because you certainly balked at running away with me. And the only reason I can think of for that was your realization that if you followed me into exile, you would lose all the advantages of being married to a man of rank and property."

Fury flashed in her eyes. "How dare you? I would have followed you to the ends of the earth, if not for Mama's being ill."

"Yet you married Trevor while she was still around."

"Because marrying *him* allowed me to take Mama with me."

That stunned him speechless.

"I didn't care about your going into exile," she went on. "I *loved* you."

Fighting to ignore the power of those words—and the fact that they were in the past tense—he clenched his hands into fists at his sides to keep from reaching out to shake the truth out of her. "You had an odd way of showing it."

"So did you, taking up with another woman. You merely saw me as one of your conquests. I daresay if I'd gone with you, I would have regretted it. It's just as your father told me: You were not—"

"My father," he interrupted, his blood going cold. "What did my father have to do with it?"

She gazed steadily at him. "He's the one who told me it was a mistress that you and Mr. Whiting fought over."

"My father," he echoed hollowly, unsure what to think. "Told you I had a mistress."

"Yes, the one time I met with him. I asked him about the rumors that you two had fought over a woman, and he told me it was true. That you'd dueled over some light-skirt."

Why would he . . . Damnation. Could Father have panicked when Bree had repeated the rumors that the duel was over a woman? Might he have said the only thing he knew would deflect the gossips from suspecting that the duel had been over Clarissa?

But Father had to have known it would also have been the only thing to poison Bree against him forever. And Niall had made it very clear how important she was to him. Father had sworn to do what he could to help her.

His heart began to pound. No—it wasn't possible. Father wouldn't have betrayed him like that. Not after what Niall had done, the sacrifices he'd made. The very idea was . . . was . . .

Unable even to consider it, he pinned Bree with a hard look. He would get her to admit the truth if it was the last thing he did. "That's a bloody lie, and you damned well know it."

Eight

The conviction in Niall's voice took Brilliana completely aback. He seemed genuinely shocked by the idea of his father telling her about his . . . peccadilloes.

Well, of course he was. Men were supposed to keep each other's salacious secrets. And a father should almost certainly keep his son's.

"It is *not* a lie, I swear." She tipped up her chin. "Perhaps you should have instructed him better not to reveal the truth."

"It wasn't the truth, blast it!" He looked like a pugilist staggering from a blow.

"Then why did he say it?"

Niall glowered at her. "I don't believe he did. He wouldn't lie like that. Not about me. Not to you. He knew how I felt about you."

"You mean, he knew you wanted me in your bed since you apparently couldn't get your paramour to go with you."

She choked down bile, remembering how news of the real reason for the duel had sent her spiraling down into despair. Until then, she'd hung her hopes on Niall saving her from having to marry Reynold, but after his father had revealed the truth, she'd begun to think that Reynold might be the lesser of two evils.

"He knew I loved you," Niall bit out.

The words sang in her . . . before she reminded herself that they were lies. "That's not what *he* said. He was very kind about why there was no point in his sending on my letter, but—"

Niall pounced on that. "What letter? He never told me about a letter."

"Well, I wrote one. Because I needed you. I met your father so I could give him the letter to send to you. But he said I had misconstrued your . . . interest in me. That sending it would be futile."

Pure shock showed on his face. "That can't be true." Though he now sounded a bit less certain. "He swore he would pass on anything you gave him, any news of you." His voice hardened into conviction. "My father was a man of honor. He always kept his word."

That unsettled her. "Perhaps he thought he wouldn't be able to find you."

"He found me well enough when he sent me money. And the newspaper announcement of your bloody nuptials."

That sparked *her* temper. "Are you saying he lied to me about . . . about how you felt?"

His eyes glittered at her. "I'm saying that you're making the whole thing up to malign his character. He's dead, after all. It's not as if he can defend himself."

"Oh, for goodness' sake, why would I do that?"

His features looked carved from ice. "I don't know. So you can make yourself look less like the adventuress you were, and more like my beleaguered sweetheart?"

The attack came so out of the blue that it snatched the breath from her lungs. "An adventuress! That's what you thought of the woman you claimed to love."

He leaned forward to stare her down. "Who married another man scant months after I left. Just today, your father told me you were 'mad for' Trevor."

The very idea of Papa speaking such an untruth made her shake with fury. "So you're listening to my *father* now, the man who may very well be counterfeiting banknotes, who only looks out for himself, who wants to take over Camden Hall and weasel his way into every aspect of my life."

That seemed to bring him up short. Temporarily.

"Fine," he said in a hard voice. "What was in this letter you wanted sent to me?"

"I thought you said there was no letter?" she spat.

He muttered a foul oath. "What do you *claim* was in the letter?"

She glared at him. No matter what she told him, he would gainsay it. Meanwhile, he wouldn't admit anything about the duel, he called her a liar and an adventuress, and he acted as if she should tell him all the humiliating little details of her life, while he pretended he had never abandoned her and had never had a mistress. Well, she'd had enough of bullying men.

She'd had enough of *him*. "You can go to the devil, you and Lord Fulkham both." She opened the door to the carriage. "I don't have to put up with your plotting and scheming and this ridiculous farce of an engagement. Nothing is worth enduring your company."

As she climbed down from the carriage, he caught her arm. "We are not finished."

She snatched her arm free. "Oh yes, we are."

Anger darkening his handsome features, he jumped out. "And your father? What about him?" With a glance up at the coachman, he bent to hiss, "Will you let him hang?"

Her stomach clenched. "No. I'll simply have to find another way."

But as she hurried into the house, she knew that finding another way was impossible. So what was she to do now?

She'd have to beg Lord Fulkham to call off this mad scheme. Surely they could put their heads together and figure out how to cut Niall out.

Because she was *not* putting up with him for one more moment.

～

Niall's gut twisted as he watched Bree disappear into the house. He'd handled that with all the finesse of a drunk playing billiards. He should have elicited her confession with subtle questioning.

Deuce take it, he shouldn't have tried eliciting anything! This mission wasn't about her and him, and the fact that he'd tangled their lives up in it showed how far afield he'd gone from investigating counterfeiting.

He'd have a devil of a time explaining to Fulkham how he'd managed to alienate the one woman who could enable them to get close to Sir Oswald.

But damnation, she drove him mad!

Throwing himself back into the carriage, he ordered his coachman to drive on, then sat and stewed. How could she accuse his father of such deceit? The idea that Father had seen her and never said a word to him about it, *knowing* how Niall felt . . .

God rot her—his father would never have told her that the duel had been over a mistress!

Unless it was to protect Clarissa.

No, how could he believe Father would have purposely cut him off from his love?

Part of their conversation the day of his departure came to him: *The last thing you need as you head off to an uncertain future is to be saddled with a wife who's unhappy about your exile. She did you a favor, don't you see? Now you can start life over abroad without such a burden.*

Niall's throat closed up. What if Father had decided to take matters into his own hands? To ensure that Niall wasn't "saddled" with the wrong sort of wife?

He recoiled. It wasn't possible. His father had promised to help her, to treat her like Niall's fiancée. He'd *sworn* it.

He'd also voiced skepticism that she would rise to the occasion and follow Niall to the Continent, but still, he'd made the vow. And Father had never broken a vow.

That you know of.

Niall drew himself up. No, blast it! He refused to believe it. Just look at how Bree had refused to answer when he'd demanded to know what was in the letter. Didn't that prove she was lying?

Or . . . protecting her dignity. Because if she really did believe that he'd fought a duel over some mistress, it was no wonder she was wary around him. And he *had* called her an adventuress.

He winced. He'd said things he shouldn't have, accused her of things he wasn't even sure she'd done. What he'd seen of her today warred with the image of her he'd built up in his head through the years.

And if she were telling the truth about the letter . . .

She couldn't be. He must stop letting her words lodge inside his brain. Not when he had no way of confirming them.

Or—did he? Fulkham might know more about her marriage and what had precipitated it. Failing that, perhaps he could get the truth out of Sir Oswald.

That thought sobered him. He still had a mission. She probably wouldn't tell anyone tonight that she'd jilted him. Surely she wasn't *that* reckless. So he could still go to the card game later and see what he could find out.

Perhaps that would be enough to give Fulkham something to go on. Or perhaps by tomorrow she would have come to her senses and realized she had to continue with this.

Either way, he still wanted to see what he could learn from Fulkham about her marriage. And he needed to discuss the new fellow, Whiting, with the spymaster before the card game, too.

With a clear goal in mind, he sought to not think about her and her accusations and focus on the mission. He changed clothes for the evening, then headed to St. George's. Unfortunately, Fulkham wasn't there, but Quinn Raines was in the otherwise empty reading room, dining on a sandwich while he scanned the evening paper.

Excellent. Why not start there? At least Niall could take his mind off Bree for a while. And Raines might have a different perspective on Sir Oswald's compatriots than Fulkham.

Being the director of his father's bank, Raines was Fulkham's prime suspect, although Niall thought that seemed too obvious. Yes, the man would be more than familiar with how to counterfeit a banknote, but would he really be so foolish as to risk his own reputation and that of his bank to do so?

Then again, Fulkham based his suspicions on the fact that Raines made a conscious effort to avoid him. That wouldn't mean anything in anyone else, since the undersecretary of the foreign office would intimidate just about anyone. But Raines dealt with foreign banks regularly. One would think he'd relish a connection to the foreign office.

Niall called for a bottle of wine from the steward, then took a seat opposite Raines. "So, I hear you'll be part of the card game at the Star and Garter tonight."

Raines gave a start and set aside his paper. "I will indeed. You too?"

Niall nodded. "Sir Oswald invited me."

"Ah, yes. I heard you became engaged to his daughter. You won the prize that many a bachelor has been eyeing."

The odd trace of bitterness in his tone made Niall bite back a hot retort. "Even you?"

"Hardly. My interest lies elsewhere." His face clouded over. "For all the good it's doing me."

That surprised him. Raines was an attractive enough fellow, despite the swarthy looks that came from his mother, the daughter of a Spanish count. Raines might not be English nobility, but his family held great consequence in the city. Another reason Niall wasn't inclined to think him a counterfeiter.

"Do I know the lady lucky enough to hold your attention?" Niall asked. "Perhaps I can put in a good word."

Raines stiffened. "I'd rather not say. Her family is unaware of my interest just now. Best to keep it that way for the moment. You understand."

"Better than you think. And let me give you a word of advice. Don't keep it secret too long." Because what if, God forbid, Niall's caution years ago had cost him his lady? What if Bree *had* been telling the truth? "That always ends badly."

He must have allowed a bit too much emotion into his voice, for Raines cocked his head. "Sounds like the voice of experience."

"You have no idea." Swiftly, Niall changed the subject. "So, this game tonight. You're Whiting's partner?"

"Temporarily. While he's been in town, his cousin has been his partner, though Pitford usually partners with Sir Oswald. Now that Whiting's cousin abandoned him for Lyons's ball, I told Whiting I'd step in, although I generally partner with Dunsleigh. You'll have the advantage of me, since I assume you've played with your future father-in-law before."

"Actually, no."

That caught Raines's attention. "Odd. He's very clannish. Doesn't let too many new fellows into our circle."

"Then I consider myself lucky to be invited."

Raines snorted. "Sir Oswald is the lucky one. I daresay he wants you for the same reason he wanted me: your deep pockets."

"I suspect the reason is merely my new family connection to him, since my pockets aren't as deep as I'd like. But I'm hoping to plump them up this evening."

"Well, don't hope too hard. Whiting is a terrific player. We both are." Raines stated it as fact. "We'll give you a run for your money."

"I have a trick or two up my sleeve myself. No pun intended."

The conversation then turned to other things. Niall itched to ask Raines about Whiting's family connections, but aside from the fact that Raines probably didn't know much, it was unwise to rouse the man's curiosity, in case he *had* heard the gossip about Niall's long-ago duel.

They were engaged in an amicable conversation about Spanish cuisine and where Niall might find a cook familiar with it when Raines trailed off. Niall followed the man's gaze to see Fulkham entering the club.

Raines's lips tightened into a grim line. "Do you know the undersecretary?"

"We've conversed a few times. Why?"

"What did you think of him?"

"That he's good at what he does."

If that alarmed Raines, he gave no sign. "No doubt he is," he said blandly, then rose. "I'll see you later at the game."

The reason for the man's abrupt departure became apparent when Fulkham approached Niall. As Raines disappeared into another room, Fulkham took the man's seat and raised an eyebrow. "You see what I mean? Always flees when I come near him."

"There might be any number of reasons for that. Could it have something to do with his mother's being Spanish?"

"I doubt it. I was posted in Spain long after she married Raines's father." Fulkham tapped his fingers on the chair arm. "It's odd. That's all I'm saying." He looked around the room, but for the moment, it was still empty. His gaze arrowed in on Niall. "So, how did it go with Sir Oswald?"

"I met him and his brother."

"Ah, yes, Toby Payne."

"You didn't mention him."

Fulkham shrugged. "He is as respectable a gentleman as his brother is not. To my knowledge, he's never been accused of so much as one infraction, in business or otherwise. Besides, the counterfeit currency appeared weeks before he showed up in London. So I'd be very surprised if he were involved."

"Ah. Still, it wouldn't hurt to look at him more closely."

"By all means, keep an eye on him. I'll see if my associates at the French embassy can tell me anything about his business affairs in Paris. After the debacle with Durand, they owe me a favor." He drew out a cigar and lit it. "Have you had any luck in your attempt to get chummy with Sir Oswald and the rest?"

"I have. Sir Oswald invited me to their card game tonight, but it's just four of us—him, me, Raines, and a man named Sir Kenneth Whiting."

Fulkham started. "Where did *he* come from?"

"Apparently, he's Pitford's cousin." Though Fulkham looked genuinely surprised, Niall fixed him with a hard glance. "Is he Joseph Whiting's relation as well?"

"If he is, it's a distant connection. I've never heard of him. But I can find out. I'm sure he's in *Debrett's*." He gazed uneasily at Niall. "If he *is* connected to Whiting, you're not going to have a problem with that, are you?"

"Not if *he* doesn't. Which he may, if they were close and he's heard that I killed his relation. Though if the latter is the case, I'm sure he'll make that quite clear tonight."

"Perhaps you should cancel. Wait until he's not one of the cardplayers. Or until I can find out more about him and why he's in town."

"I can handle it. Besides, he's as much a suspect as the rest. And tonight might be my only chance to play, anyway."

A scowl knit Fulkham's brow. "Why?"

Blast, how he hated admitting this. "I have somehow managed to . . . infuriate Mrs. Trevor. She refuses to go on with our faux engagement."

Fulkham's face cleared. "That was quick."

His reaction took Niall aback. "You don't seem upset."

The arse had the audacity to chuckle. "I'm sure you can turn her up sweet again. As the bard said, 'The course of true love never did run smooth.'"

Fulkham's mention of true love gave Niall pause. "Exactly how much do you know about my connection to Bree?"

"Bree?"

Damnation. "Just answer the question."

Fulkham shrugged. "I know that you first met her in Bath, that you courted her secretly for months . . . that after the duel you asked her to run away with you and were refused. Temporarily, anyway."

Niall blinked. "How the blazes did you—"

"I told you, I talked to her maid, Gilly. Though the poor woman was turned off shortly after you left England—the family couldn't afford her anymore—she eventually married. But her husband had lost his post, so once she learned I'd be willing to get him another in exchange for her information, she was more than happy to chat away."

His heart pounding, Niall leaned forward. "Did she happen to tell you how Bree ended up married to Reynold Trevor?"

"I didn't ask. It wasn't relevant. I only wanted to know about you and her."

"God rot you, Fulkham, what good are you?" Niall muttered.

"Don't *you* know?"

"No. And Bree won't talk about it."

"Well, you can't blame her. Her idiot husband gambled away the family's money, and then stumbled into a river drunk. Probably purposely."

His blood ran cold. "What do you mean?"

"Rumor has it he committed suicide. Can't be sure, though. You ought to ask Warren. He might know."

"He might, but he's on his honeymoon and inaccessible." Niall swore under his breath. "What else does rumor say about her marriage?"

"You know, old chap, I was only joking about the course of true love," Fulkham drawled, "but given your surprising interest in everything about Mrs. Trevor, perhaps I shouldn't have been."

"Damn you, I need to know. For the mission."

"Right. For the mission." Fulkham tapped his chin. "Well, it's not widely acknowledged, but I did hear from one of my . . . er . . . lackeys that Trevor courted her for weeks. Yet she only married him after her father lost a huge amount of money to his father, Captain Mace Trevor, in a high-stakes card game. Make of that what you will."

Niall's heart plummeted into his stomach. "Are you saying that her father *sold* her to Trevor? To pay his gambling debts?"

"No. I'm only stating what I heard."

Still, what Fulkham had heard was damning. What was more, it made perfect sense. And cast an entirely different light on her marriage. What had she said to her father, something about fulfilling her duty to the family long ago?

That scurrilous bastard. If his debts had been so massive that paying them would have crippled the family financially, and he'd forced her to . . .

Oh, God. A chill coursed down his spine. What if *that* had been the subject of the letter Father had refused to send for her? A plea for his help? To save her family, to save *her* from an arranged marriage?

No—surely she would have said something to him today, if that were the case.

Right. After he'd called her an adventuress. While she thought him a rogue who kept a mistress while begging *her* to run away with him. She believed he hadn't truly intended to marry her.

At least she *claimed* to have believed it, based on things his father supposedly had told her. Blast it all to hell. What was he to think?

He rose. "I have to go."

Fulkham glanced at his pocket watch. "It's a bit early still for a card game, isn't it?"

"Yes. It doesn't start for three more hours." But that wasn't where he was going. He had plenty of time for that later. He had to talk to her. Had to find out the truth. Had to *make* her tell him.

"If you're going to see Mrs. Trevor, I would advise you to tread lightly. We still need her."

Deuce take the man for always reading his mind. "I know. That's why I intend to, as you say, turn her up sweet. If I can."

And if she would even see him. And talk to him.

He frowned. That might be difficult to manage. She was damned angry. And though he might deserve some of that anger, she might not let him close enough to admit it.

Then an idea came to him. "Fulkham, I need one more favor." Picking up a sheet of St. George's Club stationery from a nearby writing desk, he handed it to the spymaster, along with a quill. "Here's what I want you to write. . . ."

Nine

Brilliana stood in her aunt's drawing room, staring down at the sealed note a liveried footboy had been ordered to put directly into her hand. Fortunately, that was easy, since Aunt Agatha had been taken with a horrible headache and had been resting in her bedchamber since before Brilliana's return. Thank heaven. She hadn't been looking forward to explaining why she'd gone to see Papa.

Now she had something else to deal with. And this dratted note had better not be from Niall, or she'd throw it in the fire.

But it wasn't; it was from his cursed friend, Lord Fulkham. Apparently Niall had wasted no time in asking the man to intercede.

Dear Mrs. Trevor,

I gather that Lord Margrave has behaved in
a less than gentlemanly manner and managed

to set you against him. While I understand
how that could happen, given his strong
opinions, I assure you I do not condone such
behavior.

There is still the matter of your father. So I
hope you will do me the courtesy of meeting me
in Bedford Square garden as soon as you receive
this to discuss how to handle the situation.
As I emphasized upon our last meeting, it is
imperative that we not be seen together, and
since it is dusk and the trees are thick, meeting
in the park seems the wisest course.

If you cannot meet with me, please send
a note to that effect with my emissary and
arrange some other time or place.

> Yours sincerely,
> Lord Fulkham

She glanced at the waiting footboy, who was
dressed in a livery unfamiliar to her, probably the
baron's. She'd hoped to have more time to consider what to say to his lordship. Now that the
full heat of her anger at Niall had dimmed, she
wasn't as sure of her position.

She was still furious at him for calling her an

adventuress, but Niall's reaction to her remarks about his mistress put everything in a new light. Because his father had been relatively kind, she'd believed him when he'd told her of Niall's mistress. Had she been too hasty, perhaps? Her accusations had clearly shocked Niall.

It was true he'd once been a spy and was clearly good at lying when necessary, so perhaps he was equally good at hiding his feelings. But somehow she thought there was more to it than that. He'd seemed genuinely horrified by her claim—she'd seen it in his eyes.

And surely her instincts about him hadn't been as bad as all that back then, had they? Although she'd seen evidence of the rogue in him, she'd also truly believed him when he'd claimed to love her. What if that had been the real Niall after all?

She sighed. And what if it had not?

"Mrs. Trevor?" the footboy prodded. "Do you have an answer for the master? I'm either to bring you with me to the park or carry back a response."

Might as well get this discussion over with. Perhaps Lord Fulkham knew the truth about the duel. If he did he might not tell her, but even a lack of response would tell her something.

"Let's go," she told the footboy.

With a nod, he preceded her to the door.

On the way out, she told her aunt's footman that she was going for a stroll in the park. He wouldn't find that unusual since she walked there often, and today it was lovely, with the sun setting over the houses in shades of vermilion, lavender, and citron, the vivid emerald-green plane trees standing in stark contrast below.

Perhaps when she was done with Lord Fulkham, she would return to the house for her watercolor box and attempt to capture all that beauty. The prospect of that calmed her nerves—until she entered the gates of the private park and caught sight of a gentleman dressed in evening attire with his back to her. Then her stomach knotted once again.

Because the man had sun-kissed hair and a familiar build and—

"Here she is, my lord," the footboy said.

"Thank you, Pip. That will be all."

Curse Niall to the devil. Pip was *his* servant, clearly.

As the lad disappeared out the gate and Niall faced her, her nervousness twisted into pique. "I should have known. I suppose *you* wrote that note."

"No." Niall stalked toward her. "Fulkham wrote it at my behest."

"Of course." Bitterness sharpened her tone. "He doesn't want to lose my help, so he sent his lackey to argue on his behalf."

At the word *lackey*, Niall gave a faint smile, which made her turn on her heel to head back to the gate. "Don't go, Bree," he called after her. "I've come to apologize."

She slanted a suspicious glance back at him. "Because Lord Fulkham requires it."

"No."

"I don't believe you."

"There's a lot of that going around."

That he could be so flippant about their earlier argument *really* sparked her temper. Without another word, she marched for the gate.

"I've learned what caused the rift with your father!" he cried behind her.

As her heart dropped, she paused with her hand on the latch. "Have you?" she said shakily. Oh, Lord, what had he heard? Because if he'd heard the truth . . .

He came up beside her and turned her toward him. "Although I don't know all the details, I learned enough to piece things together. Correct me if I'm wrong, but you married Reynold Trevor to keep your father and mother out of debt, didn't you?"

His pitying expression was almost as awful as his earlier insults about her being an adventuress. Feeling suddenly small and defenseless, she crossed her arms over her chest. "I suppose Fulkham told you all about it. Lord only knows how he found out."

"He's a spymaster. He hears things . . . like the fact that you only agreed to marry the man after your father lost a great deal of money to Trevor's father. So I could only think—"

"I know exactly what you think." Her throat

tightened until it felt raw. "That I was forced into it. That I'm some . . . some pathetic female who couldn't see her way out of a marriage she didn't want." She lifted her chin. "But that's not true. I went into it knowing exactly what I was getting into. So if you intend to stand there feeling sorry for me—"

"I wouldn't," he said, so fiercely that someone passing by on the street cast them a curious glance. With a low curse, he drew her deep into a secluded part of the garden. "But you should have told me."

"I *did*! At least, I tried to." Her emotions had veered so wildly all day that she could no longer resist the tears burning her eyes. Brushing away the few that leaked out, she said, "I put it all in the l-letter that you're sure I never wr-wrote—"

Tugging her into his arms, he held her close. "Shh, shh, sweeting. Forget everything I said in a temper. I'm an arse. I admit it."

"Yes, you are," she said, trying not to sniffle. She *hated* crying in front of him, especially after this afternoon.

"Tell me about Trevor," he said in a voice infinitely kind. "Please?"

It was the "please" that did her in. "What do you . . . want to know?" she muttered into his shirt.

He rubbed her back. "Fulkham said he courted you for weeks." A fractured breath escaped him. "So . . . you did care about him?"

"Of course I cared about him. He was my husband. I had his *child*."

His arms went slack. "So you were in love with him."

Oh, how she wanted to say that she had been. But even if he wouldn't be truthful with her, she couldn't lie to him. Not anymore. "I didn't say that."

Niall drew back to fix her with a hard look. "So you never loved him."

"He . . . he was my friend. And he did love *me*, poor man. He actually proposed marriage twice. The first time was a month after you left. I refused him as gently as I could. I was still hoping that once Mama had . . . passed on, I could be with you." Her voice hardened. "I hadn't yet heard the rumors about your fighting over a woman."

"They *were* rumors, Bree, nothing more," he said hoarsely, dragging her close again. "As I told you years ago, the truth was . . . *is* complicated."

Fighting to ignore her desire to believe him, she pushed free of his embrace. "Your father didn't seem to think so."

Pain slashed across his face. "My father—right." He thrust his hands into his greatcoat pockets. "Let's assume for the moment that I'm telling the truth about not having a mistress, and that you're telling the truth about what my father said. Why did you believe him?"

"He was your father. Why wouldn't I?"

He raked his hand through his hair. "Because he might have had another motive for blackening my reputation? You may recall I was initially reluctant to introduce you."

"Yes." She stared him down. "Because you never really intended to marry me. Admit it: You were ashamed of me because I was not of your station."

Anger flared in his eyes before he banked it. "I was never ashamed of you."

"You didn't even introduce me to your sister or your mother—"

"I didn't want to burden my sister with my secrets, and my mother is the most indiscreet person in the world—as you ought to know, having met her. She would have told my father at once."

"Which would have ruined everything," she said sarcastically.

"It would have indeed, if he'd disapproved of the match and cut me off financially. And back then I did worry that he might, given that *your* father—"

"Was a wastrel," she said. "Yes, I know. But your father wasn't haughty. He didn't seem to look down on me. Indeed, he was kind, even pitying. He seemed to feel sorry for me that I didn't know your true character."

"It *was* my character once," he said unsteadily, his eyes burning into hers. "But not after I met you. Then I wanted to have you—and only you—for my own." His voice hardened. "I made that very clear to him before I left for the Continent. He swore to me that if you came to him, he would help you."

She fought to breathe. "You're saying I'm lying about what he told me."

"I'm saying . . ." He released a shuddering breath. "Perhaps you misunderstood him. Perhaps—"

"I did not misunderstand him!" she cried. "Do you know what it meant to me to hear that you . . . had been deceiving me all along? My world collapsed. I walked around in a state of shock, knowing you were lost to me forever. Your father had no interest in helping me, and Captain Trevor had given Papa only two choices."

She gulped down air. "Either I accepted Reynold's hand in marriage, in which case Captain Trevor would forgive Papa's entire debt. Or I refused it, and our family, including my sick mother, would be carted off to debtors' prison."

Horror suffused Niall's features. "God, Bree, the debt was as bad as all that?"

Her hands curled into fists at her sides. "Father never could resist high stakes, drat him."

Niall paced before her, as if trying to make sense of what she was saying. Then he halted to look at her. "Did you tell my father this?"

"Of course not. And have him think me some sort of *adventuress* who was after his son's money?" When he winced to have his words thrown back at him, she went on hastily, "I did have my pride, especially after he told me about your . . . your paramour."

"Bree, there was no—"

"Anyway," she went on, unable to hear his protest again, "I'd pinned my hopes on your saving me somehow, perhaps helping to pay off the debt . . . anything that might delay the inevitable. But after your father refused to send the letter, saying that you weren't the sort of man to honor your promises, I . . . died inside. I agreed to marry Reynold, telling myself that I would grow to love him, that he was a nice man, that it was a good thing he was not *you*."

She clasped one fist to her chest. "But my heart refused to believe it. It wanted you." She glared at him. "I fought hard and long to cut you out of my stupid heart. I've spent the last several years doing so, and now you have the nerve to come here and—"

"What do you think *I* was doing all that time, damn it?" He stepped close to her. "The announcement of your marriage, which Father dutifully sent to me, ended my hopes for us. That was the real reason I went to work for Fulkham—to forget. To put you out of my mind. And my heart."

"Did you succeed?"

"Did *you*?"

She glanced away. "Will you believe me if I say I did?"

"No." He seized her hands. "Because you don't

kiss like a woman who doesn't care anymore. You don't look at me like a woman who doesn't care anymore."

Drat the man for always seeing through her defenses. "That's why I didn't tell you about my marriage! Because I knew if you heard the truth, you would use it to . . . to try to get me back into your bed. You already assume, as all men do, that a widow is eternally lonely for a man, so she would swallow any amount of pride to—"

He cut her off with a kiss. And it was every bit as glorious as the last one, long and ardent and oh so tempting.

"What do you think you're doing?" she drew back to whisper.

His eyes smoldered like wood about to erupt into flames. "Reminding us both of what we've tried and failed to forget."

"Perhaps I don't want to be reminded," she said desperately.

He merely gave her that devilish smile that always ignited her blood, then sealed his mouth to hers once more. He didn't have to call her a liar or point out her weakness. Her heedless responses to his persistent kisses did that for him.

No matter how much her mind cautioned her against giving in, her heart wanted so badly to remember, and it was her heart that had her rising to meet the wild, ravening caress of his mouth, which took hers so thoroughly that she felt the impact to her soul.

With darkness falling softly around them, she rose up on tiptoe to loop her arms about his neck. He moaned deep in his throat before dragging her to him. His hands flattened her against his body possessively, and she felt every inch of his hard muscle—and his hard arousal—through his clothing.

Heat roared up from her belly, searing away her objections and fears. Oh, unfair. He knew precisely how to make her remember.

Except that now he was making new memories, sweeping her body with his fingers as if to memorize her curves . . . or perhaps just mark them for his own. And the hunger of those hands made her want to touch him, too, to slide her fingers inside his tailcoat and up beneath his waistcoat to where only a thin linen shirt separated his flesh from hers.

"Damn it, Bree," he whispered, "you don't know how I've missed this—being with you, touching you, kissing you."

Next thing she knew, he was walking her backward until she bumped up against a plane tree. Then his mouth was on hers again and his hands fumbling with her shawl, and she was reveling in every moment. His body covered hers as he drank of her mouth and she drank of his.

Niall's eyes gleamed in the dark. "I want to touch you." He removed her fichu, then tugged her clothing down to expose one breast. "Here."

"Yes . . . please . . ." she breathed, hardly conscious of what she said.

Need flaring in his face, he covered her breast with his large hand, and started caressing it, kneading it, thumbing the nipple to a fine point that shot sensation down to her toes.

Goodness gracious, that felt *amazing*. She must be out of her mind. Anyone could happen into this corner of the garden, evening or no. And if they found her and Niall doing this . . .

What kind of wanton creature was she, to allow such madness?

The kind who'd once dreamed of doing this with him in their marital bed.

"Do you like my hands on you, my beautiful rose?" he asked.

"Mmm," she managed. "Delicious."

He brushed kisses over her cheeks, her eyelids, her temples. "I love how you blossom beneath my touch."

She'd never guessed this could feel so wonderful. It had never been like this with Reynold, her rather formal, correct husband, who'd made love to her in the dark with furtive efficiency.

There was nothing furtive about Niall's caresses, and certainly nothing efficient. They were luxuriously blatant, driving her into more of a frenzy by the moment.

"I've waited years for this," he said hoarsely. He kissed his way down her breast. "I want to taste you."

"Oh yes," she breathed, and buried her hands in his hair to urge him down to her bosom.

That was all it took to have him seizing her breast in his mouth, laving and sucking and turning her mind to mush. Every part of her felt liquid and hot, boiling beneath his avid attentions.

As he teased her nipple with teeth and tongue, she moaned and pressed against him, wanting more and more. With a triumphant groan, he dragged up her skirts so he could reach beneath them and between her legs to the part of her aching for him, already drenched for him.

Part of her was shocked by that sudden intimacy. Part of her was fascinated.

And the latter part was winning. "We probably . . . shouldn't do this," she said feebly. "Someone might . . . stumble across us."

"No one's coming in here, Bree," he choked out against her breast. "Pip is standing guard outside the gate."

That really did shock her. "Niall!" She pulled his head back from her breast. "Did you plan this?"

His eyes glittered at her. "I planned a private discussion with you. This is an . . . unexpected reward for managing it."

Reward? The audacity of the man! "You deserve no rewards, you scoun—"

He cut her off with a kiss so thorough that her argument melted away, and she gave herself into his hands. Oh, how magical they were! One took over fondling her damp breast, while his other continued to delve through her curls until he found her slick flesh.

Then he teased and rubbed her down there like the reckless rogue he was.

"You're so warm for me, sweeting," he whispered against her lips. "And so damned wet, it's hard for me to bear."

Feeling wild and shameless, she cupped his arousal through his trousers. "Yes, I can see how hard it is."

He jerked back to gape at her. "You're not the Bree I used to know."

Because he brought out the wanton in her. Lord only knew why.

She felt heat rise in her cheeks. "Does that . . . bother you?"

"Are you out of your mind? Not one whit." With a knowing look, he thrust his hips against her hand. "Show me what you've learned while I was gone."

Not this, to be sure. Reynold had never encouraged her to explore him, so doing such . . . wicked things felt enormously freeing. Because she'd been curious. She'd always wanted to feel and stroke and explore, but Reynold had seemed disapproving of that idea.

Niall was downright eager for it. He swiftly unfastened his trousers and drawers so he could draw her hand inside, then returned to making her insane with his own hands.

So they explored together, finding each other's most sensitive spots, relishing each other's soft responses.

And hard responses, too, for the more she caressed him, the firmer and thicker he grew, until his member was sticking out of his trousers like a hound sniffing out its pleasure.

"I want to be inside you, sweeting," he growled against her throat, which he'd just been tonguing. "Now. I beg you."

"You're . . . already . . . inside me," she teased.

"Don't be coy. You know what I mean."

She did. And she wanted him inside her, too. Which was odd, since she'd never really enjoyed the act with her husband, so she doubted she would enjoy it with Niall, but . . .

He cupped her face in his hands. "Do you want me or not, my wanton wench?"

No one had ever called her a wench. Or a wanton. She rather liked it. It fed her urge to rebel, to let him take her right here against the tree.

"Because if you don't want me—" he went on.

"I do." When an expression of pure raw hunger filled his face, she added, more softly, "I've always wanted you."

"No more than I wanted you."

Catching her legs behind her knees, he dragged them up to encircle his hips, so he could slide inside her.

She grabbed his shoulders. My word. It was

so . . . intrusive. Rigid. *Good*. It felt exquisite, even though it had been over a year since she'd done this. She knew from experience that the feeling wouldn't last and the exercise of lovemaking would grow tedious, but for now, this was enough.

"God, you're tight as a virgin," he ground out.

He drove into her up to the hilt, and she gasped. She didn't *feel* like a virgin. There was no pain, no awkwardness. It even seemed natural to let Niall take her up against a tree, probably because she had loved him once.

But not anymore. She stifled the very thought. She couldn't let herself be that foolish again. It always hurt too much when it was over.

"All right?" he asked.

The question took her by surprise, especially since she could feel the strain in his muscles as he held her in place. In her experience, men didn't care whether the woman was . . . comfortable. "Yes."

"Good," he said hoarsely. "Because I couldn't let go of you now if my life depended on it."

She barely had time to be thrilled by that before he was kissing her again, fondling her again, thrusting into her with hard bursts of energy that should have hurt or chafed her.

But the more he drove into her, the more heated she grew. Then he shifted her so he was pounding her in an unfamiliar way, rousing her in an unusual manner. It made her hot and hungry and eager for the next thundering thrust.

"God, Bree," he rasped, "you enslave me."

"Good," she said saucily. "Someone . . . should."

"Watch it, wench. Or I'll enslave *you*."

He already had. With every lunge inside her, he heightened her need, tightening the chains that held her to him and wrapping her in the wild heat that was Niall in full arousal.

He might as well have put shackles on the arms looped about his neck, for she couldn't let go of him. And the more he drove into her, the more enslaved she felt. Like some harem girl, she rode out her pleasure with her strong, commanding sheik, and every inch of her felt joined to him, part of him . . . needing him.

Then her blood began to rise and her heart to hammer, and she felt herself reaching for an elusive something she'd never felt before. Unable to help herself, she shimmied and arched against him.

"Yes, sweeting," he whispered. "That's it. Come for me. Come *with* me."

In her feverish state, she wondered fleetingly where he wanted her to go, but then he was thrusting and thundering and she was reaching, reaching up and up . . . and suddenly, as if shooting over a hill into the unknown, she caught the stars she was reaching for.

Then he drove deep and groaned her name against her lips, and the stars exploded all over her, inside her, around her . . . setting her adrift in a sea of pleasure. With him.

Ten

Though Niall released her legs so she could stand once more, he refused to let go of her, not yet ready for that. He couldn't believe he'd taken her like a whore against the tree, here in a garden where anyone might find them. He couldn't believe she had *let* him.

But he'd do it again without hesitation. Because it was Bree. His, at last.

He brushed kisses over her cheeks and eyelids, basking in the contentment of having her after all these years.

She stirred in his arms. "What was *that*?"

"What?" He drew back to look at her. "What we just did?"

"No." She colored fetchingly. "What it . . . did to me. I . . . I had the strangest sensations. Like I might faint . . . or fly or . . . something."

Uh-oh. "Pleasurable sensations?" he asked warily.

"Oh yes!" When he began to chuckle, she added

hastily, "Not that I haven't felt something . . . close to that before, but not—"

He cupped her cheek. "I take it that Trevor never made you come."

"'Come'? Ohhh, *that's* what you meant when you said, 'Come with me.' You meant that feeling."

"Yes. When a man 'comes,' he . . . er . . . puts his seed inside you. When a woman does, she feels those things you felt. Or so I'm told."

"Seed?" Panic crossed her face and she pushed him away, going off a little distance so she could straighten her clothing. "Oh, Lord, you could have put a child in my belly!" There was just enough light from the streetlamps for him to see her desperate expression. "You said there were ways to avoid that. Can you—"

"I'm sorry, sweeting—any method of that sort would need to be arranged beforehand." Swiftly, he buttoned up his breeches and trousers. They were obviously not going to renew their sensual interlude. "I didn't come here intending to do as we did. But you were married to Trevor for a few years before you bore a child, so I doubt that our one time—"

"That's what men always say." She stared him down. "Then they prove to be wrong, and next thing you know, they've gotten a woman with child and they're running away as fast as they can."

"I wouldn't do that, damn it!"

"You did it before."

"Not after giving you a child, for God's sake! And I had good reason for leaving, no matter what you think." He walked up to grab her by the arms. "I'm not having this argument now, when we just shared the most magical moment of our lives."

She gazed at him, her face softening. "It *was* magical, wasn't it?"

"Yes, it was." He smiled at her. "We should do it again."

Now looking distinctly wary, she drew away from him once more. "I don't think that's wise."

"Why not?"

"Because I can't be your mistress, Niall."

"I'm not asking you to be my mistress." He stared at her. "We could marry. Turn this into a real betrothal. I need a wife, and you—"

"I don't *want* to marry you!" she cried.

The words cut through him like a knife of ice. "Ah," he managed to eke out.

"Don't you see? I can't do it again. You broke my heart the first time. You can't just . . . come back after seven years and take up where we left off, as if nothing ever happened."

He fought the urge to pull her back into his arms and kiss her senseless again. "Is there someone else?"

"Of course not."

"Then it's only your fear talking. And I see no reason either of us should give in to it."

"It's not fear; it's caution. I have good reason to be cautious. We're different people now, you know. I've already been married to one man who treated me like his Botticelli, and I don't want another. Besides, my son is his heir, and I can't take up with anyone without considering how it would affect him. Especially a man who still keeps secrets, who still won't—"

"Listen," he broke in, "I'm only asking you to give me a chance. You're right. We *are* different people now. But not so different that we don't still have *this* between us. So why not take it slowly? Continue with our pretend engagement, but actually treat it as a courtship. Get to know each other as we are now."

She eyed him warily. "Is this your round-about way of getting me to comply with Lord Fulkham's scheme again?"

"Damnation, it has naught to do with—" He choked down a string of angry words. She was intentionally provoking him. Because she didn't yet trust him not to break her heart again. And truth be told, he wasn't entirely easy with her yet, either.

All the more reason they should take some time to be together. So he forced himself to be calm and not rise to her barbs. "I don't give a damn about Fulkham's scheme. If you don't care if your father hangs, then I bloody well don't, especially after what he did to you."

Catching her hand, he lifted it to his lips for

a kiss. "But even if you refuse to help Fulkham, I *will* court you. I'm not giving up on us this time, Bree." He sucked in a ragged breath. "Unless that's what you really want, and then I'll honor your wishes. But I don't think it is."

The fact that she didn't instantly refuse emboldened him. "Look at it this way. We have a unique opportunity. We're already considered betrothed by the world. So we can court without anyone thinking twice about it. If it doesn't succeed, then you can do as you initially planned and jilt me. Go back to your estate and closet yourself away from me and the world."

He pulled her closer. "But if we can find what we once had, wouldn't that be worth it? If you can come to trust me . . ."

"So I can have my heart broken again the next time you decide to . . . to fight a duel and flee the country?"

That made him laugh, in spite of everything. "I'm not fighting any more duels, sweeting." He grinned. "Unless they're fought over you, and then you can come with me."

She eyed him askance. "And take my son, too? And have him leave his inheritance behind? And his family?"

Bloody hell. "All right, bad joke," he said sourly. "The point is—"

"The point is that you haven't considered *my* life, *my* situation. You want to start again as if nothing happened. Yet so much has happened to *me.* It has changed me. I don't think you realize how."

"Then let me find that out. What's the harm in it? That we might fall in love again? That doesn't sound awful to me."

"Of course it doesn't. Love isn't the same for a man." She made a vague gesture in the direction of his trousers. "For men, it's just about *that*. For women—"

"I don't think women are as different from men as you suggest," he said softly. "I never forgot you, Bree, and that was without ever having you in my bed. I never stopped missing you. And I daresay you were the same. You never learned to love Trevor, after all."

"No, but I tried. Hard." She drew her hand from his, and wandered over to the plane tree. "Has it occurred to you that perhaps my heart is . . . permanently broken, which is why I could never love my husband? That after fighting so hard to cut you out of it, I can never let you—or anyone else—back in?"

He refused to let her see how her words tore at him. "No, that has not occurred to me, because it's absurd."

She flashed him a wan smile. "That's the problem. You truly believe it's absurd. But perhaps you shouldn't."

A voice came from beyond the garden. "Brilliana? Are you still out here?"

Lady Pensworth. Deuce take it.

Bree shot him an apologetic glance. "I'll be in shortly, Aunt Agatha!" she called out.

There was a long pause before the old battle-ax answered. "All right. But don't be too long."

Stepping up to him, Bree whispered, "She'll question your poor footboy until she gets the truth out of him, and then she'll be in here demanding to know what we're up to. I'd better go."

He caught her by the arm. "Just think about what I said, Bree. Give yourself tonight to consider my proposition." When she looked as if she might make some protest, he added, "We can court respectably. No bed play."

A rueful laugh escaped her. "You really think you can manage that."

"I can manage anything for another chance with you."

That wiped the humor from her face. She looked lost, unsure of her bearings. He understood. But that didn't mean he had to take her reticence as the last word.

He knew he wouldn't hurt her again. Now he just had to make sure she knew it, too.

"I'll give you my answer as soon as I can," she said. "Now, I really must go."

This time he let her. Because he had to. Not because he wanted to.

But long after she disappeared, he stood there, replaying everything they'd said, and it occurred to him that he hadn't stopped to examine his own feelings in the matter. He'd just stormed in as always, with his eye on the prize, not considering whether the prize was what he truly wanted.

He'd spent only one day with her—she might really be as different as she'd said. She did seem more guarded about her feelings. And he wanted a wife who could love him freely.

What if, God forbid, she *couldn't* love him again?

He snorted. This wasn't about love. He wouldn't let it be about love. He'd gone that route once, and it had nearly destroyed him. Love was as tumultuous as war, and he'd had enough of both. He wanted a wife who would give him peace. Children. A pleasant life.

And yes, passion. He and Bree had that, at least.

But was that enough? It might not be for her, especially if her years with Trevor had set her irrevocably against marriage.

No, he couldn't believe it. All women wanted husbands, didn't they? She was still merely chafing over her notion that he'd fought the duel over his mistress. A notion she'd had from his own father.

He winced. He'd have to accept that if he were to trust her.

As for her conviction that he'd betrayed her with another woman, she would never come to trust *him* until she could believe him on that score.

He scrubbed a hand over his face. He'd have to handle this with great care. He could ask Edwin about Clarissa's present state of mind. According to Warren, Edwin knew everything about the rape and the duel, so Niall wouldn't be speaking out of turn.

Yes, that was what he should do. Speak to Edwin in the morning and see if the man thought Niall could approach Clarissa without alarming her during her pregnancy.

"I didn't tell her nothing, sir. Just so you know."

Niall glanced up to see Pip standing there. "Who?"

"Lady Pensworth. I played dumb when she asked who was out here with Mrs. Trevor."

That made Niall laugh. "Trust me, she'll know before the hour is up. Lady Pensworth is nothing if not resourceful." He handed the boy a guinea, and the lad's eyes went wide. "Tell your master I appreciate his lending me your aid. And tell him it was successful."

He hoped it had been, anyway.

"Is there anything else I can do for you, my lord?"

"Not unless you can tell me which of the windows in that town house belongs to Mrs. Trevor's bedchamber. I could use a way to reach her without going through Lady Pensworth." And he wouldn't be averse to throwing a few pebbles at her window the next time he wanted to talk to her.

"I'm sorry, sir, I don't know which one. But I can find out." He held up the guinea. "For another of these."

Niall laughed. "Cheeky devil. All right then, see if you can discover it." He held out the guinea, then drew it back when Pip reached for it. "But do it discreetly, mind? If Lady Pensworth hears about it, you'll only make matters worse."

Pip looked wounded. "I know how to keep quiet, sir. I do work for Lord Fulkham, after all."

"Good point." And that gave him an idea. "Here's your guinea, and there'll be another if you find out what your master has learned from *Debrett's* about a man named Sir Kenneth Whiting and bring the information to me at the Star and Garter at ten."

"Very good, sir. It will be done."

"That's all then. Thank you."

The boy walked off.

It would be good to go into this game fully armed with information. Because if Sir Kenneth *was* related to Joseph Whiting . . .

He'd cross that bridge when he came to it.

～⚬〰

Brilliana should have known that the moment she walked out of the garden, her aunt would be waiting.

"My footman informed me that you went out to meet someone while I was napping, but that other young fellow wouldn't say whom." Disapproval laced Aunt Agatha's tone as she walked alongside Brilliana. "So, who was it?"

"You do realize I'm a grown woman and not some chit out of the schoolroom," Brilliana said irritably. "I can meet with whomever I please. For goodness' sake, I'm engaged—"

"Which is precisely why you should not be dallying with Lord Fulkham."

She blinked. "Lord Fulkham? What would make you think—"

"My servant said he recognized the footboy's livery as that of Lord Fulkham."

Brilliana couldn't help it—after everything that had transpired earlier, the fact that Niall had gone so far as to use the baron's servant in order to allay her own suspicions started her laughing.

"I don't find it remotely amusing, my dear." Aunt Agatha narrowed her gaze. "You're not playing the two men off each other, are you?"

That only made Brilliana laugh harder. As Aunt Agatha began to scowl, Brilliana fought to restrain her laughter. "N-no," she choked out. "Not in . . . the least, believe me." She could barely handle the one tiger she had by the tail, let alone two of them.

"Then what did Fulkham want?"

Oh, Lord, what to say? Perhaps a version of the truth? "For one thing, it wasn't Lord Fulkham. It was Niall. My fiancé and I argued this afternoon, and he knew I wouldn't admit him. So he got Lord Fulkham to write me a note requesting a private meeting in the park, and Niall had it delivered by the man's servant to further my assumption that I was meeting with Lord Fulkham."

"Yes, but why did you even go? Didn't you stop to question why Lord Fulkham would want to meet with you in private instead of simply calling on you like a respectable gentleman?"

Drat it—she couldn't tell Aunt Agatha the real reason Baron Fulkham might have for wishing a private meeting. "Lord Fulkham said he didn't want the neighbors speculating about why he was calling on me when I was newly engaged."

"And you believed that havey-cavey story."

"Why wouldn't I?" To keep from having to look Aunt Agatha in the eye while she spun her tale of half-truths, she headed up the steps. "I figured the man was overly cautious. He *is* a member of the government, you know."

"Hmm." Aunt Agatha followed, keeping pace with Brilliana quite easily for a woman of advanced years. "So what did Lord Margrave want?"

"To apologize, of course."

"That certainly took a while," her aunt said dryly.

Brilliana nearly missed a step. "What do you mean?"

"The footman said you'd been out there in the garden a half hour or more."

Fighting a blush, Brilliana fumbled for how to answer. "Well, he didn't *start* with the apology, believe me. First he attempted to . . . finish hashing out our argument from earlier."

"I'm not surprised. I did wonder how he would react once you told him the truth."

Brilliana paused at the top of the steps. "The truth?"

"About your father. And what he did to you."

"Oh. Of course." Brilliana had entirely forgotten how she and her aunt had left things earlier.

"That *is* what you were arguing about, isn't it? You said you were going to tell him later. Or did you turn into mush once you saw Sir Oswald and then decide to put the past behind you?"

"Hardly."

"Good, good. You shouldn't."

Hoping to put an end to the conversation, Brilliana hurried into the house, but Aunt Agatha was right on her heels and caught her in the foyer before she could head for the stairs. "So what did Lord Margrave say when you told him about your wretched father?"

Oh, Lord, would this never end? And how was she to answer? In Aunt Agatha's eyes there would be no good reason for her to reconcile with Papa. Yet she and Niall *had* to continue their efforts.

It suddenly dawned on her that she hadn't yet told Niall for certain that she would go on with this farce. She'd said she would think about it.

But she'd mostly meant that she would think about letting him court her. Because the truth was, she'd already made up her mind about Papa. There was no sense pretending she could stand by and watch him hang, not if she could prevent it. After seeing him look so ill today, after hearing the yearning in his voice when he asked about Silas, she *had* somewhat turned into mush.

A pox on Lord Fulkham for putting her in this situation. She'd safely packed away her feelings for Papa—and Niall—years ago, and now the dratted undersecretary was forcing her to experience them all again.

"Well?" her aunt prodded. "What did Lord Margrave say when you told him?"

Brilliana hated that she was so bad at subterfuge. And leave it to Aunt Agatha to make things even more difficult than they needed to be. "Niall said that although he thinks what Papa did was deplorable, Silas is still Papa's grandson and it's important to stay involved with one's family."

Aunt Agatha snorted. "Then it's no wonder you argued. I hope you stood firm."

Oh, dear. "To be honest, once Niall made his case, I saw his side of things. He pointed out that after not having had his own family for so long, he appreciated them all the more. Blood is still blood, after all."

"And bad blood is still bad blood," her aunt retorted. "Besides, your fiancé is the one responsible for not 'having had his own family.' He's the one who fought a duel, and for what? The gossips said it was over some woman."

Brilliana cringed. "You heard that, too?"

Aunt Agatha scrutinized her. "Was the woman you?"

"No. And I don't want to talk about it," she said.

Her aunt scowled at her. "You have become decidedly uncommunicative of late. This betrothal seems to have you at sixes and sevens."

What an understatement. "I don't want to talk about it because there's no time, if I'm to dress for the ball."

That clearly took her aunt off guard. "We're going?"

"If you feel well enough."

"It was just a trifling headache," Aunt Agatha said with a trace of petulance. "But I thought perhaps you might not *want* to go now that you're betrothed. Unless Margrave is attending?"

"He's not invited," she lied. "So of course I'm going. After I marry, he and I will be retiring to the country and I'll miss all the balls. So I must kick up my heels while I can."

Then she fled, desperately needing to be away from Aunt Agatha's incessant questions. Because how could she admit that she didn't know why Niall had fought? That his refusal to tell her chafed her?

Indeed, it was the main thing that kept her from agreeing to his proposal that they court.

And how *could* he expect her to fall in with his plans when he was keeping so much from her?

She groaned. He expected it because he knew how susceptible she was to him. And oh, but he was right. She still couldn't believe how wonderfully naughty it had been to be seduced against a tree by the scoundrel.

Well, it didn't matter. She refused to *let* it matter. She must think of other considerations while she made her decision. She must think of Silas and Camden Hall. She must be absolutely sure that Niall could happily be part of her life before she fell in with his plans to court her.

Because if he could not, she could not allow his seductions to go any further. No matter *how* deliciously enticing they might be.

Eleven

Niall sat in the taproom at the Star and Garter, staring down at his cards. They were excellent. But so far, Sir Oswald hadn't impressed him with an ability to take advantage of good cards. No wonder the fellow lost money routinely.

The question was, did he use counterfeits to make up for that?

"Sir Oswald?" Mr. Raines asked. "What's your bid?"

"Leave me alone. I'm thinking."

Which, from what Niall could tell, the man didn't do terribly often.

Sir Kenneth leaned back in his chair. "Margrave, could you please get your partner to move this along?"

"Why?" Niall countered. "Have you somewhere else to be?"

Pip had met him earlier to say that Sir Kenneth was Captain Joseph Whiting's second cousin.

Which had made Niall automatically dislike the baronet.

"You tell him, Margrave," Sir Oswald said. "Some of us like to take our time when playing cards."

Niall resisted the impulse to point out that having plenty of time didn't seem to help Sir Oswald's bids one whit. But it did make Niall wonder how the man could be the mastermind of a counterfeiting operation. He wasn't the brightest star in the sky, to be sure.

At last Sir Oswald bid, and the rest of the table was able to do so as well. Niall only hoped his partner's bid was based on the cards and not wishful thinking. So far, they hadn't done very well against Raines and Sir Kenneth.

Sir Oswald was an indifferent player, heedless and impulsive. Sometimes he shone. Other times he sank like a lead weight, taking his partner with him. Thank God Niall wasn't as poor as he was pretending, or he'd be destitute after his stint with Sir Oswald.

Meanwhile, Raines had shown himself to be a thoughtful and careful player. Indeed, he seemed to lack the kind of reckless character Niall would have considered necessary for a counterfeiter. Then again, a clever man would hide his true character if it were devious, and Raines did seem to have a brain.

The gentleman he couldn't make out was Sir Kenneth. The baronet's playing was all over the place . . . as was his character. The man was enigmatic, to say the least.

"So," Niall said, deciding he couldn't lose anything by being blunt, "I understand you're related to Captain Joseph Whiting."

Sir Kenneth blinked. "I am, indeed. How did you—" His eyes narrowed. "Ah, right. I forgot. You fought my late cousin in a duel years ago."

Niall nodded, wondering what Sir Kenneth would say to that.

"Why did you duel?" the man asked.

"Don't you know?" Niall countered.

Sir Kenneth shrugged. "I heard it was over some paramour the two of you had shared."

Niall stifled a groan. Had everyone in England heard that nasty gossip?

"But honestly," Sir Kenneth went on, "you could have fought for any number of reasons. Joseph was an arse. I nearly called him out myself once."

That took Niall by surprise. "Did you?"

"The man insulted the oldest of my sisters, for God's sake. He tried to kiss her in our conservatory." Sir Kenneth rearranged his cards. "She complained to Mother, who banned him from the house."

"Good for her," Niall said, then tensed. He didn't want Sir Kenneth making any sort of connection between his sister and Clarissa.

But Sir Kenneth was oblivious. "That man was incapable of keeping his prick in his trousers."

To say the least.

"Some men are like that," Raines said. "And the ones who aren't assume that other men are all like that."

And some women assume the same.

No, that wasn't fair. Given the gossip, was it any wonder that Bree believed that Niall had betrayed her? He *had* fought a duel over a woman. Just not the kind of woman she'd been told.

Sir Kenneth scowled. "But my sister was only fifteen at the time. What was the man thinking?" He arranged his cards. "Good God, who wants to dally with a schoolgirl, anyway? I personally prefer a woman with more experience. A Cyprian, a bored wife, a merry widow." He flashed his partner a conspiratorial look. "And I'm not the only one with such a preference, am I, Raines?"

Raines tensed up. "I don't know what you mean."

"Right," Sir Kenneth said with a sly smile. "So it's just me, then."

"Are we going to play or not?" Sir Oswald broke in. "It's your lead, Sir Kenneth."

"Of course." The baronet laid down his card, and the game was on.

As they went around the table, Niall turned to Raines. "How long have you been coming here?"

"Two years or more," Raines said. "I enjoy the game. It takes my mind off my . . . troubles."

Niall couldn't help wondering what those

troubles might be. "I confess I have a weakness for card games," he said, to establish his pretend character. "I can't seem to stay away."

"Exactly!" Sir Oswald cried. "They're quite entertaining. And they can be lucrative."

Sir Kenneth took the trick. "Only when one wins. I don't care for losing, myself."

Hmm. Perhaps Sir Kenneth was willing to win at any cost. And the sort who'd cheat would also be the sort who'd pay his debts with counterfeit money.

Niall would have to keep an eye on the baronet's playing. "I understand that you only recently came to town, Sir Kenneth. What brought you here in summer, other than this latest, uncharacteristic sitting of Parliament?"

Sir Kenneth shrugged. "My youngest sister's debut will be next season, so I figured I'd take my seat and also squire her and my mother around while they shopped for her coming-out."

"That sounds costly," Niall said.

"It is, though I don't mind. She's the last of three to need a husband, so I'll spare no expense to make sure she finds one. It won't take much, I daresay. She's the sort of girl every man wants for a wife."

"Oh?" Niall asked. "What sort is that?"

"Pretty. Eager to please. Malleable."

Odd, but that didn't sound as appealing to Niall as it once had. Now that he'd been dealing with a more prickly sort of female, he realized he liked the challenge of a woman with her own opinions.

"So," Niall said, "are you in the market for that kind of wife yourself?"

"I'm not in the market for any kind of wife at the moment—at least not until I get my sister settled." Sir Kenneth grinned. "Although if I had *your* situation, I might be."

Niall tensed. "What do you mean?"

"Well, you have the best of both worlds. A pretty young woman who's also an experienced widow with a fortune. Cream of the crop, as far as I'm concerned." He smirked at Niall over his cards. "First time I saw Mrs. Trevor, I thought about throwing my hat into that ring myself. Then you beat me to it. If I were you, I'd guard that woman jealously. There's a line of bachelors stretching from here to Almack's just waiting to have a go at your little filly if you should choose to discard her."

Only with an effort did Niall resist the impulse to tell the man to rein in his comments about the "little filly"—that she was now off-limits to any other bachelor. Instead he forced himself to focus on what Sir Kenneth's comment said about his character.

And how curious that the man would speak of her that way in front of her father. Did Sir Kenneth have some idea of marrying her so he could feed Sir Oswald more counterfeits?

"Watch your tongue," Sir Oswald snapped.

"That's my daughter you're talking about in such a rude manner."

"You have a daughter?" Sir Kenneth said, clearly shocked.

Ah, *that* was why the fellow hadn't governed his tongue. Which also meant that the baronet wasn't angling for a closer connection to Sir Oswald. It didn't stop him from being a counterfeiter, but it gave him one less reason to be so.

Sir Oswald slapped down a card. "I told you when I introduced his lordship that I invited him to join us because he's going to be my son-in-law."

"I'm afraid I wasn't paying attention," Sir Kenneth said. "I was trying to catch the taproom maid's eye."

That only slightly mollified Sir Oswald. "Well, you can be sure that my daughter is too good for the likes of *you*, sir."

The vehemence in Sir Oswald's voice took Niall by surprise. Perhaps the man wasn't as heedless of Bree's welfare as it seemed.

"Forgive me, Sir Oswald," Sir Kenneth said in a tone that showed he was clearly unrepentant. "To be honest, I thought you were childless. You never mention your daughter or even your wife."

"My late wife." Sir Oswald hunched over his cards. "And a man don't have to go on and on about his family all the time, you know. It don't mean anything."

After that, Sir Oswald was cranky, Sir Kenneth was embarrassed, and Raines was concentrating on his cards, so Niall had trouble turning the conversation back toward anything that might give him an idea of who the counterfeiter might be.

But he did surreptitiously mark with tiny creases or tears the banknotes used for wagering, so he'd know who'd used what to pay. Then he set about trying to win—no small feat with Sir Oswald as a partner—so he'd be able to scrutinize the banknotes later.

About halfway through the evening, their luck turned, thank God, and Sir Oswald apparently paid closer attention to his cards, as if determined to impress Niall. Which made sense, given that the man had just practically admitted to never speaking of his own daughter to his friends.

Some hours later, Niall and Sir Oswald were doing so well that they already had the pot of two hundred pounds in the bag. And since his friends had agreed that this was to be the final game, Niall and his partner were going to be leaving with money in their pockets.

"Well, well," Sir Oswald crowed as Niall took the final trick. "I should have *you* for my partner from now on, Margrave. You've clearly got the devil's own luck."

"To be fair, Sir Oswald," Sir Kenneth drawled, "there was *some* skill in the man's playing."

"All the better," the old man said. "A skillful player *and* a lucky one." He leaned toward Niall. "Promise me you'll partner me again tomorrow night, sir. Pitford will play with Whiting anyway."

"What about me and Dunsleigh?" The question came from Raines. "You're choosing Margrave over one of us?"

Sir Oswald shrugged. "Pitford has been choosing his cousin over me. Seems only fair that you two sit out and give me and my future son-in-law a chance. Eh, Margrave?"

"I wouldn't wish to intrude," he lied.

"Ignore Raines," Sir Oswald said. "It's no intrusion. If he don't want to sit the game out, then he can play with Sir Kenneth again, and the other two can watch. Serves them right for abandoning us tonight."

Raines looked irritated. "Fine, old man, Margrave may join us again if you prefer. It's better than listening to you grouse about not winning."

This whole conversation grew more interesting by the moment. Was Raines simply annoyed to be pushed out by Niall, or annoyed to lose his chance at passing off some counterfeits?

Niall wouldn't know for sure until he could get a good look at their winnings. Despite the paltry sum, the pot contained a variety of notes for Niall to examine later. It included some of everyone's money, along with at least one fifty-pound note and several twenty-pound notes.

Unfortunately, Niall had to split the winnings

with Sir Oswald, but he'd come prepared for that. With a little sleight of hand, he was able to switch out notes he knew were genuine for the ones they'd won in the card game, before giving Sir Oswald his winnings.

Niall watched all the gentlemen to see if they noticed, but none seemed to, not even Sir Oswald, who shoved the genuine notes into his purse without looking at them. That made Niall wonder even more if the man had realized he'd been using counterfeit currency all this time.

On the other hand, there might not be any counterfeits among the currency at all. In which case, Niall would be no closer to the truth than before.

But he wouldn't mind it if this investigation took a while. The longer it lasted, the longer he got to court Bree, and he needed all the time he could get.

If she would even let him court her. Because right now she didn't seem that keen on it.

That worried him. Most women would jump at the chance to be courted by an earl.

But Bree had always been her own person. So perhaps he'd assumed too much about her feelings yet again. Perhaps her marriage, flawed as it had been, had still made her too cautious to wed.

It didn't matter. He wouldn't let it. Somehow he must change her mind, make her see that theirs would be a good match. Because he was beginning to think that the only match he wanted was with Bree.

～～

The next morning, Niall headed for his brother-in-law's, praying that Edwin had risen early as usual. Having tossed and turned half the night remembering his argument with Bree, Niall was determined to find out how the couple felt about his revealing the truth about Clarissa's past.

But the moment he entered the Blakeborough town house he was informed that Clarissa and Edwin were both gone.

"Gone!" Niall said. "Gone where? Why?"

The footman colored and mumbled something about fetching Clarissa's lady's maid, then hurried off.

When the maid appeared, her morning cap was askew and her apron streaked with dust. "Forgive me for looking so disheveled, my lord, but I'm in a rush to pack for her ladyship. It's all very sudden, I'm afraid."

That didn't sound good. "What has happened?" he asked, his gut knotting.

"Yesterday her ladyship had a bit of a scare concerning the babe, and Dr. Worth insisted that she be taken to the country, away from the upsets of town. So the mistress and master left for Stoke Towers at dawn this morning."

Niall's heart sank at the idea of Clarissa having complications this early in her pregnancy. She was only six months along, for God's sake! "Is she all right?"

"The doctor says she will be. It was only a little blood, but still . . ."

"Blood!" Damnation. "Is there any chance she may . . . lose the child?"

"The doctor says no, sir, but his lordship doesn't want to take any chances and neither does she."

Niall could well understand that. Clarissa and Edwin had been so thrilled about the child's approaching birth that Mother had taken to complaining that all they ever talked about was the baby.

God only knew what they'd do if Clarissa lost the baby. The very thought of that sent his stomach roiling.

"Is Dr. Worth attending her in Hertfordshire?" he asked.

"He says there's no need," the maid said. "He has explained to me and his lordship what must be done. And he promised to drive out to Stoke Towers whenever summoned. In the meantime, he means to visit her once a week, more often if necessary, though he says he feels certain it won't be necessary."

That relieved Niall enormously. If the doctor didn't think the situation dire, then perhaps it was simply one of those freakish things that happened to women while they were breeding.

Still, this newest development didn't help his situation. There was no way in hell he dared speak to Clarissa of the rape now. Though perhaps he could talk to Edwin about it. Edwin might be able to say whether Clarissa would care if Niall revealed the truth to Bree. In strictest confidence, of course.

"My lord?" the maid said, dragging him from his thoughts. "Do you wish to send a message with me? I hope to be following the master and mistress shortly in the second carriage."

It was a none-too-subtle attempt to point out that she had things to do, and he needed to leave her to them. "Do you think his lordship would mind if I rode out there to speak with him? I should like to find out more details about her condition, for my own peace of mind."

"I'm sure that would be fine, though I doubt he will let you see her ladyship." She flashed him a rueful glance. "His lordship would wrap the mistress up in cotton until the day of the birth if he could."

"Yes, he is nothing if not overprotective. And under the circumstances, I wouldn't expect him to let me see her anyway. But thank you for telling me what you know. I'm relieved to hear my sister is in such good hands."

With a bob of her head, the maid started to walk away. Then she paused. "If you would keep this under your hat, I'm sure his lordship would much appreciate it. He doesn't want a slew of concerned friends running out to the estate to attempt seeing his wife."

"Of course."

"And . . . er . . . if you could delay telling Lady Margrave for a while, that would be good, too. Your mother . . . can be . . . well . . ."

"Difficult. Trust me, I know." Niall smiled. "I'll put off mentioning it to her as long as I can."

It wouldn't be that hard. Yesterday Mother had spent her time paying calls on her many friends to wax poetic about the upcoming wedding of her son to a rich widow. It would take her a good week more to tire of *that* enterprise, and by then, perhaps Clarissa would be feeling well enough for visitors. He could only hope.

Niall left with his head in a muddle. He'd intended to call on Bree this morning, but he also wanted to head out to Stoke Towers as soon as possible. And since he couldn't explain to her why . . .

A thought occurred to him. He'd promised to help Bree learn how to manage her estate. And his own manager had sent him a note only this morning asking when he'd be coming to Margrave Manor, since they needed to discuss a few items of business.

Why not invite Bree to the estate for the day? They could make an outing of it, chaperoned by her aunt, and even bring the lad, if she wished. Then, at some point, he could slip away to speak to Edwin at the adjoining estate, and return before she even knew he was gone.

Of course, all of this was assuming that Bree had made up her mind to let him keep courting her. God, he hoped she had. Because the urge to see her, kiss her, touch her, was suddenly overpowering.

He glanced at his pocket watch. Nine o'clock. It was a trifle early to pay calls, especially if Bree and her aunt had gone to the ball last night, but neither of them struck him as the sort to lie abed half the day. And he wanted to leave for the country at once.

With that decided, he headed straight for Lady Pensworth's town house. But before he could knock, he heard a child's laughter coming from the Bedford Square garden across the street.

Turning to look, he spotted Bree sitting on a bench with Silas gamboling nearby, accompanied by the nurse. Perfect. Now he needn't deal with the aunt at all until he got Bree's approval.

He strolled over and paused at the gate to watch the domestic scene, his heart flipping over in his chest. She was so good with the boy, and the lad clearly adored her. What a mother she would make to their own children. And God, how he wanted to see Bree's belly heavy with *his* child, the first of many.

He began to understand a little of his brother-in-law's overprotectiveness. Because if it had been Bree instead of Clarissa having difficulties with her pregnancy . . .

No, he wouldn't think of that. Bree had already

had one child with no trouble; he didn't see why she couldn't have another. And Clarissa would be fine, too. The maid had as much as said so.

"Silas!" Bree called out. "Stop pulling up the verbena. They're for everyone to enjoy."

"That's his favorite color," the nurse said. "You should paint him holding some, mistress. The purple would make a pretty picture."

"It would," Bree said. "But I'm not doing watercolors just now. I'm working on another Wedgwood, now that they've shown some interest in my designs."

"You heard from them?" the nurse asked.

Bree nodded. "Just this morning. They said they'd like to see more, and they gave me some ideas of what they're looking for."

"Congratulations, mistress!"

"Oh, they haven't accepted them yet, but the letter was encouraging."

He sucked in a breath as a long-forgotten memory of finding Bree sketching a classical statue of Aphrodite in a park rose to his mind. Years ago, she'd dreamed of designing for the famous pottery. Apparently that dream had never died.

Slipping through the gate, he came up behind her to look over her shoulder at her sketchbook. More than ever, he was humbled by her talent. She had a knack for black-and-white images. He could easily imagine her sketch of Cupid appearing on a Wedgwood vase.

The nurse glanced up and gave a start to see him there, but young Silas broke into a grin and toddled toward him.

Niall pressed a finger to his lips, then leaned over Bree's shoulder. "Silas makes an excellent Cupid."

She jumped, then turned to lift an eyebrow at him. "You, sir, are very sneaky."

"Yes, well, you knew that about me already."

He tipped his head in the direction of the secluded area where they'd made love the evening before, and she rolled her eyes before returning to her sketching.

"Why have you come here so early?" she asked.

"To watch you draw."

She snorted. "Somehow I doubt that."

He laughed. "Actually, I'm here to invite you to join me for an outing."

Her hand paused mid-stroke. "What sort of outing?"

"A jaunt to Margrave Manor. I have urgent business there, and I did promise to give you lessons in running an estate."

Her expression softened markedly. "Nurse," she said to the servant, "why don't you take Silas over to the fountain and let him throw some pennies in it for good luck?"

"Yes, mistress. He do love throwing pennies, our lad."

Once they were well away, Bree asked, "What about Papa and your mission?"

Niall took a seat beside Bree and laid his arm across the back of the bench. "We *will* have to return by evening, since I agreed to play cards with him and his friends again tonight." He ran a finger down the back of her neck. "But before then, I want some time alone with you."

"Stop that," she murmured, though she didn't move away. "Did you learn anything about the counterfeiting last night?"

"Not so far. Your father and I won, but none of the notes were fakes. I went through them carefully, then sent them off to Fulkham to be sure. I doubt he'll find anything. Giving counterfeits to tradesmen is one thing; distributing them among one's friends is quite another. Besides, the card games may not be how your father is passing the notes on. *If* he's even the one passing them on."

"You think he's innocent?"

"I damned well hope so, for the sake of you and Silas." When her face clouded over, he changed the subject. "Anyway, I have the whole day ahead of me to spend with my fiancée. And I thought we'd use it productively at Margrave Manor."

A sigh escaped her. "You know I can't run off to your estate unchaperoned."

"Which is why I intend to include your aunt in the invitation. And young Silas, too, if you wish." He bent close to add in a whisper, "I figure that the lad will keep Lady Pensworth occupied, so I can keep *you* occupied. If you know what I mean."

She eyed him askance. "You're a very wicked fellow, Lord Margrave."

"Not as wicked as I hope to be once we reach my estate."

He was rewarded for that rakish comment when she colored prettily. Her blushes never ceased to rouse him. She knew just how to make a man yearn. And he was yearning something fierce for her just now. "Say you'll go, Bree."

"Not if you're planning to be wicked. You promised to behave." She tapped his hand with her pencil. "I knew you wouldn't be able to stick to your promise. But I warn you—I will hold firm in my determination not to give in to any attempt at wickedness on your part."

"Shall we place a wager on that?" he said with a grin.

"I never gamble."

"Then you lead a very dull life."

Her gaze turned earnest. "I do indeed. And I like my dull life."

"Do you? Is that why you blush so whenever I threaten wickedness?"

She swallowed. "I just happen to blush easily."

Even the motion of her throat captivated him. "I never saw you blush with anyone else."

"That's because you haven't been around to see me with anyone else," she said tartly. "Our first courtship was secret, while our second—"

"So there *will* be a second courtship, then."

She sniffed. "You didn't let me finish. I was

going to say that our second courtship is pretend."

"It doesn't have to be."

"Niall, there are still things you aren't considering."

The doom and gloom in her voice got his back up. "Like what?"

"Like Papa, for example. What if he's guilty?"

"What if he is? I don't give a damn what happens to him after what he did. Do you?"

"No, but I don't think you've considered how it will affect *you* if he's guilty. There will be a trial and gossip in the press, and you'll be part of that. So if you marry me you'll *have* to give a damn. As a widow with little at stake, I can weather the scandal simply by retiring to the country and living a quiet life. But that's impossible for you. An earl must move in society."

"An earl can do pretty much as he pleases," he countered. "Besides, my name is already tarred with scandal because of the duel. One more is hardly going to hurt me."

"That was a duel of honor, which isn't held in contempt in your circles. But counterfeiting?" When he let out a coarse oath, she added more gently, "You have family you're not going to want to see suffer if Papa is convicted. And as long as you're connected to me, they *will*. Delia can distance herself from her former sister-in-law to a certain extent, but Clarissa cannot distance herself from her brother. Only imagine what effect the gossip would have on her."

"Trust me, that isn't the sort of gossip that would faze my sister." He searched her face. "Or is this another excuse for why we shouldn't marry?"

"I'm just saying—"

"You told me you'd give me your answer soon." He rose from the bench to stare down at her. "So is it yea or nay? Because I'm in no mood to continue this dance without knowing where it's heading."

"I need more time to consider everything— Papa and Silas and all of it."

He suppressed a curse. "I've waited seven years for this," he said irritably. "I'm not inclined to wait seven more."

Heading for the gate, he fought to tamp down his temper. Enough of this. If she thought to drag him about by a leading string, she would be sorely disappointed. He wanted her, but not at the cost of his dignity.

"Wait, Niall!" she cried out behind him.

He halted, then turned to glare at her.

Her expression fraught with uncertainty, she stood up. "If you wish, I shall talk to my aunt about your invitation to an outing, perhaps sometime later in the week—"

"I have to go to Margrave Manor *today*, Bree. Now, if possible."

She blinked.

"I told you," he went on, "my business there is urgent. Will you go with me or not? Because you and I both know that your aunt will do whatever you wish." He crossed his arms over his chest. "So it's time for you to decide. What exactly is it that you wish?"

Twelve

Brilliana's stomach knotted. He was the most impatient fellow she'd ever met.

Sometimes she adored that boldness. And sometimes she wanted to throttle him for it. Because it smacked a bit too much of bullying, and she'd had more than enough of that from Papa.

"I don't *know* what I want, don't you see?" she said. "I've never before had the chance to choose."

"Yes, apparently Trevor couldn't resist gaining you at the expense of your choice."

That was certainly a hit direct. And perversely, she felt compelled to defend her late husband. "It wasn't like that. Reynold loved me. He was upset that his father forced my hand, but he was as trapped as I. If he'd refused to marry me, Papa and Mama would have gone to prison. He couldn't let that happen. And neither could I."

Niall snorted. "*I* gave you the chance to choose all those years ago. You could have chosen me." He scowled at her. "Instead, you chose your family—your mother."

"She was ill, and you weren't. Of course I chose her."

Apparently that argument held some sway with him, for he let out a frustrated breath. "Damn it, Bree. I hate this."

"So do I." She *wanted* to throw caution to the winds. But the last time she'd done that, she'd ended up with a man who'd fought a duel over another woman. Or so the gossips—and his own father—had said. "Fine. I'll go with you. We'll take Aunt Agatha and Silas, and we'll see what happens."

It would give her a chance to see how he was with Silas over an extended period of time. And to see if Niall would make a good manager—or help her to be a good manager—of Camden Hall.

To see if he cared about her beyond the bed-chamber. So far, he'd said lots of nice things, but nothing about love.

Not that she blamed him. This wasn't about love for her, either. Because loving Niall was what had landed her in trouble the first time. If she hadn't fallen so hard for the scoundrel, she might have learned to love Reynold later.

But Niall had spoiled her for any other man. So if she let him court her again, it would merely be because it was practical. She refused to give him her heart only to have it trampled upon again. She'd never survive that twice.

He eyed her warily. "And after our 'outing,' you'll give me your decision about my courting you?"

"Yes." She supposed she owed him that much. "I promise."

That seemed to mollify him. "Very well. That sounds fair." An enigmatic expression crossed his face. "And after our outing, I may be able to . . . help your decision along."

She assumed he was speaking of using his "wickedness" against her again. "We will have Silas and Aunt Agatha with us. So there will be no wickedness."

"If you wish," he said.

That was a noncommittal answer if she'd ever heard one, but it was enough. Because she didn't want any more seductions. Truly, she didn't.

You can lie to him, but you can't lie to yourself.

Oh yes, she could. She'd been doing it for years. "Then I suppose we should go speak with Aunt Agatha."

His broad smile gave her pause, but she refused to dwell on it. He was going to teach her how to manage an estate. And perhaps from that she could deduce his true character. That was all that mattered.

Or so she told herself.

An hour later they were in his carriage, headed for Margrave Manor. It was just her and Aunt Agatha and Silas. Brilliana had left Nurse behind.

But not because of what Niall had said about letting Aunt Agatha be occupied with looking after Silas, and thus unable to chaperone *them*. Certainly not.

Liar.

"So, Lord Margrave," Aunt Agatha said. "I understand that you've been suffering some financial difficulties at Margrave Manor since your return."

"What?" Brilliana exclaimed.

When he lifted an eyebrow at her, she belatedly remembered what the gossips were supposed to be spreading around. Drat it, this subterfuge of Lord Fulkham's grew more onerous by the day.

"That's what I've heard in town," Aunt Agatha said.

Niall flashed the woman a bland smile. "It's nothing I can't handle."

"I should hope not." Aunt Agatha stared him down. "I wouldn't wish to see my niece forced to deal with an estate mired in debt when she already has a struggling estate of her own."

Brilliana choked back a laugh. Niall was clearly going to regret having invited Aunt Agatha along.

"Surely it's not 'of her own,'" Niall said. "Doesn't it belong to young Silas?"

Hearing his name mentioned, Silas, who'd been bouncing happily up and down on the seat beside Niall, crawled onto his lap, then sat staring up at the earl with rank curiosity.

The expression on Niall's face was priceless. It was obvious he'd never had to deal with a small child, for he shot her a helpless glance, as if to say, *What the devil do I do with him?*

"Silas, come here," she said.

Silas simply cocked his head and continued to regard Niall with interest. "Jack." He held out his hand. "Jack. Jack."

"I'm sorry, lad," Niall said. "But my name isn't Jack. It's . . . er . . . Margrave."

Brilliana and Aunt Agatha burst into laughter, which elicited a scowl from Niall.

"That's what he calls his jack-in-the-box," Brilliana explained. "He remembers that you helped him with it, so he thinks you can get it for him."

"Ah," Niall said. "Sorry, lad, no Jacks here."

"I told you we should have brought it along," Aunt Agatha said. "The lad is very attached to it."

"Literally," Brilliana said. "And I didn't want to deal with his catching his fingers in it all the time."

"What about this, lad?" Niall pulled out his pocket watch. "It makes music just like your 'Jack.'"

He turned it over to wind it, then pushed a button. As a familiar tune from *Eine Kleine Nachtmusik* began to play, Silas clapped his hands. His pleasure was so infectious, even Niall smiled.

When the song ran out, Silas grabbed the watch, scrambled off Niall's lap, and brought it to Brilliana. "Jack," he said. "Jack."

"Give it here, lad," Niall said.

"It's fine—I can do it," Brilliana said as she wound the music-box portion of the watch and pressed the button. "Looks like 'Jack' has become his word for 'make it go.'"

She started to hand the watch back to Niall, but her aunt took it instead. "Is this one of those automaton watches?"

An odd look of alarm crossed Niall's face, but before he could answer, Aunt Agatha had opened the watch to look at the inside panel. Then she froze.

"What is it?" Brilliana asked.

Aunt Agatha snapped the watch shut and held it out to Niall, her features as stiff as her starched pelerine. "Perhaps you should take this back, sir."

Brilliana got suspicious when a flush rose over Niall's features. Snatching the watch from her aunt's hand, she opened the panel to stare at it. Then she, too, froze as she saw what was inside.

Opposite the exposed inner workings of the watch was a little scene of a naked man standing between the legs of a reclining naked woman and doing *that* with her in perfect time to the music.

"Oh, good Lord," she muttered.

She couldn't take her eyes off it. It was so very *awful*. The man was freakishly well-endowed, with ballocks the size of oranges and a *thing* the size of a club. Worse yet, the woman's breasts were the size of cantaloupes, with badly rendered nipples.

The artist in her rebelled. "Whoever drew this has no sense of anatomy whatsoever."

Niall's bark of laughter shook the carriage. "*That's* what concerns you about it? The quality of the art?"

"Jack!" Silas cried and tried to take the watch. "Jack!"

She snapped the watch shut and tossed it to Niall. "Oh no, my lad, there will be none of this sort of Jack for you. Not now, not ever."

Niall only laughed all the harder, while Aunt Agatha muttered, "Good luck, my dear. I daresay Silas will grow up to be as incorrigible as the rest of them."

As if to prove his great-aunt right, Silas climbed up on the seat next to Niall, crying, "Jack, Jack!"

"Sorry, lad," Niall choked out. "Your mama says 'no Jack.'" He leaned over to murmur, his eyes twinkling at her, "Not until you're twelve at least."

She bristled. "If you think you are going to corrupt my son as early as twelve, Niall Lindsey, you have another think coming! I will throw that thing away first, I swear."

A strange look crossed his face. "When we marry, sweeting, you can throw away every watch I own. Including this one."

Oh, dear, she'd as much as said that he would be in her life when Silas turned twelve.

Then he added, rather gleefully, "Although, to be fair, it's not mine. It belongs to Warren."

"Of course it does," she snapped. "The two of you are peas in a pod."

"Warren asked me to hide it now that he's married—at least until he can convince Delia that he's *not* the rank scoundrel everyone believes she married. If you want it gone, I'll give it back to him. Or to Edwin, who gave it to Warren when they were both bachelors."

Now she was truly shocked. She wouldn't put anything past Delia's husband, but Clarissa's? "Lord Blakeborough made *this*?"

"No, I think he picked it up in some shop. You know how he likes automatons."

"Well, he ought to have better taste in them. That rendering is horrendous."

"Not as bad as some," her aunt put in. "My late husband had a Swiss one. Dreadful artwork. He used to leave it open to shock the maids, until I gave him a piece of my mind." She polished her spectacles with her handkerchief. "Men are children, my dear. The sooner you learn that, the better off you'll be."

That sobered Niall a bit. "I don't think there's any harm in having fun from time to time. For men or for women."

Brilliana snorted. "I prefer other entertainments, myself."

"Right." A sudden twinkle appeared in Niall's eyes. "Like a stroll in a garden, where you can observe the bark of the plane trees up close—for your sketches."

The blatant allusion to their activities yesterday was beyond the pale. Infuriating.

She tipped up her chin. "I do enjoy a good stroll—especially a *solitary* one."

He flashed her an impish smile. "I should think you'd have had enough of solitary strolls after the past year."

"Reynold wasn't much for strolling, anyway," Aunt Agatha put in. "My nephew preferred to drink."

Brilliana gaped at her. "Aunt Agatha! Don't tell him that. You mustn't speak ill of the dead."

"Why not? It's the truth. My nephew always drowned his sorrows in spirits. I never understood it. What did he have to be sorrowful about? He had a wife he adored, an estate of some consequence, and a son and heir. Yet he couldn't be content."

The comment sliced through Brilliana, because she knew why her husband hadn't been content. He'd never gained her love, and at the end he'd realized he never would. Even worse, he'd found out whom to blame for her damaged heart.

"Reynold simply wasn't like other men, that's all." Brilliana gestured to the pocket watch in Niall's hand. "He certainly would never have carried one of *those*."

Niall's eyes narrowed on her, but before he could retort, Aunt Agatha said, "Of course not. My nephew was rather stodgy, my dear. Everyone knew that."

Brilliana covered Silas's ears. "Don't say things like that in front of his son."

The woman sniffed. "Silas doesn't know his father from a peddler. And if Reynold had wanted to be known as anything else, he should have stayed around to raise the boy. For that matter, if he'd wanted to be known as a man of character, he shouldn't have tried to force a woman into wedding him."

Swallowing hard, Brilliana looked out the carriage window. She could feel Niall's gaze searching her, and she just couldn't meet it.

"So he really did buy Bree's hand in marriage," Niall said. "In exchange for his father discharging Sir Oswald's debt."

"He did." Her aunt sighed. "Though apparently he had to convince his father to agree."

The words caught Brilliana off guard. She swung around to stare at her aunt, her blood thundering in her ears. "What do you mean?"

"Captain Mace Trevor never cared about anything but money, my dear." Compassion mingled with guilt in her features. "I suppose I should have told you before. I didn't want to muck around with your relationship to my nephew, but the truth is that Reynold was the one to suggest that the debt be repaid by a marriage between you two."

That took Brilliana entirely by surprise. She'd known that Reynold was a bit obsessive about her, but he'd characterized their arranged marriage as something that had been cooked up by their fathers because of his interest in her and the gambling debt. According to him, he'd merely gone along with what their fathers proposed.

Apparently that had been a lie. As had so many other things in their marriage.

"Reynold was nothing if not resourceful," Brilliana said bitterly. "He tended to want his own way in everything."

"Yes, well, that's a characteristic of men, too, my dear," her aunt said.

"Not all men," Niall gritted out.

He said that a great deal. As if he were different. As if he would never betray her the way her husband had apparently betrayed her.

Hah! She knew better. "And *you* never want *your* own way," Brilliana said sarcastically. "You're perfectly happy to go along with whatever I want."

He smiled. "As long as what you want includes marriage to me, yes."

She told herself the words were merely part of their subterfuge, but the look in his eyes said otherwise. Unfortunately, his eyes lied.

Or did they? No matter how much she told herself that they did, she wanted to believe they didn't.

"My point is," Aunt Agatha broke in, "my dear niece has already had a husband who regarded her as nothing more than a beauty to show off to his friends and a means to produce his heir. She does not need another."

Niall tore his gaze from Brilliana. "And she won't get one. Because while I admire her beauty, I also regard her as a woman of intelligence, capable of great things. Why do you think I want her to produce *my* heir? Because any child would be lucky to have her as a mother."

Lord, but the man did know how to make a woman swoon.

He glanced out the window. "And speaking of that, we've reached the estate that my heir will inherit. Lady Pensworth, I do hope you'll be willing to keep an eye on young Silas this afternoon. Once I'm done with my business, I've promised Bree a tour of Margrave Manor, and I don't imagine it's something that Silas would enjoy."

Aunt Agatha regarded him steadily. "I quite agree."

And just like that, Niall managed to get his own way yet again.

Except that this time Brilliana could not resent him for it.

Thirteen

As it turned out, Niall's business only took as long as it took for Brilliana and Aunt Agatha to eat. Though he was still waiting to hear from an important associate, he told her he'd take her around his estate until word came that the man was available.

So now the two of them were surveying his property. Brilliana was in awe. The closest she'd ever been to Niall's estate had been when she'd attended the house party at Stoke Towers next door, and she hadn't actually seen it. She'd never imagined it could be so big.

Niall pulled up his gig and pointed to a large whitewashed building. "This is our dairy. We produce our own cheese from our own milk."

She sighed. "How I wish we could do the same. But we closed our dairy because we had to sell the cows to keep the estate afloat after Reynold's death."

"That's a damned shame," he said.

Ignoring the pity in his voice, she said, "We do have sheep, however, so we can sell our wool. Just no cheese."

"Actually, you can make cheese from sheep's milk, too. The English don't do it much, but it's common on the Continent. There's a delicious one called *queso manchego* that I ate often in Spain."

The hint of wistfulness in his voice arrested her. "You sound as if you miss being on the Continent."

"Not entirely. I don't miss Portugal." Something dark glittered in his eyes before he masked it. "But I do occasionally miss Spain. England will always be my home, and I'm glad to be back, but I miss the pleasant days and nights of summer in Corunna. It's rarely bone-chillingly cold, as it is here in winter. And I miss the spicy food, not to mention the friendly people."

"And the pretty women?" she asked, unable to help herself. That ridiculous watch had reminded her that he was a rogue at heart.

As if hearing the jealousy in her voice, he turned to face her on the seat. "Trust me, there wasn't a single woman in Spain or Portugal who held a candle to you. And no, I didn't spend my years there going from bed to bed, as you seem to have assumed."

"I know I have no right to complain about whom you might have bedded while on the Continent. I shared Reynold's bed for years, after all, but—"

"I had little time for women, Bree." His expression hardened. "I was too busy keeping up with Fulkham's tasks and trying not to get myself killed. And there were *no* other women until you married another man."

His jaw tightened. "I won't lie to you—I didn't handle that well, especially at first. So I tried to prove to myself that I was still the dashing fellow I believed myself to be." He stared off into the distance resolutely. "That I didn't care about being tossed aside."

For the first time, she realized how much her marriage so soon after his departure must have wounded him. And despite the fact that his admission to having bedded other women wounded *her*, she could hardly chide him for it. She'd married another man, and he'd known about it the entire time he was abroad. How could she blame him for finding solace where he could?

He slanted a glance at her. "Admit it, you were probably feeling much the same as I—it was why you accepted Trevor's courtship. You could, after all, have rebuffed him so entirely that he wouldn't have bothered you anymore."

"I did rebuff him at first, by not accepting his proposal of marriage."

"Yes, but you let him continue to court you, didn't you? So some part of you must have enjoyed being the center of his attention."

She examined that idea and realized there was

some truth to it. Reynold had been so very adoring of her—or at least of her looks, though she
hadn't realized how shallow his interest was at
the time. She'd ignored his attentions when she'd
been focused on waiting for Niall's return, but
after she'd begun hearing the rumors, her confidence had faltered.

"Yes, I suppose I did enjoy it a bit, especially
after your father told me the duel had been
fought over a mistress," she said. "Reynold treated
me like a princess, and he was relatively well
educated and able to engage in intelligent conversation. Aunt Agatha called him stodgy earlier,
and there's some truth to that, but at that point
all I could see was that he wasn't a rogue."

"Like me," he said tightly.

"Exactly. He didn't duel over mysterious
females. He didn't duel at all. He lived a perfectly respectable life." She shook her head. "It
was only after our marriage, when I realized that
his respectability had its roots in a contempt for
anything creative or unusual or unlike *him*, that I
found it harder to be with him."

And once Reynold realized she couldn't be as
adoring of *him* as he thought she should be, he'd
grown even more determined to make her love
him.

"I tried my best to hide my true feelings," she
went on, not sure why she was telling Niall all
this. "But I failed. As I said before, subterfuge
isn't my strong suit."

"That's because you, my dear, are a rebel."

She drew herself up. "I am not!"

"Oh yes, you are. A rebel is anyone who cannot help but be true to his or her own nature, no matter what society tells them."

When he reached over and rubbed her thigh through her skirts, she couldn't keep her breath from quickening or her heart from beating faster.

As if he could hear her reaction, he chuckled, then released her. "Consider this." He began ticking things off on his fingers. "One, you used to meet me in secret—because you *wanted* to and because you liked me, rogue or no. Two, you did your best to avoid marriage to Trevor, and three, when that didn't work, you refused to love him."

"All right, I suppose I was a bit of a rebel in my marriage."

"Not just in your marriage. Even when I first knew you, you aspired to draw things for money, when society would say you should only draw them for your own pleasure, like the rest of the ladies." His eyes gleamed at her. "And today, when confronted with a naughty watch, you didn't throw it out the window. Instead you critiqued the workmanship. You must confess that at heart, you're as much a rebel as I."

"That's nonsense," she said with a sniff, annoyed that he knew her so well. "We should go on. Silas is napping now, but once he gets up—"

"Whatever you wish," he said, laughter lurking in his face as he picked up the reins. "So tell me, what would you like to see next, my Lady Rebel?"

She ignored his teasing. "Show me everything. Or as much as you can before Silas wakes up and begins trying Aunt Agatha's patience."

For the next hour, he showed off his estate with obvious pride. He took her by a well-stocked conservatory, a stable full of prime horse-flesh, a working tannery, and several pretty little tenant cottages.

How she wished Camden Hall could be so extensive and well run. No one who'd visited Margrave Manor would believe Fulkham's manu-factured gossip about Niall's needing money, so it was a good thing Niall didn't entertain.

Yet, anyway. That would surely change once she married him.

She caught herself. *If* she married him. Lord, she had to watch that. If she let something like that slip in front of him, he would be relentless in his pursuit, and she needed time and space to think.

They moved on to the fields. He told her about the equipment he'd bought to increase his barley production, then took her to where the corn was being harvested.

He fairly strutted around the fields. Clearly, he was rather proud of his crops.

And she couldn't blame him. "What are your yields?" she asked.

When he rattled them off, she gazed at him

in awe. "From what I understand, that is very impressive."

"You don't have to sound so surprised," he said dryly. "I'm only a rogue when *you're* around. The rest of the time, I try to be a responsible land-owner."

She arched an eyebrow. "Who carries a naughty watch."

He smirked at her. "As I said, a man needs a bit of fun." With a quick glance at the nearby workers, he smoothed his hand down her backside.

"Don't do that *here*," she whispered.

"*Here* is the perfect place for it. All this fertility is in the air, giving rise to thoughts of plowing and planting and—"

"Stop that," she said, struggling not to laugh. He was such a . . . *man*. Moving away, she strolled along the edge of the fields. "And you still haven't explained how you got such grand yields. You've only been back in England a month. How did you manage it?"

"The planting was overseen by Warren, who managed Margrave Manor in my absence. But while he did his best, he had his own properties to run. So in trying to bring the estate up to snuff, I've instituted some new harvesting methods, which have helped to improve our yields a bit." He led her away from the fields. "I've got plans to do much more. Margrave Manor has great potential. As, I imagine, does Camden Hall."

"I certainly hope you're right."

They walked to the top of a hill, and she halted as the vista spread out before her took her breath away. "Are those apple orchards?"

"And pear." He smiled. "We make our own cider and jam."

"This would be a perfect spot for drawing, with the fields behind and the orchards below. And look, we can even see the stream that borders your property! Not to mention the folly over at Stoke Towers. So many subjects to sketch!"

His eyes gleamed at her. "You can come here whenever you like. We can have picnics. Silas can slide down the hill, as boys like to do—"

"Oh, he's much too young for that."

"Now, perhaps, but in a few years . . ."

The words hung in the air between them, a promise of their future together. Oh, Lord, she was already thinking of them as married. She shouldn't encourage him. And yet . . .

"Could we see the orchard?" she asked, unable to keep the excitement out of her voice.

With a grin, he offered her his arm for descending the path that wound down the hill. She tucked her hand in the crook of his elbow, trying not to show how the intimacy of that small act was affecting her.

As they strolled down the path, he asked, "So, what do you grow at Camden Hall?"

"Flax. That's what Reynold preferred."

"You're better off with corn. It's in high demand just now."

"Is it?" A sigh escaped her. "I confess to not knowing much about markets and such, though I seem to recall that corn doesn't grow well in our part of Cheshire."

"I can help you find out for certain. And also determine what other crops might be profitable at present."

"That would be exceedingly useful. But what about drainage? And where do you get your fertilizer? Oh, and . . ."

Encouraged by his willingness to teach her, she peppered him with questions about all the things that had perplexed or confused her. He answered each one, appearing to grow more bemused by the moment.

After she voiced her concern about the feasibility of having a dairy at Camden Hall, he said, "You know more than you let on about estate management."

"I don't know nearly enough. But I'm trying to learn."

"You seem to have a clear picture of what your estate needs."

"It was hard-won, believe me. After Reynold lost so much at the gaming tables and . . . died, Delia and I couldn't afford a manager—so it was either sink or swim. And since Reynold had never taught me how to run the place . . ." A lump stuck in her throat. "He would never have explained to me the things you did today. He didn't trust me that much."

"I doubt it had to do with trust. He probably just thought he should be the one to handle estate matters, so you could take care of other ones. Like raising his son."

A harsh laugh boiled out of her. "Yes, he was so concerned about the well-being of his son that he—" She choked back the impulse to tell Niall about the suicide. "It doesn't matter. Why are you defending him, anyway?"

"I'm not. I agree with your aunt—he shouldn't have gambled away so much of Camden Hall, or stumbled off a bridge drunk, leaving you and his sister to handle his property without any training. An estate needs a person at the helm who knows what he—or *she*—is doing."

She narrowed her gaze on him. "And you would be fine with having the person at the helm be a woman."

"Of course. Warren wasn't the only one who looked after Margrave Manor, you know. Clarissa had a part in it as well. Did a damned fine job with what she handled, too."

"That doesn't surprise me one whit," she said stoutly.

"Me either." He smiled down at her. "Rather like your late husband, my sister is nothing if not resourceful."

"Yes, but Clarissa is the good sort of resourceful. Reynold was the bad sort—he was only canny when it came to *his* needs."

"But clearly not when it came to yours." He

searched her face. "You really didn't know that the arranged marriage was his idea, did you?"

"No. You probably think I'm an idiot for it—"

"I could never think you an idiot. Naïve sometimes, perhaps, but not an idiot."

"You may change your mind when you hear that I truly believed he felt as trapped as I, embarrassed to be forced into proposing to the woman who'd already refused him once." She gazed down at the path. "I don't know why it has taken me so off guard. In truth, nothing I've learned recently about Reynold should surprise me—not his secret machinations, or his losing all that money to Warren's brother, or—"

"Warren's brother!" Niall stopped short on the path. "What the blazes are you talking about?"

She gaped at him. "You didn't know?"

The shock on his face made that perfectly clear. "How could I have known?"

"Didn't Warren tell you?"

"He damned well did not."

That's when it dawned on her. Warren and Delia had only found out about the Lord Hartley connection right before they left for their honeymoon. That was when she'd learned of it, too.

"Which of Warren's brothers are you talking about?" Niall persisted, now clearly agitated. "He has five."

Goodness gracious. She probably shouldn't have said anything. "Lord Hartley. I think they call him Hart."

"Hart." Niall scrubbed a hand over his face. "My cousin Hart is the one to whom your husband lost all his money? How the deuce did *that* happen?"

"Reynold wagered three thousand pounds on a game of piquet in exchange for Lord Hartley wagering a piece of information Reynold wanted very badly."

"What piece of information?"

Oh, dear, now she *really* wished she hadn't mentioned it. "Um. Where you were in Spain." She gave a shuddering sigh. "You see . . . it turns out that when Reynold went to London, it wasn't because he had a burning need to gamble. He went because . . . well . . . he was looking for *you*."

Fourteen

For a moment, Niall could only gape at her. "He was looking for *me*?" he repeated inanely. "But what . . . why . . ." He dragged a hand through his hair. "How the bloody hell did your husband even *know* about me? Did you tell him?"

"Of course not." She wrapped her arms over her waist. "He found out on his own."

"How? And how much did he find out? That we'd been in love? And had planned to marry?"

"Everything. He . . . saw some sketches of you that I kept in the bottom of my trunk."

That arrested Niall. "You kept sketches of me." Which said more than anything that she'd never stopped caring about him. Missing him.

"A few," she admitted. "So he demanded to know who the sketches were of, and I . . . told him. I made it sound as if our association was casual, that we were merely friends, but as you know, I'm not very good at—"

"Subterfuge, yes," he bit out. "You've made that abundantly clear."

"That's why my answer didn't satisfy him. He kept badgering me for the truth, and I kept sticking to my story. So one day while I was shopping with Delia, he turned my bedchamber upside down looking for something to confirm his suspicions, and he found the sealed letter I'd wanted your father to send to you."

"You kept that, too," Niall said, incredulous.

"It was my reminder not to . . . trust my heart again." She glanced away. "Reynold opened and read it. So he learned everything. How I'd begged you to return. How I . . . felt about being forced to marry him. The truth that I'd struggled so hard to hide from him."

"Oh, God," Niall said hoarsely.

He actually felt a bit sorry for Trevor. He could only imagine how *he* would have reacted to such a letter. To have this gorgeous angel telling him that he'd always been second choice would have destroyed him.

Then again, *he* would never have forced into marriage a woman who didn't want him.

"We had a horrendous row over it," she admitted. "He demanded to know what had happened between you and me, and I had no choice but to tell him."

"And as a result he ran off to London in search of me?"

"Not right away, no." She picked nervously at

her pelerine. "He brooded for a few weeks first. I couldn't bear it. So I sat him down and pointed out that you had betrayed me, that I no longer cared about you, that I'd lost all feeling for you years ago. I told him he and Silas were my whole life, and that wasn't ever going to change. I honestly thought that was the end of it."

Niall shook his head. "Did you tell him you loved him?"

Her face closed up. "No. But he knew I didn't from the day he proposed. I made that very clear."

"Back then, it wouldn't have mattered to him *what* you said. No doubt he'd kept hoping he could change your mind." The way Niall kept hoping that he could convince her to take a chance on him again. "But after he learned about me and you didn't profess your love for *him*, no amount of proclaiming that you were done with me would have convinced him I was out of your life for good. He knew he would never have your heart."

"He already had the rest of me! And it wasn't as if I could have . . . taken up with you again if you'd returned. Plus, there was no chance of your returning, which I also made perfectly clear."

God, she understood men so little. "Sweeting, what he heard was, 'If my former love were here, I'd be with him, but he's not, so I'm content to be with you.'"

"But how could he think that?" she cried. "I told him I hated you!"

"You didn't get rid of your sketches of me. Or

the letter." Which gave him hope. "*Somewhere* in your heart you kept me close, and I daresay he realized that. Hate is the flip side of a coin to love. Indifference is just . . . indifference. And death to a marriage."

Hurt and guilt shone in her face. "I couldn't help that I didn't love—"

"I'm not saying it's your fault. Just that knowing you didn't love *him* probably made hearing about me even worse. Because it meant there was a reason you couldn't love him. A reason you would never change your mind."

She turned to walk blindly down the hill. "I thought he accepted that our marriage was the only thing I allowed myself to care about. He never let on that he didn't believe me."

He strode alongside her. "Because he didn't want you to know. A man has his pride, after all."

"But it was another month before he went off to London. By then I'd thought the matter settled, since he never mentioned it again."

"I assure you, it was festering all that time." When she stared at him, her eyes stark, Niall gentled his voice. "I'm judging from how *I* would have reacted."

They walked to the edge of the orchard in silence. He wanted to take her in his arms, kiss and touch her, and remind her how much he cared about her. But this probably wasn't the time.

"So," Niall ventured, "what explanation did he give for his trip to London?"

"He said he needed to take care of estate business and would be back in a couple of days. Instead, he was gone a fortnight." She fiddled with her pelerine. "When he returned, he was despondent over his loss of three thousand pounds. To pay the debt, he'd had to mortgage the estate to the hilt."

"He didn't tell you why he'd lost the money?"

"He only said a man had cheated him at cards." She let out a shaky breath.

"Hart cheated? That doesn't sound like . . . Well, I mean he *could*, but I wouldn't expect—"

"You'll have to ask Warren why. But I think Lord Hartley believed, because of the questions Reynold asked about you, that he was looking for you because he wanted vengeance for Joseph Whiting. There'd already been another of Mr. Whiting's relatives looking for you, after all."

"True. And that makes sense. Hart would have protected me at all costs." He shoved his hands in his pockets. "No doubt your husband was too embarrassed to admit he was seeking the rival for his wife's affections."

"Too proud, more like."

"That, too." Niall glanced at her. "But what did he hope to accomplish by learning my location?"

"I'm not sure." She sighed. "All I can think is that he wanted to . . . find you and discover why you'd had my heart and he hadn't? Or perhaps he meant to call you out. I doubt we'll ever know. He must have had *some* plan, but he never revealed it.

Not until after Delia and Warren's wedding, when Lord Hartley admitted what had happened, did I even learn that Reynold had gone there for the express purpose of finding out where you were."

A pang of guilt seized Niall. Because of *him*, she'd lost her husband and been saddled with a debt-ridden estate. Because of *him*, Silas had lost a father. According to Fulkham, rumor had it that the man had committed suicide.

He wondered if she knew, but he didn't dare ask—not when she was this upset over what Trevor had done by arranging their marriage without her knowledge. If it were true, then Niall had *that* on his conscience, too. And yet . . .

If not for what her husband had done, she wouldn't be free again. And it might be selfish of him, but that was all that mattered to him.

Although one thing still disturbed him about her tale. "So, your husband loved you so much that he wagered everything he had to find his rival."

"If you can call it 'love.'" She wandered into the orchard, walking aimlessly among the apple trees that hung heavy with fruit. "That's what *he* called it. But . . ." She shook her head. "Do you remember saying, 'A man pursuing beauty will pay anything to gain it'? That's how it was with him."

He followed her into the trees. "He saw you as his Botticelli." Who wouldn't? Here in this verdant green, she was a succulent fruit any man would want to devour.

"A Botticelli that he'd realized he didn't own.

All that mattered was that no one else have his Botticelli."

"I can't say I blame him. When I heard you'd married him, I wanted to march back here and steal you away." He gave a shuddering breath. "But then I let myself be swayed by my father's words about your being interested in me only for my title, and I realized—or thought I realized—that you didn't *want* me."

Her eyes luminous in the shaded orchard, she halted to face him. "Your father said that about me?"

"Why do you think I called you an adventuress? Father was the first to use the term."

She planted her hands on her hips. "Why, that . . . that . . . *liar*. He sounded so sympathetic to my concerns. So sincere! I *believed* him when he said you truly wouldn't want me to follow you to Spain. And all the while, he was playing with us both! Toying with us! Lying to us!"

"It appears so, yes." Niall could no longer cling to the image of his father as a man of honor who would never betray him. To do so would mean that everything she'd said was a lie, which he simply couldn't accept.

Clearly Father had been so obsessed with protecting Clarissa that he hadn't cared who else he hurt. Which in itself felt like a betrayal.

Niall lifted his hand to cup her cheek. "We were just too young and foolish to see past my father's machinations to the truth."

As he smoothed his fingers over her flawless skin, her breathing grew ragged. "I wouldn't have listened to him at all . . . if I'd known the truth about why you dueled. He was able to persuade me precisely because *you* kept that secret."

Uh-oh. He wasn't ready to discuss that further, not until he met with Edwin.

So he did the only thing he could think of—tugged her close and kissed her the way he'd been wanting to since this morning. Deeply. Thoroughly. With tongue and teeth and all the raw, hot need churning inside him.

And for a moment she opened up to him, his lovely rose, grabbing him by the shoulders and straining against him to kiss him back, giving as good as she got.

Then she caught herself and tore her mouth free. "Niall . . . what I'm trying to say is . . . you *still* keep secrets from me."

"None that matter," he countered.

When he tried to cover her mouth with his again, she turned her head. So he shifted to kissing her jaw, her throat . . . the few bits of pure, sweet flesh that weren't covered up by her demure carriage gown.

When he tongued the hollow of her throat, she moaned. "My husband . . . kept secrets, too. And I hated it."

He scattered kisses over her cheeks and nose. "You kept secrets from him, as well."

"Just the one. And I shouldn't have. Perhaps

if I'd told him about you from the beginning . . . he'd still be alive."

"Then God forgive me," he growled, "but I'm glad you didn't."

"Don't say that." The words were a thready whisper.

"It's the truth." He tightened his arm about her waist. "If he hadn't died, I'd now be looking for a wife in society and comparing every woman to you."

"No, you wouldn't. You thought me an adventuress. Some part of you still does, or you would tell me the tru—"

He attempted to kiss her again, but she caught his head to stay him. "My point is," she whispered, "you know every one of my secrets, but you won't tell me yours."

"I will. Eventually."

"Why not *now*?"

With firm purpose, he walked her backward toward an apple tree. "Because right now I want only one thing—to make love to you. To remind you that there are things between us that transcend the past. I know how to make you yearn and burn. I know how to give you pleasure." He lowered his voice to a harsh rasp. "And you want me to. You know that you do."

When she swallowed hard, he exulted. She wasn't as immune to him as she tried to pretend.

"I—I said no bed play."

"I see no bed."

She eyed him askance. "You're splitting hairs, you devil. You knew what I meant." When he pressed her up against the tree, she lifted her eyes heavenward. "What is it with you and trees, anyway? My maid still hasn't worked the stains out of the last gown you ruined. And why must we do this *here*, where anyone might find us?"

"Because we can," he rasped against her lips. "Because we want to. Because I own every inch of this land, and I want to take you in the place where I mean for us to build a life together." He dragged up her skirts. "I'll buy you a new gown, sweeting. But all these apples hanging from the trees are making me hunger for something sweet, and I simply have to indulge."

Even her look of confusion bewitched him. "What are you talking about?" she asked.

He dropped to his knees. "You, Bree. I want to feast on *you*."

Holding her skirts bunched up at her waist with one hand, he used the other to part the opening in her drawers so he could view the lovely flesh he meant to kiss and devour. He suspected that her stodgy husband had never done *this* to her, and when he leaned forward to place his mouth on her and she gasped, he knew he'd guessed right.

"What the devil are you . . ." She released a shaky sigh as he licked her pretty mons, then delved deeper with his tongue. "Oh . . . my . . . *word*."

God, she was as luscious and juicy as ripe fruit. He could dine on Bree for hours. Or at least long enough to show her that there was so much more to making love than her arse of a husband had shown her.

"Hold this." He thrust her gathered skirts into her hand, and miraculously, she did his bidding.

Then he set about giving her delicious honey-pot the attention it deserved. He'd always loved the taste of a woman fully aroused, but God, Bree tasted better than anything. And she was so receptive, too, clutching at his head to hold him to her as she pushed her cleft against his tongue.

"Niall . . . heavens . . . that is so . . . so . . . *naughty*."

"For my naughty wanton, yes." He licked and teased and tormented, relishing her sighs and moans and eager little thrusts of her pelvis against his mouth. "I love when you're naughty, sweeting."

He thrust a finger inside her, and she murmured a soft, "How *marvelous* . . ." that shot his arousal to new heights. He didn't know how he'd control himself until he'd brought her to release.

But he must. Because he refused to be the sort of selfish lover she was used to. He intended to make her blood race and her head spin, to make her forget about anything but how this felt, how they felt together.

It was the only way he could think of to reassure her that they would make a good match.

That they could start again. Together. No matter what secrets he had to continue keeping.

She was panting now, making little mewling sounds that turned him harder than the trunk she leaned against. Feeling the blood rising in his cock, he increased the strokes of his tongue across her hard little pearl as he drove into her with one finger, then two, in his desperate bid to bring her to *la petite mort*.

Soon she was shimmying and pushing against him like a greedy urchin eager for more, until he could hear her moaning and feel the spasms signaling her release against his tongue.

It was all he could do not to crow his triumph as she pulled him hard against her and let out a low cry of pleasure. At least he could make her feel this, damn it. Perhaps for now, that would be enough for her.

While she gasped and shuddered, he relished the taste and smell of her as he brushed kisses to her bared thighs, smoothed his hands over her silk-clad calves . . . indulged himself in the glory that was Bree's body.

Once she calmed, he wiped his mouth on her petticoat, then rose.

"You are . . . full of . . . surprises . . ." she choked out as she clung limply to him.

He drew her arms about his neck. "You've scarcely seen a tenth of what I can do, my dear Lady Rebel." He rubbed against her, knowing she could surely feel his hardened cock even through his drawers and trousers. "Shall I show you more?"

Her eyes softened, and he was sure she was about to agree to more wild and woolly swiving, when a faraway cry arrested them both.

"Lord Margrave? Are you down in the orchard?" came a voice from the top of the hill.

Bree tensed up and Niall groaned. "Don't answer," he ordered her. "He'll move on."

"But it might be important." She fixed him with an anxious gaze. "It could have to do with Silas, who has surely been awake for some time. Or it could even concern Aunt Agatha."

"Damnation. I can't wait until the day I can have you to myself, whenever and wherever I please, without all these cursed interruptions."

She shot him a sad little smile as she pushed down her skirts and straightened her clothing. "That day won't come until Silas—and whatever other children we have—are grown and have moved away. So you'd best get used to interruptions."

Nothing could have reminded him more effectively of how different they both were now. Although he was still a carefree bachelor, she was no longer the virginal innocent. She was a mother with responsibilities he couldn't begin to fathom, as well as a landowner who must take care of her own people.

He must do the same for his, which would mean juggling the needs of his estate with the needs of hers. Somehow he'd have to make sure that by marrying him, she didn't lose any more than she already had as a result of her husband's selfishness. He would have to accept the messy circumstances of her situation and Silas's, to make room for all of it in his life, if he was to gain her.

"Very well," he said. "Let's go see what the blasted fellow wants."

At least she'd spoken of possible children with him. That heartened him.

After making sure they both looked presentable, they left the trees and headed up the hill. Spotting his underbutler coming over the top of it, Niall called out, "Down here! We were touring the orchard."

The servant hurried down the hill to meet them. "You said to let you know at once if Lord Blakeborough answered the message you sent to him at Stoke Towers earlier, sir, and it just arrived. So I came right out after you."

He'd completely forgotten that he'd sent a note to Edwin asking to meet with him at his earliest convenience.

As the servant handed over the sealed missive, Bree gazed up at Niall. "Why is Lord Blakeborough at Stoke Towers?"

Gritting his teeth at the need to evade the truth with her yet again, he said, "Edwin thought my sister could use a respite from the excitement of town, so he brought her out here to take the country air for a while."

Bree frowned. "But at the party, I got the distinct impression that she meant to stay in town until close to the end of her time."

He didn't answer right away, so intent was he on reading the message. It said, *Come whenever you can. I have no set engagements.*

Good. Niall had been worried that he might have to return to town for the card game tonight before he'd had a chance to see his brother-in-law.

Shoving the note into his pocket, he told his underbutler to go fetch the gig and bring it to the top of the hill. As the servant scurried off, Niall offered Bree his arm. "We must return to the house. I need to go over to Stoke Towers and discuss something important with Edwin before you and I get back on the road this evening."

Bree took his arm and let him lead her up the hill. "We can stop on our way back to town. Aunt Agatha and I would love to visit with Clarissa while you're closeted with her husband. And I'm sure Clarissa would enjoy seeing Silas."

"Absolutely not," he said without thinking. When that seemed to startle her, he cursed his quick tongue. "I mean, Silas is a bit too boisterous for a woman in her condition, don't you think?"

She narrowed her gaze on him. "We took him on a visit to Clarissa's only last week."

"All the same, I'd prefer to be certain of your welcome before we descend on them en masse."

Halting to face him, she lifted one eyebrow. "What's going on, Niall?"

God, how he wanted to tell her about Clarissa's difficulties. But he'd promised his sister's maid that he would respect Edwin's wishes, and so he must. At least until he was sure Clarissa and Edwin didn't mind Bree knowing. "Nothing's going on."

He strode up the hill ahead of her to where the gig was already waiting, with his underbutler at the ready. "Please take our guest back to the house," he told the servant, "and make sure she and Lady Pensworth and young Silas have a good tea."

Bree came up alongside him. "Niall—"

"I'll be along presently, I promise," he told her firmly. Taking her hand, he pressed a kiss to the back. "It's just some business matters."

"Then why can't—"

He released her hand and strode off toward the stream that separated the two estates. He'd had enough of this secrecy. He would meet with Edwin and be done with the prevarications and evasions once and for all.

Then he and Bree could finally start making plans for their lives together.

~∞~

The ride back to the manor house began as a silent one, which was fine by Brilliana. She wasn't sure she could trust herself to speak civilly right now, even to one of Niall's servants.

When it came to her, Niall could be a very bad liar. And the fact that he could show her such sensual delights, then shut himself off from her yet again, drove her mad.

She must have made some frustrated sound, for Niall's underbutler slanted a glance at her. "You mustn't let his lordship upset you, ma'am. I daresay he doesn't mean to be curt. He just has a lot on his mind these days."

"I'm sure he does." *As do I.*

They traveled another half mile in silence.

"Your boy Silas is a sweet lad," the underbutler went on. "Already got our housekeeper wrapped around his finger, and that's saying something."

The words softened her. "I do hope he hasn't been too much trouble."

"Not one bit. Reminds us of his lordship at that age." When she looked at him curiously, he said, "I was a footboy then. The master and I practically grew up together, we did. He had a stubborn streak that fairly drove his father mad."

"I can only imagine," she said dryly, remembering what Niall had said about his father. "Was the previous earl strict with his son?"

"Oh yes, ma'am. Hired a tutor who made the young master toe the line until he went off to school. Then the old earl tried to keep him from mixing with the rakish blades there by having him live with a fine family all by himself, instead of on the premises at Eton."

"Did that work?"

"Hardly. You know the young gentlemen, always up for a jolly time."

"Yes." A jolly time that generally involved naked females.

Still, she had to admit she was benefiting from Niall's education in the art of pleasing women. She fought a blush. How could she have known that a man putting his mouth down there might be enjoyable?

Or, for that matter, that making love could be so pleasurable. Eminently pleasurable. Only imagine if she and Niall were to do that often. . . .

She frowned. She mustn't think only of their physical encounters; there was more at stake than a few moments of passion. Of very delicious, enticing . . .

Oh, Lord, she was becoming such a ridiculous wanton.

"So," she said, to put such thoughts from her mind, "you were saying that his lordship's friends were all rakish blades."

"Not all. There was Lord Blakeborough, the only one that the earl approved of, on account of his being a responsible sort. But the earl found even some of the young master's cousins suspect. Like Lord Knightford, who wasn't allowed at the house in those years. The old earl disapproved of the marquess's reputation."

"I can see why, though I gather that his father's disapproval didn't stop my fiancé from going out on the town with the marquess in their later years—at least before he left the country."

"Oh yes, those two gentlemen were thick as thieves for a while. Had some wild times, from what I hear." He clucked his tongue at the horses. "But the young master changed in that last year before he got sent away. Started paying better attention to the estate and even reconciled with his father. So that duel he fought took us all by surprise. Didn't seem like something he'd be wont to do anymore."

She eyed him closely. "Do you know *why* he fought the duel?"

"Afraid not. The whole thing was kept hush-hush." He looked at her. "But don't you believe what the gossips say about it. He wasn't the sort to fight over a mistress. We never heard nary a word about a mistress until he fled the country."

That didn't mean he hadn't had one. "Why are you telling me this?"

The servant shrugged. "If you're going to marry his lordship, I think you should hear how he really is, not who the gossips say he is." He shot her a veiled look. "He's not a fortune hunter. I don't know who cooked up that non-sense about him, but it's a lie. He doesn't need to marry for money."

Fulkham had done his job so well that word had trickled down to Niall's servants. Well, at least they didn't believe it. Nothing like a loyal servant to take the true measure of a man, no matter what the world said about him.

"Besides," the underbutler went on, "I can tell that the master truly likes you. That's why he's marrying you, I daresay."

She bit back a smile. "I hope you're right. Because I truly like him." Except for when he was being so secretive.

Meanwhile, his servant seemed perfectly willing to tell every secret he knew about his master. Perhaps she could get him to reveal more. "Do you happen to know what his meeting with Lord Blakeborough this afternoon is about?"

The underbutler shrugged. "It might be about her ladyship's condition."

"Clarissa?" Her heart caught in her throat. "Is something wrong?"

He blinked at her. "He didn't say?"

"I'm sure he would have if he'd had the chance," she said quickly, not wanting to squelch his eagerness to tell all. "But we were too busy discussing the estate to talk about his sister."

"Well, she's having a bit of trouble with the babe. From what I hear, it's nothing to be overly concerned with, but Lord Blakeborough isn't taking any chances. That's why he brought her out here. To get her away from the city and visitors and such."

Visitors like her and Aunt Agatha and Silas, who might be "too boisterous" for a woman in her condition. Did Niall really think she would do anything to jeopardize the health of his sister?

Goodness gracious. The man was a piece of work, keeping everything close to his chest while she confided in him regarding everything.

You didn't tell him about Reynold's suicide.

She scowled. That was different. It had naught to do with him.

It had everything to do with him. If not for what your husband found out about you and Niall, Reynold might still be alive.

A plague on her noisy conscience for being right. And, Lord forgive her, she was glad Reynold *wasn't* still alive. What did that say about her?

It said that she wanted what Niall was offering—passion, family, a future. She wanted to be his wife, to share his thoughts, to have his heart. She wanted to have picnics with him and engage in scandalous outdoors lovemaking and, yes, give him children, lots and lots of children who'd be playmates for Silas and a comfort to both her and Niall in their old age. It was all she'd ever wanted.

The question was, did she want those things so badly that she was willing to overlook his secrets and his youthful peccadilloes and his refusal to trust her?

Of that, she wasn't sure.

Fifteen

If Niall's argument with Bree hadn't already killed his erection, this visit to Stoke Towers would certainly have done so. The servant who'd shown him to Edwin's study had walked as if on eggshells. The very air in the manor house was subdued, as if its denizens were holding their breaths for Clarissa.

Had her situation worsened? God, what would he do if it had?

Edwin walked in, looking even more somber than usual. "I suppose you've come because you heard about your sister's troubles."

Niall braced himself for anything. "Yes, when I came by your town house this morning, her lady's maid told me. How serious is it?"

"Dr. Worth says that a woman can sometimes have a little blood at this stage, that it's not unusual." Edwin let out a shuddering breath. "But I can't stop thinking about the possibility that she might lose the babe." His eyes looked a bit wild. "I don't know how I'd bear it. How *she* would bear it."

"If Dr. Worth says she'll be fine, then she will be," Niall said to soothe the man's agitation. "You trust him, don't you?"

"With my life—but it's not my life at stake. Still, he says that if the bleeding doesn't become heavy, then it's naught to be concerned about."

"So, where is Clarissa now?" Niall asked.

"In her bedchamber. The doctor says she needs plenty of rest."

"Of course." Niall eyed his friend closely. "I don't suppose I could see her?"

Edwin's face closed up. "No visitors for a while, Dr. Worth said."

"Even family?" Niall said, though he wasn't entirely surprised by Edwin's answer. He'd already known he might not be able to talk to her.

"Yes, even family. And especially not your mother. At least not until Dr. Worth can be sure this isn't anything more than normal. He was very firm on the 'no visitors' rule."

"It's probably a good one."

"Yes," Edwin said absently.

"She doesn't mind, does she?"

"No, she doesn't want to risk the baby any more than I do." Edwin stared out the window. "I only wish there was something more I could do to help. I feel so . . . bloody useless."

If ever Niall had been in doubt about his

brother-in-law's feelings for Clarissa, those doubts were dispelled. The man was obviously distraught. "I'm afraid this is one area in which a husband isn't much good to a woman, other than to keep her company—which might be more helpful than you'd think. Clarissa's unaccustomed to being cut off from people, so she probably welcomes your companionship."

Edwin snorted. "You'd think so, but no. She says I fuss over her too much, that I'm as bad as an old woman."

Niall let out a laugh that made his brother-in-law scowl at him. "Sorry, but that sounds exactly like something Clarissa would say."

With a distracted nod, Edwin walked toward the door. "I don't mean to be inhospitable, old man, but—"

"Actually, I didn't just come to find out how Clarissa is doing," Niall put in. "I need to speak to you about something important."

That arrested Edwin. "All right. I can spare a little time." He walked over to a brandy decanter. "Something to drink?"

"Oh yes," Niall said. In some ways, discussing Clarissa's assault would have been easier with her than her husband. Now that the moment was upon him, he wasn't sure how to begin.

He waited while Edwin poured them each a finger of brandy, then took a drink to steady his nerves. "Warren told me that you know why I fought that duel with Joseph Whiting."

Though Edwin's gaze darkened, he nodded.

"I realize this is difficult to talk about," Niall went on, "but here's my situation."

As succinctly as possible, he laid out the details of the aftermath of the duel. Niall revealed everything that had happened between him and Bree years ago, including telling Edwin the lies Father had told Bree in an apparent attempt to save Niall from himself.

He even explained Fulkham's scheme, and how that had brought him and Bree back together again. Niall knew he could trust Edwin with *that* secret, since Edwin was indebted to Fulkham for the latter's refusal to let Edwin be prosecuted for the death—in self-defense—of Whiting's other cousin, Durand.

Edwin asked more questions about Fulkham's scheme than Niall expected, and Niall answered impatiently, wanting to get to the important part of the discussion—his desire to tell Bree the truth about the past.

But at last, Edwin seemed satisfied with Niall's answers. Only then did he discuss what Niall had revealed about his past with Bree. "Clarissa and I guessed that there'd been something between you two, but we had no idea of the full extent of it. She'll be astonished. *When* I can tell her, that is."

That arrested Niall. "What do you mean?"

"I'm not about to reveal any of it now. She already feels guilty that you went into exile because of what she sees as her 'error in judgment' by letting Whiting get her alone."

When Niall tensed at the very idea, Edwin added hastily, "Trust me, I've fought to disabuse her of that notion. You and I see that bastard for what he was—a rank blackguard—and I think I've convinced her that she wasn't at fault for what happened."

"Thank God. I have *never* blamed her for my exile. And I have certainly never regretted fighting that duel. If you could have seen her lying there beneath Whiting, crying and bleeding—" He caught himself as Edwin paled. "Sorry—I don't know how much of it she told you."

"Everything, I think. But it took weeks, even after we were married." His voice hardened. "That man nearly destroyed her. And I refuse to let him take one more thing from us. Which is why I'm not telling her any of this until after the babe is born."

"That's fair," Niall said. "I had hoped to gain her permission to reveal the truth about the duel to Bree, who still believes that I fought over some mistress, but if you think Clarissa shouldn't be bothered with it—"

"I do. If she learns that you lost your only love because of what happened to her that night, it will eat at her, and she doesn't need that burden right now."

The finality of the words struck a chill through Niall. "I understand. And you're probably right."

He stared his brother-in-law down. "But I hope I at least have *your* permission to tell Bree the truth."

When Edwin said nothing, merely turning aside to gulp a generous portion of brandy, Niall's blood pounded in his ears.

"Edwin," Niall said firmly, "Bree believes I betrayed her with another woman. She's balking at marrying me precisely because she knows I'm keeping secrets from her. I have to tell her."

"Of course you do. Just not yet."

"Damn it, man—"

"This is my *wife* we're talking about!" Edwin faced Niall, a hint of desperation in his features. "And my child, possibly my heir. If any of this got out, if people knew that Clarissa was raped all those years ago—"

"Bree would never jeopardize Clarissa's health or reputation. They're friends, for God's sake."

Edwin glowered at him. "Not close ones. Not the way Clarissa and my sister are friends. All it would take is one word from Mrs. Trevor to the wrong person, and Clarissa could be embroiled in an enormous scandal. You *know* that."

"She would never speak of it to anyone. She cares about your sister—about *me*—too much to do such a thing."

"Really? The woman married another man instead of waiting for you."

"To save her family from debtors' prison."

"Exactly—and she's bound to resent you because you left her to endure that. For all you know, she may eventually resent you for helping to get her father prosecuted as a criminal."

"After what that bastard did to her by gambling her future away, she'll probably cheer when he's arrested."

"And what about after her name is dragged through the mud and her reputation permanently besmirched? After her son is forced to live with the ensuing scandal? No matter what Fulkham promised, if her father proves guilty, there will be a trial and, no doubt, a conviction. She'll have to endure gossip and rumor—"

"She doesn't care about that."

"She should. And so should you, for that matter, if you mean to marry her."

That shook him a little. "I would brave any scandal to have her."

"You say that now. You may not be so easy about it when it dogs you—and your family—for years." He looked grim. "Trust me, I know."

It dawned on Niall then that Edwin's brother Samuel had put the family through quite a number of scandals. No wonder Edwin was being so wary.

"My point is," Edwin went on, "if she grows to resent you for it, she may grow to resent Clarissa, too. All of this—the duel, your exile, her being forced to marry another man—began with Clarissa's rape. You may not resent your sister for it, but you don't know that Mrs. Trevor will feel as you do."

Niall frowned. "Don't be absurd."

"When you tell her the truth, you're taking a chance. You can't be absolutely sure of her."

"But I can." At least he was fairly sure he could. Granted, Edwin had a point about her resentment, but Bree would never hurt Clarissa to strike back at him. Would she?

We're different people now.

He scowled. Yes, they were. But surely not *that* different.

Edwin crossed his arms over his chest. "I'm sorry, I can't be quite as sure of Mrs. Trevor as you. I simply don't know her character well enough for that, and since you're thinking with your cock, I daresay neither do you." Even as Niall bristled, Edwin added, "Promise me you won't tell her yet. You're putting not only your own life and future at stake, but Clarissa's and mine. After the babe is born, I don't care what you do, though it will be on your head if Mrs. Trevor lets one word of it slip to anyone. But until then . . . I can't risk it."

Though Niall understood Edwin's caution, it made him angry that the man couldn't trust *him* to know what was best. "And if I lose Bree?"

"You won't," Edwin said firmly. "If you do, then she didn't truly care for you in the first place. I married Clarissa without knowing anything of her past, after all."

Niall gritted his teeth. "You married Clarissa because it was the only way to keep her safe from Durand. And while I'm enormously grateful for that, it doesn't change the fact that neither of you thought you had a choice. Bree does have a choice. And right now, she's not inclined to make it in my favor."

"All the more reason you shouldn't be spilling secrets to her."

"For God's sake—"

"This matter with her father may go on for weeks, anyway, and Mrs. Trevor has to stay engaged to you until that's done, right? So just let it ride for the time being. I'll see how matters progress with Clarissa's health, and if I feel that it's safe for you to reveal everything to Mrs. Trevor, I'll tell you."

Niall glared at him.

Edwin glared right back. "I should hope you would care enough about your sister to protect her."

"That's a low blow, given what I *did* to protect her," he clipped out. "If not for my keeping her secrets all these years, you two wouldn't even be married, I suspect."

"Then you suspect wrong," Edwin said hotly. "I loved her long before I realized it. I would have married her even knowing what that bastard did to her."

"So you say. But none of us can ever be sure what we'd do if circumstances were different."

Edwin stiffened. "If you will not do this for your sister, then do it for me. I ask you, as my closest friend in the world, to keep quiet about the truth until Clarissa has the babe."

Damn him. Edwin knew that Niall owed him more than he could ever repay, for saving Clarissa from Durand. "I'll think about it. That's all I can promise."

With his heart in his throat, he headed for the door.

"Niall!" Edwin called out.

Niall halted to glance back at him. "What?"

"I know I've been lax in thanking you for fighting Whiting all those years ago, but you have my eternal gratitude for that. If he had lived, she would have suffered a great deal, her reputation dragged through the mud at his hands. And I do recognize that your silence is what has enabled Clarissa to live scandal-free all these years." He rubbed his temples. "I'm merely asking you to keep her secrets a short while longer. Three more months at most."

Bitter words threatened to boil out of Niall, but there was no point. Edwin would not be reasoned with. "Tell my sister that I hope she feels better soon." He stalked out the door.

But as he walked back to Margrave Manor, he weighed his choices. He had to decide if he was willing to ignore his brother-in-law's demands in order to gain the woman he desired. Did he trust Bree enough to risk his sister's health and reputation? His connection to the family he'd so desperately missed?

Much as he hated to admit it, Edwin had made some good points. Bree *did* resent him—that was clear from her guilt over her husband's death. Niall wanted to believe her resentment stemmed only from not knowing the truth about the duel, but what if it ran deeper? What if it had to do with how he'd handled his escape from England, treating her concerns as trivial and not making better plans for a way for her to reach him?

Because Edwin was right about those long-ago mistakes, too—everything that had happened to Bree had been a direct result of Niall's actions on Clarissa's behalf.

If Bree resented Clarissa for it, made any remark to a maid or her aunt or anyone that somehow got out, Edwin would never forgive him. Niall would never forgive himself. The possibility of Clarissa's being hurt was something he couldn't just set aside.

Still, he honestly didn't know how much longer Bree would wait for him to be open with her. If he lost her by being overly cautious, he wasn't sure he could ever get her back. And that price was so high, he didn't think he could pay it.

Brilliana had never seen Niall so quiet. While the carriage raced back toward town long after sunset, he stared out the window, seemingly oblivious as Silas rolled about and chattered and made a general nuisance of himself on the seat next to Niall.

Had Niall heard some bad news regarding his sister? Brilliana dearly hoped not. But did she dare bring it up after he'd been so reluctant to share her condition?

"I pray that Lady Blakeborough is well," Aunt Agatha said, as if reading Brilliana's mind. "And the babe."

Niall looked startled. "Yes, my sister is well," he said warily. "Why do you ask?"

"Your servants were quite concerned. They even asked *me* how she might be faring." Her aunt sniffed. "I had to admit that I had *no* idea. Which shocked them, since they knew you were completely aware of her recent difficulties. I can't imagine why you wouldn't tell us of such things. We are about to become your close rela—"

"Enough, Aunt Agatha," Brilliana said curtly. "His lordship is clearly distraught over the situation. I'm sure he didn't tell us about Clarissa's health because he didn't want to worry either of us."

With a sharp breath, Niall settled back against the seat. "Clearly, I am going to have to have a word with my servants."

"They're merely concerned," Brilliana said. "Don't chide them for that. They adore Clarissa as much as we do."

An odd expression crossed his face as he gazed

at her. "I would have told you, but I was sworn to secrecy in the matter. She's very popular in society, as you well know, and Edwin didn't want all her friends trooping out to bother her just now."

"Understandably," Aunt Agatha said, softening only a fraction. "But I should think we are more than mere 'friends.' Lady Blakeborough will become my niece's sister when you marry, after all."

Her lecturing tone brought a faint smile to his lips. "Duly noted, Lady Pensworth. I shall keep that in mind the next time I am sworn to secrecy. And if it makes you feel better, my brother-in-law warned me not even to tell Mother. So I could hardly reveal the secret to you in good conscience." He flashed Brilliana a veiled glance. "Edwin tends to be cautious."

"Not telling his mother-in-law about her own daughter's difficulties?" Aunt Agatha retorted. "I would box the impudent fellow's ears."

"I'm sure you would." His tone turned ironical. "Fortunately, my mother would probably prefer not to know. She isn't the sort to sit by a sickbed, even her daughter's. And believe me, Clarissa would consider her not being there as something of a blessing."

My mother is the most indiscreet person in the world, Brilliana remembered him saying. Perhaps that hadn't been quite the exaggeration she'd assumed.

Aunt Agatha crossed her arms over her bosom.

"Then you have a most peculiar family, Lord Margrave."

"Indeed I do," he said, obviously not the least insulted. "In any case, I'm glad that the two of you now know of Clarissa's situation. I am entirely ignorant about women's . . . matters, and you may be able to enlighten me as to how serious my sister's condition actually is. I keep hearing differing accounts."

With that, he proceeded to give them a thorough recitation of what the doctor had said about Clarissa. Though it still chafed Brilliana that he hadn't confided in her before, she could see how he might be reticent under the circumstances.

"What do you think?" he asked.

"I think the doctor is right," Aunt Agatha said. "It doesn't sound terribly serious yet. Still, he was wise to have her sent to the country. In my day, women were not as active as they are now in the weeks before their confinement. I honestly don't know what some of them are thinking."

Brilliana laughed. "If you'll recall, Aunt, the day before Silas was born, I attended a dinner party with twenty guests. And his birth went perfectly well."

Silas bounced energetically on the seat, as if to confirm her assertion.

Niall's gaze narrowed on her. "There were no difficulties at all?"

"None."

"You needn't worry, my lord," her aunt said. "My niece is of sturdy enough breeding stock for anyone."

"Aunt Agatha!" Brilliana cried.

"What?" the baroness said. "That's what he wanted to know—whether you could produce his heir without incident."

A flush spread up Niall's neck. "Actually, I was . . . er . . . that is . . ."

"Pay my aunt no mind." Brilliana flashed the woman a quelling glance. "She has a tendency to treat all men as boors who must be chided routinely."

Aunt Agatha sniffed. "Lord Margrave does keep an erotic watch at the ready."

Niall scowled. "I swear, I will throw the damned thing out the window if you two don't stop bringing it up."

He drew it out of his pocket, and Silas jumped up. "Jack, Jack!" he cried.

"Oh, for God's sake," Niall muttered and hid the watch once more.

Brilliana couldn't help but laugh, and after a moment, her aunt joined her, which broke the tension.

From then on, the conversation was more amiable. Niall entertained Silas by bouncing the boy on his knee. Brilliana entertained Aunt Agatha by relating the entirety of their tour of the estate. And Aunt Agatha entertained Niall with her usual droll comments.

By the time they reached the Pensworth town house, all was well. Unfortunately, it was nearing ten o'clock, when Niall was supposed to join Papa for a card game, so after he saw them inside, he merely brushed a quick kiss to Brilliana's cheek before dashing back out.

As Brilliana watched him hurry down the steps, her aunt came up next to her. "He's got rather more in his favor than he lets on, doesn't he?"

Brilliana bit back a smile. "That's high praise, coming from you."

"Yes, well, I still don't like his reasons for marrying you—all that nonsense about needing a wife for his heir and your needing a father for Silas. But if *you* don't mind those reasons, who am I to protest?"

Her aunt started to turn for the drawing room, then paused to look back at Brilliana. "Besides, I would take a rogue with a sense of humor and a genuine concern for his sister over a selfish, stodgy fellow any day. Good choice, niece."

Then she marched off, leaving Brilliana to stare after her with her mouth hanging open. Her devil-may-care fiancé had somehow managed to charm even Aunt Agatha out of her disapproval.

Could the end of the world be far behind?

Sixteen

After the frustrating encounter with Edwin, Niall was in no mood for playing cards and trying to unmask counterfeiters. But that hardly mattered. He'd promised Fulkham. And too much was at stake if he stopped doing this now. So as he strode into the Star and Garter, he attempted to hide his agitation.

He hadn't even reached the taproom before he ran into someone he knew.

"Good day to you, Mr. Payne," he said as Sir Oswald's brother strode into the hall.

The man looked startled to see him. "Are you playing again, then? Since they already have four, I figured you'd seen the light after one game with my hapless brother and his ridiculous friends."

"I believe some of us are merely watching tonight, since we're expecting six players. Would you want to join our merry band after all? We might be able to drum up a fourth for you and get two games going."

He snorted. "Not on your life. I merely came to retrieve some funds from Oswald that I need for a business venture."

Odd. "I thought *you* were generally the one loaning money to *him*. Or so your niece told me."

A bland smile crossed the man's face. "Precisely why I had to retrieve funds. The fellow is always borrowing and has tapped me out. Fortunately, he's been flush lately, so I figured I'd get my money while I could."

"Very wise."

"Well then," Payne said, "enjoy your game. I understand that I have you to thank for Oswald's good fortune, so try to make sure he wins again, will you? He still owes me money, and the longer he keeps winning, the more chance I have of getting it back."

"I'll do my best," Niall said with a rueful smile.

He watched as Payne hurried from the inn, obviously in a temper. Not that Niall blamed the man. This was what Bree had endured all these years from her father, a man who would take from everyone in his circle until they bled. It was a wonder Payne had put up with it so long.

For Payne's sake, Niall hoped he'd "retrieved" genuine notes from his brother and not counterfeit ones. Assuming that Sir Oswald *was* the counterfeiter. Niall began to pray otherwise. It would make matters easier for Bree and Silas.

Silas? God, he was already thinking of the imp as his charge. And the odd thing was, the idea of that didn't alarm him as much as it had two days ago.

The boy was lively, to be sure, but not as difficult as one would have thought. Silas would make an excellent older brother to the children Niall intended for him and Bree to have one day.

Which reminded him of Lady Pensworth's outrageous remarks, and the rest of their journey home. He was still smiling over that when he walked into the taproom.

"Here he is!" Sir Oswald was already shuffling the cards. "I told you he'd be here in time, Raines."

Raines gave a long-suffering sigh. "I never doubted it, sir."

Sir Kenneth was there, too, and Pitford, whom Sir Oswald immediately introduced to Niall. Apparently Dunsleigh was the only one who hadn't arrived.

"So," Niall said as he sat down opposite Bree's father, "which of you three is playing tonight?"

"Dunsleigh is ill, so he's out," Sir Kenneth said. "And I told Raines I'd sit out, too, since he'd like to play. After last night, I'm not sure I wish to take on you and Sir Oswald again, Margrave."

"Fine by me." Niall removed a card from the pack that Pitford had cut and laid it faceup on the table. "But your luck might change."

"I've stayed solvent all these years by not clinging to that gambler's hope," Sir Kenneth said.

"Very wise of you." Or very cautious. Niall wasn't sure which.

They each chose cards until the first diamond showed up, which determined who dealt. It turned out to be Sir Oswald.

"Besides," Sir Kenneth said, motioning to a tap-room maid, "I prefer to drink, especially when a chit as fetching as that one is bringing the tipple."

The saucy girl sashayed over with a smile that said she knew Sir Kenneth was most interested in a tipple from her nipple, and she meant to satisfy his thirst.

"Then it's probably just as well you're sitting this out," Raines drawled as Sir Oswald began to deal the cards. "With a distraction like her, you're bound to play badly, eh, Pitford?"

Pitford winked at the barmaid. "Ah, but it would be worth the distraction."

"Not if we lose," Raines said irritably.

"If you don't want to partner me, step out so my cousin can step in," Pitford said. "Otherwise, let me have my little enjoyments."

Raines hunched over his cards. "Fine. Just see that you pay attention to the game."

Interesting. Why was Raines so determined to play? Perhaps so he could pass off some counterfeits?

The game began, and Niall had to fight to

keep his mind on his cards. He didn't necessarily have to win this time. He'd brought plenty of assorted banknotes so he could switch out his good ones for those in play, no matter how he and Sir Oswald did at the tables.

Now he just had to pray that *something* turned up. He was tired of waiting for things to happen. This group could go for weeks without his so much as seeing a fake pound note, which was maddening.

Several hours of play later, Niall finally got his wish. Or he thought he did, anyway. Sir Oswald laid down a twenty-pound note that looked slightly off, though it was hard to tell in such dim light. Fortunately, Niall and his partner won that time, so he raked the note over to his side and made sure to mark it and then exchange it for a good one, sliding the suspicious one into his coat pocket.

He would have to show it to Fulkham to be certain, but if it were indeed a counterfeit, then Sir Oswald was probably part of the criminal enterprise.

Damn it all to hell. Niall had been praying that Sir Oswald had merely passed on counterfeit notes he'd received from someone else at these games. But Niall had seen the man take the note out of his own purse. Since it was highly unlikely that the man had received such a large note in change somewhere, and equally unlikely that he'd picked it up at his bank, Sir Oswald was at best distributing the notes and at worst producing them.

Either way, it was getting harder to believe that Sir Oswald didn't know they were counterfeit.

So that must be the next step in Niall's investigation—learning where Sir Oswald had gained the notes. With the exception of Sir Kenneth, who hadn't been in town long enough, any one of these men could still be a suspect, since they were his friends.

The rest of the game went by in a fog, with Niall scarcely caring whether he won or lost. Because now he had a decision to make, one he hadn't anticipated having to make before.

Should he tell Bree?

She was on this mission with him, so he ought to tell her. But how would she react? Sir Oswald was still her father—she might not be so sanguine anymore about seeing him arrested.

Edwin's words kept clattering about in his head: *No matter what Fulkham promised, if her father proves guilty, there will be a trial and, no doubt, a conviction. She'll have to endure gossip and rumor. . . .*

Damn Edwin. And Fulkham. And bloody Sir Oswald, for being a bastard who didn't give a farthing for his family. Niall wished them all to blazes.

"You're not playing as well tonight, Margrave," the arse had the nerve to complain. "Mind your cards, for God's sake, or we're going to lose the pot."

Niall grunted some answer and tried to concentrate.

But it was no use. A short while later, they lost it all.

"Shall we play again, gentlemen?" Sir Oswald asked hopefully as Raines gathered up the winnings and began to split them with his partner.

"I'm done in for the evening." Pitford grinned. "As my cousin here says, it's always best to quit while one's ahead. Eh, Sir Kenneth?"

Sir Kenneth didn't answer, too busy nuzzling the ample breasts of the barmaid who sat giggling on his knee.

Raines frowned. "I'm surprised you could keep your mind on the game, Pitford, with your cousin making such a spectacle of himself. Might as well end the night. I can't stand one more minute of this nonsense."

"Indeed," Niall said. "Ah, well, Sir Oswald. Perhaps tomorrow night we can get some of our own back, eh?"

Sir Oswald glared at him. "Only if you promise to play better."

"I'll play better if you bring enough luck for the two of us," Niall said mildly. "I had abysmal cards." He rose. "Well then, fellows, I'm off."

"Me too." Raines stood up. "I'll walk out with you, Margrave."

As the two of them strolled out of the Star

and Garter, Niall wondered if he should take another stab at assessing Raines. The man *could* be in league with Sir Oswald. Raines was, after all, a banker.

"I suppose I'll see what's going on at St. George's," Niall said. "Care to join me?"

"I'll walk that way with you, but I'm not going in. Fulkham is supposed to be there tonight."

Why would the man assume that? Could Raines have caught on to Niall's association with the baron? Was he feeling Niall out on the subject? "Ah, did he say he would be there?"

"Not exactly. I . . . er . . . heard it from someone close to him."

What could that mean? Was there someone spying on *Fulkham*? "Oh? Who?"

Instead of answering that, Raines tensed and said, "You seem to know the man relatively well. What do you know of his . . . relationship to Mrs. Vyse?"

That threw Niall off. "She's his sister-in-law."

"I *know* that," the man said irritably. "But do you think there is something more between them?"

"Something romantic, you mean? I doubt it. I suppose they could have an affair, but they could never marry. He's her brother-in-law."

"They *could* marry, if no one in the family objects. It's only the Church that forbids it. And there are ways around that."

"Even so, *he* wouldn't do it. Fulkham's career

is everything to him. He would never risk that to marry his brother's widow, knowing that the world sees it as incest."

"Still, he and she are very close."

"I suppose." And why did the man care anyway? Then it dawned on him. "So *she's* the woman whose family doesn't know of your interest. The woman you're courting."

Raines stared grimly ahead. "It's not so much courting as . . . God, I don't know what it is, except that she's driving me insane. She's dragging her feet on the subject of marriage, yet she acts as if she cares about me." He muttered a curse. "Please don't tell anyone, especially Fulkham."

So Raines's avoidance of Fulkham had nothing whatsoever to do with the counterfeiting. He just happened to be a banker who fancied Fulkham's relation.

Although that raised other questions. "Why don't you want Fulkham to know?"

"Because she says we must keep it secret, that he won't approve." They were nearing the club, so Raines slowed his pace. "But I'm worried that her reason for keeping our . . . association quiet has more to do with her feelings for Fulkham than anything else."

"I've not seen any indication of that, but I don't know the two of them well. And the only way *you're* going to know for certain is to ask her."

"And risk losing her for good? If she does want him, I can't bear it. I can't share her. I know some men do that, but not me."

"So you'd rather not know the truth?"

"Yes. No." He grimaced. "Once I know . . . it's over. I'm not ready for it to be over." Raines halted just short of the entrance to St. George's. "I suppose you think I'm acting like a fool."

"No. I think you're acting like a man smitten by a woman. Women are devilishly tricky creatures, and sometimes one can't help but be at a loss as to how to catch them."

Raines snorted. "Clearly, that doesn't apply to you. You've caught your woman."

He forced a smile. "I'm not so sure. I won't be sure until the day we stand at the altar and say our vows."

A day that he feared might never come. He and Bree still had so many difficulties to get past—the situation with her father, her inability to trust him, his inability to reveal his secrets . . .

"My point is," Niall went on, "dealing with a woman is hard enough without adding needless speculation about what might not even be a problem. Ask her for the real reason she's dragging her feet with you. Just be prepared for the consequences if the answer isn't one you want to hear."

A pity he couldn't take his own advice. Because he *knew* why Bree was dragging her feet. He just couldn't do anything about it without betraying his family's confidences. And the vow he'd made to his father.

Not that he much cared about that anymore. If Father had broken his promise, Niall could damned well break *his*.

"Thanks for the advice, old chap," Raines said. "I'd best be going. I daresay the ball that Mrs. Vyse was planning to attend is still going on. And given that her pesky brother-in-law will not be there—"

"You plan to play while the cat's away. Good luck."

After Raines left, Niall hesitated at the entrance to St. George's. He ought to go in and report to Fulkham. They needed to discuss whether the banknote was indeed forged, and whether Fulkham had learned more about Sir Kenneth's reasons for being in town. The man might even have some advice on how to proceed with uncovering Sir Oswald's cohorts.

The trouble was, Niall didn't *want* to talk to Fulkham tonight. He wanted to talk to Bree first. Edwin's words about what her father's arrest might do to her and Silas still haunted him. It had been one thing to postulate such a thing when Niall had misunderstood her past actions and when Sir Oswald's guilt was more uncertain. But now, with what he'd found out about how she'd suffered at the man's hands . . .

He *had* to see her before this went any further. Consulting the damned watch he was keeping for Warren, he grimaced. Past 2:00 a.m. She was probably tucked up cozily in her bed, dreaming of Wedgwood vases and fields of flax.

Or *him*. God, he hoped she was dreaming of him.

Then again, she *could* still be awake. Unlikely, but a possibility. And thanks to young Pip, Niall knew which room was hers.

Seventeen

Brilliana couldn't sleep. She tried, but it was futile. She kept wanting to do naughty things to herself—to touch her body in her most private places, all while reliving her afternoon with Niall.

Determined to squelch her scandalous impulses, she got out of bed, lit a candle, and went to her writing desk to pull out her sketchbook. But as she did so, another one fell to the floor.

Her breath caught. It was her *old* sketchbook, the one with drawings of Niall. That was the last thing she should be looking at right now, yet she couldn't help herself.

With a sigh, she flipped through the images. On the one hand, she was pleased to see how her abilities had improved from those early days. On the other, those first drawings catapulted her right back to the naïve hopes of her youth. She'd drawn Niall as impossibly handsome, with a look

of love in his eyes and a sensuality that had captivated her even then.

The pesky devil. Even in sketches, he seduced
her.

She understood now why some women relished marital relations. She'd always seen being
bedded as a chore to be endured. But that was
because Reynold had always roused her without
making her "come," which had only succeeded in
frustrating her.

She even remembered telling Delia a few
months ago that the pleasures of the marital bed
were only pleasurable for the man. Brilliana dearly
hoped that her sister-in-law hadn't listened to her
nonsense and was having a fine time on her honeymoon with lovemaking. Her new husband was
even more of a rogue than Niall, so he undoubtedly knew a thing or two about pleasing a woman.

Unlike Reynold. Brilliana sighed. He had been
more concerned about his own satisfaction than
hers, and not just in the bedchamber. He'd never
encouraged her sketching or her ambition to
design for Wedgwood or even her burgeoning
interest in matters concerning the estate.

And why? Because that might have taken
time away from her catering to *his* needs. Selfish
wretch.

Meanwhile, Niall—

A noise very near made her jump. It sounded
almost as if something were knocking against the
French doors of her balcony.

She turned to look and nearly came out of her skin. A man was silhouetted there, peering into her room. But before she could raise an alarm, he said, "Open the door, Bree. Please."

"Niall? Goodness gracious!"

She flew to do as he asked. While he entered the room, she peered outside. "How on earth did you get up here?"

"I climbed the downspout."

"That tiny thing? Are you mad? You could have fallen to your death!"

He chuckled. "Not likely. I'm an expert at climbing buildings." He dusted off his coat. "I saw the candle burning in your window and figured that since you were up, we could talk."

"It's two in the morning!"

"Yes, but you're awake."

Well, she could hardly refute that. She should put on her wrapper, make him go, or do something other than stand here in her nightdress drinking in the sight of him. "Why didn't you want to wait until morning?"

"We can't have a discussion about your father's situation in front of your aunt."

Oh, right, he'd played cards with Papa earlier. "So what's he done now?"

"He paid for his losses with a counterfeit twenty-pound banknote."

She raised an eyebrow. "And that surprises you?"

"Some, yes. I'd hoped he might not be guilty. But clearly he's in this up to his neck." Taking off his coat, Niall threw it over the chair by her desk. "At the very least, he'll probably end up standing trial and being transported abroad for his crime."

"We knew that was possible."

"Possible, yes. Certain, no. And now that I consider the result of such a scandal once it becomes public—"

"Oh. I see." She crossed her arms over her chest self-consciously. He was starting to reconsider marrying her. She didn't blame him, but still, it hurt. "I've made my peace with it, but I can see why it might give *you* pause. You won't want to marry a woman who will drag your family through the mud."

"What?" he said, clearly shocked. "That's not what I meant at all. It's you and Silas that worry me." He strode up to where she stood near her bed. "I came here to tell you that if you want me to save your father from prosecution, I might attempt it. I can confront him with this banknote and tell him I'll turn him over to the authorities unless he reveals everything about the operation. And then I can do my damned best to keep him out of it."

"Have you lost your mind? You do that, and you risk making an enemy out of Fulkham! Or worse, being forced to keep working for him."

He shrugged. "Not necessarily. I'm sure I could negotiate something with him."

Her heart leapt into her throat. "No, you are *not* doing that."

"It's not for *your father's* sake, but yours and Silas's. The way I see it—"

"Absolutely not! I lost you once. I couldn't bear to lose you again."

"You won't lose me. We could work the matter out so that—"

She shook her head so violently, her unbound hair swung about her shoulders. "We're not discussing this anymore. If you're truly only concerned about me and Silas, then we'll stick to the original arrangement."

He got that stubborn look on his face that told her he meant to keep beating at this until he changed her mind, and desperation seized her. So she took a page from his book and did something outrageous to distract him.

She kissed him. Right on the mouth. With all the pent-up need she'd been feeling from the time she'd left him this afternoon.

He jerked back to grab her by the arms. "What the blazes are you doing?"

"What do you think?"

"But we need to discuss—"

"I don't want to talk right now, and especially not about Papa." She flung her arms about his neck. "I want to do this." Then she kissed him again.

He froze, but only briefly before kissing her back so ardently that it made her swoon. He was such a luscious kisser, and tonight she wanted nothing more than to revel in his experience at seduction.

But cursedly he came to his senses and broke the kiss. Sweeping her with a quick, heated glance, he muttered an oath under his breath before putting her aside. "We have to *talk*."

"Not now."

"Bree—"

"Aren't you supposed to be a rogue?" She planted her hands on her hips, perfectly aware of how the motion thrust her breasts forward, and reveling in the dark interest in his eyes. "Why don't you behave like one?"

He gritted his teeth. "That's not what I came here for."

She lifted an eyebrow.

"All right, so . . . perhaps I had that in the back of my mind, but—"

"Good." Feeling every bit the Lady Rebel he called her, she grabbed his hand and drew it to her breast.

He let out a harsh breath. As if in a trance he rubbed her there, softly and silkily at first, and then with a firm touch that had her nipple tightening to a hard point.

"God help me," he murmured. "I'd swear you have the most supple breasts in all England." Then, growling her name, he swept her up in his arms and tumbled her onto the rumpled bedcovers with a low cry of exultation before covering her body with his.

And it was *glorious*, like being consumed by a magnificent beast. Which was precisely what he

was, her reckless rakehell. With all the ferocious-
ness of a Bengal tiger, he devoured her mouth
while his hands fondled her breasts through her
nightdress.

She plucked at his clothes, desperate to touch
bare skin and hard muscle, and that seemed to
give him pause. "Aren't you worried your aunt
will hear us?"

"She sleeps like the dead, trust me."

That was a *slight* exaggeration, but she didn't
care. Niall was her fiancé. What was Aunt Agatha
going to do—force him to marry her? At this
point, even that sounded appealing.

"Besides," she went on, "I want you."

"Do you?" He stared down at her a long
moment. "Well then, who am I to protest?"

He rose to dispense with his clothes as she
watched in avid anticipation. Their hurried lovemaking against trees hadn't allowed her a chance
to see him naked, so when he started to climb
back into bed, she whispered, "Wait. I want to
look at you."

His eyes glinted in the light of the fire. "Does
this mean that my Lady Rebel is making an
appearance?"

"Apparently." In the morning, she would undoubtedly rethink her rebellion, but right now
she delighted in it. She wanted him in her arms
and in her bed. *Now.*

"Then I want tit for tat. Literally." He crossed
his arms over a chest that was as broad as it was

sculpted. In the firelight the hair dusting it glimmered golden, making her want to smooth her hands over every inch. He must have realized it, for he cast her a cocky grin. "Take off your nightgown, sweeting."

Heat rose in her cheeks. She'd never been fully naked for anyone, even her husband. Yet her answer was decisive. "All right." She rose up on the bed just enough to tug her nightdress over her head and toss it to the floor.

It left her totally exposed before his hot perusal, which ought to have made her nervous. Yet somehow Niall's ravening gaze, touching on her breasts, her belly, her thighs . . . her privates, only aroused her further. Niall had experienced all of her body in furtive touches, but this blatant conquering with his eyes was so much more intimate. Erotic. *Thrilling*.

With her blood pounding in her ears, she surveyed every inch of his male beauty. Lord, but he was fine. He was taut where Reynold had been soft, lean where Reynold had run to fat. He was as different from her late husband as a wolf from an overfed dog. Heaven help her, but that made her desire him all the more.

She held out her hands. "Come to bed, my wild rogue."

He approached, but didn't join her. "Is that how you see me still?"

"Do you mind?" she asked, surprised by the disappointment in his voice.

"Not at present," he said, utterly serious. "But I may in the morning."

"Then we'll deal with it in the morning. For tonight, however, can you just be my wild rogue?"

He reached up to stroke her hair, then wrapped a hank of it lightly around his hand so he could then draw it over her nipple repeatedly, until she was gasping at the tantalizing caress.

Firelight caught his smile. "I can do anything, if it means having you. Like this, aching for me, gasping for me. Wanting me as much as I want you. Say it again. That you want me."

"When you look at me like that, I want you more than you can ever dream."

"I doubt that," he said, running his hands down her sides to her waist. "I have pretty vast dreams of you wanting me, sweeting."

She drew his hand between her legs. "So do I."

With a sharp intake of breath, he cupped her down there, then took her mouth with a fierceness bordering on savagery. Next thing she knew, he was pressing her back onto the bed so he could lie on top of her. The feel of him surrounding her was so exquisite that she arched up against him, hungry for more.

"Ah, my lovely, wanton girl," he murmured.

"Take me, Niall," she whispered against his throat. "The way you do in your dreams."

"This is ten times better than any dream," he

said hoarsely. Then he filled her with his flesh in one sleek stroke.

She'd have expected such haste to make their joining unsatisfying, but instead it was ferocious and exotic and absolutely wonderful. He drove into her and she felt every thrust to the depths of her soul. She fondled him, and he moaned with each touch as if she'd caught the essence of him.

With silent caresses, they made the sweetest love she could imagine, and she relished every moment. *This* was what she'd expected of marriage, this union of bodies and pleasure and passion and . . . oh, everything.

"Niall," she whispered, her heart so full of joy that she wanted to share it with him. "Make me yours, my darling."

"You've always been mine, whether you knew it or not."

And then he was driving her forward to that lovely place of bliss, and she was clutching him to her and straining upward until he gave a few quick thrusts that sent her leaping toward the stars.

He must have followed her there, for he groaned so feelingly that it tipped her over into heaven.

"My dearest rogue," she cried. "My darling Niall."

"Yes, sweeting." He thrust hard, then spilled his seed inside her with a long, aching moan. "Mine," he murmured against her lips. "All mine."

And in truth, she wanted nothing more than to be his. For the rest of her life and beyond.

Lord help her.

~~⁓~~

Niall lay on his side next to Bree, his head propped up on one hand as he stared down at her nude form. He couldn't stop looking at her. Like some elusive goddess in a painting, she lay drowsing, with her hair spilling out over the pillow, rumpled velvet lit by candlelight.

Her plump breasts were topped with cheeky pink nipples he wanted to ravage all over again. Entranced by her beauty, he skimmed a hand down the soft contours of her body. Satiny skin, hips lush enough to tempt a man, and between them . . .

God, he had to stop thinking of it, or he'd take her again, and they still had things to discuss. He couldn't believe that she'd seduced *him*. It was so unlike her.

Or perhaps not. She *was* his Lady Rebel, after all.

He brushed a kiss to her rosy cheek, wishing he could stay here until morning, wishing he never had to leave her bed. But since they weren't married, that wasn't a choice.

She nuzzled his chin. "You need to shave."

"That's all you have to say to me?" he teased.

"What did you want to hear?"

"That I made you swoon. That I'm an excellent lover. That you can't believe my astounding capability to—"

"Enough," she said, a soft laugh escaping her. "You know perfectly well that you made me swoon and shiver and shake. As always."

"That's more like it." He cocked his head to listen, but heard nothing in the house. "All seems quiet. We might have gotten away with this."

She shot him a bemused look. "Since when do you care?"

"Since I first laid eyes on you."

"What fustian!" She smoothed her hand over his chest. "You've always been a rogue and will always be one, no doubt."

The words cut him deeper than she could know. "Don't say that."

She blinked. "Why not? I don't mind it, honestly. It's what makes you . . . interesting."

He sighed. "It's what makes you think I betrayed you years ago."

Her gaze grew shuttered. "It doesn't matter. We're different people now, and I use 'rogue' only in the best sense. It's what makes you so very good at *this*."

"Ah. So you've decided to overlook my past because I give you pleasure."

"That's not what I—"

"Bree, I didn't betray you back then," he said earnestly.

He had to tell her the rest. Clearly she wanted

to forgive him without knowing the truth, but the festering sore of her misconception would poison their future, whether she realized that or not.

And in his heart, Niall trusted her to keep his secret. And his family's.

Because he loved her.

He always had. Even when he'd believed the worst of her, some kernel of him had clung to the hope that she wasn't the woman his father had made her out to be.

She settled the restlessness in him as no one else ever had, offered him respite from the tumult in his mind. One look at her with Silas, and he knew that together they could make a very happy family.

But she could only learn to trust him again if he trusted her. So he had to tell her the truth—because he couldn't go on without her.

He took a deep breath. "The duel all those years ago was indeed fought on behalf of a woman—but not the sort of woman you think. I fought Joseph Whiting to gain justice for Clarissa."

Eighteen

Brilliana gaped at him. He'd fought the duel over his *sister*? But she had barely been out at that point. "Did Whiting insult her? Harm her somehow?"

A hard look entered Niall's eyes. "He raped her."

"Oh, my Lord. And she . . . told you?" Most women would have hidden it, if only to preserve their reputations.

"She didn't have to. I came upon them just as he finished using her most brutally." A haunted look crossed his face as he slid from the bed to pull his drawers on. "If you could have seen her lying there in the orangery that night, broken and bleeding and sobbing her heart out—"

"Your poor sister! How awful!" She could only imagine how terrible it would be to be taken against her will. Reynold might have been abrupt, but he had never hurt her.

Niall slanted a wary glance at her. "You don't blame her, do you?"

"Of course not! How could I? One hears of scoundrels who try to get girls alone to kiss them, or put their hands where they shouldn't. But this goes beyond the pale."

Suddenly, the full significance of his confession hit her. He had never been involved with a mistress. He had never betrayed her. As he'd said back then, he'd had good reason to duel.

"But why didn't you tell me this years ago, when you asked me to run away with you?" she whispered.

His face closed up. "My father swore me to secrecy to save Clarissa's reputation. Whiting hadn't told his seconds what the duel was about, hoping he could force Clarissa into marriage since he'd taken her innocence. Indeed, he made an offer for her when I discovered them together. But I wasn't about to sentence my sister to life with such a villain."

Brilliana shivered. "Certainly not."

"Once I'd killed him and it was clear that no one but Clarissa and I knew the truth, I turned to Father for help. He pointed out that we could preserve Clarissa's reputation as long as we prevented her from having to testify to what had happened. The only way to avoid a trial was for me to flee England, so I did—to ensure she could have a future."

Crossing his arms over his chest, he stared at Brilliana. "I don't regret it. I did what I had to."

She rose from the bed to slip her nightgown

on. "Of course. I don't dispute that. But . . . I know you made a vow to your father, but you said I was your true love. Surely you could have told *me*."

His gaze was stark. "How would that have changed anything?"

"For one thing, your father's lies to me wouldn't have swayed me. I would have clung to the hope that you might return. I would have tried harder to reach you." Her voice dropped to a whisper. "I wouldn't have married Reynold."

He shook his head sadly. "Your circumstances forced you into that, as surely as mine forced me into fleeing. Your father gave you no more choice than mine gave me."

"But if I'd known you were waiting for me, I might have—I don't know—tried to find out from your mother where you were. Or from your sister. I might have gone abroad with you and taken Mama, too."

"Bree," he said gently. "Your mother could never have managed such a trip, and you know it."

"Still, I would have held firm against Papa," she protested. "I would have waited for you."

"And stood by while your mother went to debtors' prison? I doubt that."

She winced. He had a point. And yet . . . "We'll never know, will we? I might have managed something, but you didn't trust me with the truth, so I believed your father and made my own arrangements."

"It wasn't a matter of trust."

"Wasn't it?" Her throat aching with unshed tears, she drew on her wrapper. "You didn't tell me the truth because you believed your father when he said I was an adventuress." A fractured sigh escaped her. "I cut my father off when he betrayed me." When he'd abandoned her to Reynold. "Yet you . . . you trusted yours. Instead of trusting your heart."

"But I wasn't the only one. I told you I'd had good reason to fight the duel, but my word wasn't enough. You chose your mother's happiness over mine, so you can hardly blame me for choosing my sister's happiness over yours."

His voice softened. "And anyway, the problems between us didn't stem from a lack of trust. Your mother was very ill, and you were caught between a rock and a hard place. So was I—I wasn't free to divulge someone else's secret. We both did what we thought we had to. We can't alter the past, but can't we put it behind us?"

She wanted to. She really did. But every time she put her faith in someone, she ended up being hurt. "You're the one who kept all the secrets. I didn't keep any from *you*."

A shadow crossed his face. "Didn't you? Fulkham says your husband purposely drowned himself. Yet you've said naught of that to me. Is it true?"

Shame swamped her. "I didn't learn of it until recently—but yes." Tears threatened to choke her.

"He did it because of me and you. He realized that you had my heart when he did not. And after he lost so much money . . ." She shook her head. "It was all too much for him."

"Damned fool." Niall approached to take her into his arms. "None of it was your fault, Bree. Not the arranged marriage, not the fact that you couldn't love him, and certainly not his actions near the end. You have to stop blaming yourself for it."

She stared up at him, looking haunted. "But because of what I did, Silas will never have a father."

"Not because of what you did—because of what *Trevor* did. And Silas *will* have a father. I mean to be his father, if you'll have me."

The words hung in the air. Niall truly wanted to marry her. Apparently he'd always wanted to marry her. She could scarcely believe it. Believing it was dangerous.

She pulled free of him. "Tell me this. Once you realized yesterday *why* I married Reynold, why didn't you reveal your reasons for the duel? Your father is dead, so why not tell me?"

He pushed his fingers through his disheveled hair. "Because it wasn't my secret to tell. It was Clarissa's. And Edwin's. I wanted their permission before I said anything to you."

A lump caught in her throat. "I guess they gave it to you, or you wouldn't be here telling me this."

"Actually, they didn't. Edwin wouldn't even let

me see my sister. He begged me not to reveal the truth about the duel, because he was afraid that if you couldn't be trusted with the secret and it got out, the scandal might cause Clarissa to lose the child. He insisted that I keep quiet."

She stared at him, scarcely daring to breathe.

He reached up to wind one of her curls about his finger. "But I knew I could trust you, that it was time we put this behind us. Keeping the secret from you has been intolerable, and I couldn't do it any longer." His heart shone in his eyes. "I've sacrificed enough for my family. I will not sacrifice *you*. Ever again."

She wanted desperately to believe him. But . . .

He cupped her cheek. "I hope I've made it clear where my loyalties lie. I risked my sister's health and my friendship with Edwin to tell you the truth. Because I know, in my heart, that I can trust you implicitly. The question is, do you trust *me*?"

"How can I?" she burst out. "You left me once—for noble reasons, I know. But the end was the same. I was left alone, with no one to help me deal with Mama." Her throat constricted. "Or to stop Papa from tossing me to another man. Then *Mama* left me, too—not that she could help it—but I still ended up in a marriage to a man I didn't love."

As Niall stared at her, his face full of compassion, she couldn't stop the tears from rolling down her cheeks. "And even *he* left me in the end. Don't you see? Everyone leaves me eventually, whether I want them to or not. So how can I be sure you won't do it, too?"

He brushed away her tears. "Because I love you, sweeting. I always have. And you love me, too. I know it."

After running his thumb over her lips, he gave a sigh, then released her. "Unfortunately, you don't trust your own heart. You're so afraid of being hurt that you won't take a chance on being happy." He headed over to finish pulling on his clothes. "So you're the one who has to choose, Bree. Will you give in to your fear? Cling to your anger over my abandoning you to Trevor all those years ago? Tell yourself that you're doing what's safest, when really all you're doing is running away?"

He stared her down. "Or will you choose *us*? I've chosen us over everyone else. I want you as my wife, no matter what happens with your father or my sister or Edwin. Now it's up to you to decide what *you* want. I can't make the decision for you. If I could, we would be heading for the altar right now."

When she just stared at him, her mind racing and her heart pounding, he said, "I'll give you time to think about it, but not very much. I'll be here tomorrow to officially ask you to marry me. And I'll need your answer. Because I can't go on loving you, knowing that you're too afraid to love me. Reynold might have been willing to do that. I am not."

And with that, he went out the balcony door.

She hurried out to watch, to make sure he didn't kill himself. As he climbed nimbly down the side of the town house, the words, "Wait, come back, I want to marry you!" were on the tip of her tongue.

Yet still she held back. What if she and he could not make it work in spite of their love for one another?

Will you give in to your fear? Cling to your anger over my abandoning you to Trevor all those years ago? Tell yourself that you're doing what's safest, when really all you're doing is running away?

She *was* running away. Because not running away meant facing an uncertain future. She'd done that and had it turn out badly so many times that she was afraid to do it again.

At the edge of the garden Niall stopped to blow her a kiss, and her heart lurched in her chest. She loved him so much.

But he didn't understand that love wasn't always enough. It hadn't been enough to keep him at her side. It hadn't been enough to keep *anyone* at her side. And then she was inevitably left bleeding where no one could see.

She choked down her pain. Niall didn't understand that trusting your heart, opening it to love, could destroy you. And right now, that terrified her more than even the thought of being without him.

Nineteen

Niall went straight to his study, knowing he wouldn't be able to sleep. Frustration gripped him, not only with Bree but with the whole damned situation. He loved the woman to distraction, and if she didn't accept his proposal tomorrow, he didn't know what he'd do.

For one thing, to finish his agreement with Fulkham he'd have to continue their fake engagement, and the idea of being with her as some polite pretend suitor . . . He couldn't do it. Not anymore.

Meanwhile, this counterfeiting scheme made less and less sense. Sir Oswald wasn't the master criminal type; the man could barely win a game of whist, for God's sake!

Raines wasn't a viable suspect anymore, unless the tale about his interest in Mrs. Vyse was just to throw people off, and somehow Niall doubted that.

Niall wanted the culprit to be Sir Kenneth, but that was merely because of the man's association with Joseph Whiting.

Gritting his teeth, he sat down at his desk and took out the banknote he'd snagged earlier in the evening to examine it under a magnifying glass. It was definitely a counterfeit. But if Fulkham hadn't told him how to recognize the fakes, Niall would never have caught it. The art was quite well-done. Which, according to Bree, ruled out Sir Oswald as the person who created the forgeries.

Niall sat back. He'd send this off to Fulkham with a note arranging to meet tomorrow at the club. That would give the man time to consider their next step. In the meantime, Niall would talk to Sir Oswald. Not to confront him, but just to see what information the fellow might let slip.

And perhaps in the process, he would read Sir Oswald the riot act over what the man had done to Bree. It was something Niall could do for her that she seemed unable to do for herself. So at the very least, it would make him feel better.

With that plan in mind, he was finally able to sleep for a few hours. But as soon as he'd awakened and sent off the note to Fulkham, he dressed and headed for the Payne town house on foot. He needed to clear his head, and a brisk walk was good for that.

He was half a block from the place when he spotted a coach pulling away from the door.

Blast, was Sir Oswald leaving already? It was awfully early for the man to be out and about.

Then the coach rumbled past, and Niall realized it was a hackney carrying Toby Payne somewhere. Good. That would give him more privacy to speak frankly with Sir Oswald.

As Niall neared the entrance, he heard a loud commotion emanating from the open windows on an upper floor.

Sir Oswald was apparently on the warpath. "Who is *he* to tell me how to live?" the man raged. "All he gives me is grief every bloody day. I didn't *ask* him to come here and make my life a misery!"

The sound of someone murmuring soothing, indistinct words drifted out to Niall.

"What am *I* supposed to do about it?" Sir Oswald said. "Bloody arse. Be damned glad you don't have a brother, Jenkins. They're nothing but trouble!"

Niall approached the door, but before he could knock, it opened to reveal a harried footman. "Thank God you've come, my lord! Perhaps you can settle the master down."

"Bring me up to him. I'll see what I can do."

The footman hurried up the stairs ahead of him to announce him.

They ended up in Sir Oswald's study, where poor Jenkins was being forced to play the role of reassuring friend, probably because Sir Oswald's so-called friends were mostly bounders who only cared about him as a potential source of revenue.

The minute Niall entered, Sir Oswald turned all his anger on him. "This is *your* fault, Margrave, for not playing better last night. My brother is furious at me, and why? Because we lost. Because the money he loaned me is gone."

The money Payne had loaned *him*? That gave Niall pause. "Leave us," he told Jenkins and the footman, who beat a hasty retreat. Then he approached Sir Oswald. "What are you talking about? I ran into your brother last night on my way into the inn, and he told me he had come to get money from *you*. That you had paid him back for some past loans."

Sir Oswald's mouth fell open. "Don't be absurd, man. I have no blunt at present. Everything I get goes right to paying my creditors. I sure as hell don't give it to my brother."

What had Bree said the first day they'd come here? *If my father is part of this conspiracy, I warrant it's only because he owes money everywhere.*

"I don't understand," Niall said. Why would Payne have lied about that?

"Toby came to the inn to bring *me* funds," Sir Oswald went on. "Then he apparently regretted it today, for he was just here demanding the money back from me. I told him you and I lost it all, and he was none too happy."

One of the two men had to be lying. And if Payne had given Sir Oswald money last night

instead of the other way around, then the counterfeit note might have come from *him*.

But how could that be? Fulkham had said
Payne hadn't been in England long enough to be
responsible for the counterfeiting.

Could Sir Oswald be the one lying?

Possibly. Except that the fellow was clearly
agitated and not governing his speech. And he'd
been raging over the matter before Niall entered
the building. "What exactly did your brother say
to you?"

"All sorts of things. He kept asking me about
twenty-pound notes and how many I put in the
pot and who had won them." Sir Oswald scowled
at Niall. "As if that matters. Who gives a bloody
damn whether the notes were ten or twenty or a
hundred? The money is lost."

Niall's pulse quickened. A counterfeiter would
care what notes were used. And where they'd
ended up. And Niall could definitely see Payne
as a master criminal; the man seemed far more
clever than his brother.

By God—what if Payne had brought Sir
Oswald money last night for the man's gambling,
and had *accidentally* put some counterfeits in?
The banknotes that were originally discovered
had been used for various creditors, making them
harder to trace since tradesmen received money
from so many places. But a counterfeit in a gambling pot was a bit easier to trace back.

Once Payne realized he'd accidentally given

his brother the counterfeits, he must have grown worried enough to demand the notes back from his brother.

"And he's not just furious at me, you know," Sir Oswald went on. "He's none too happy with you, either. Seems to think you're not good enough for Brilliana. A man of your rank! I don't know who he *does* think is good enough."

Sir Oswald began to pace his study, his cane tap-tapping. "And why must the bloody arse always be mucking about in our affairs? He should leave her be. Didn't he cause enough trouble for her and me the last time? Why, if it hadn't been for him—" Sir Oswald caught himself. Blanching, he turned away from Niall and headed for a decanter of brandy. "Anyway—"

"Wait a minute," Niall broke in, a suspicion chilling his blood. "'If it hadn't been for him,' then *what*?" As Sir Oswald shakily poured himself a glass of brandy, Niall walked up to take it from him. "I want to know *exactly* how your brother caused trouble for you and your daughter 'the last time.'"

"Well . . . I mean . . . it's thanks to *him* that she hates me now. My own daughter. I should never have listened to the bloody arse."

Narrowing his gaze on the man, Niall said, "Listened to him about *what*?"

Sir Oswald tugged at his cravat. "He's the one who said I should take Captain Trevor's offer all those years ago."

The bottom dropped out of Niall's stomach. It took every ounce of his control not to show that he knew what the man was talking about. "Captain Trevor's offer?" he echoed.

"Don't pretend you aren't aware of how her marriage to Reynold Trevor came about. I know Brilliana. She *had* to have told you, if only to rail against me." Sir Oswald scowled. "She hates me for arranging that match. That's why she cut me off. Won't even let me see my grandson. My own grandson!" He eyed Niall closely. "You *do* know about that arrangement, don't you?"

I know you sold your daughter to Trevor.

No, he needed more information, and he wouldn't get it by antagonizing the man. "I know a little." Niall handed the glass of brandy back to the man. "But I don't see what your brother had to do with it. You didn't have to heed his advice."

"Oh yes, I did. I wrote to him in France—asked him for money to pay off Mace Trevor, so I wouldn't have to . . . convince her to marry the man's son instead." Sir Oswald brooded a moment. "Toby said he was tired of loaning me funds every time I found myself in dun territory. He said I should take Captain Trevor up on his offer. Because he wasn't giving me a penny more."

Damnation. "Was Brilliana aware of her uncle's part in it?"

Sir Oswald swigged some brandy. "I didn't tell her. I was afraid that if she knew I'd lost so much money that even my own brother wouldn't help me anymore . . . well, she wouldn't agree to the marriage, either, and her mother and I would go to debtors' prison. Her mother was ill." He got a faraway look in his eyes. "So dreadfully ill."

So dreadfully ill that Bree had sacrificed her future for her. Anger at the man roiled in Niall's gut.

When Sir Oswald remained silent for several moments, Niall prompted him. "So you didn't tell her about your brother's part in forcing your hand."

"No." He drew himself up. "None of her concern. I explained to her the circumstances, and she agreed to the marriage." He glared at Niall. "If I'd known she wouldn't speak to me after that, I damned well would have told her how little choice I had in it. But she would only talk to her mother, who didn't know any of it anyway. And after her mother died, Brilliana stopped coming here entirely, so I had no chance to tell her." He shook his head. "She hates me now."

"Can you blame her?" Niall clipped out. "She feels betrayed. I should hope you'd understand why."

Guilt crossed his face. "I suppose." The old fellow waved a hand in the general direction of the outdoors. "But it was all Toby's fault for refusing to give me any more money. Coldhearted bastard. What was I supposed to do?"

"Not lose it in the first place."

"You're one to talk. Toby says you're in dun territory yourself. Anyway, Toby refused to help me ever again. Until a few months ago, when he sent me some money out of the blue."

Niall caught his breath. That fit with when the bills had started showing up in London. "He sent you the money from France, I take it?"

"Aye." Sir Oswald eased into a chair. "Though I should have known it wouldn't last. He's back to being angry with me, and threatening to cut me off once more."

"So what happened a few months ago to make him change his mind?" Niall asked.

"It seems he heard I'd put the family property up to let. Guess he didn't like the idea of that, since his line will inherit it when I die. So he agreed to lend me money if I'd just pay off some of his debts here with banknotes he sent me. So I did." The old man touched a finger to his nose. "He didn't want to have to pay the duty on the cash, you know. Wanted me to get around that by saying I was taking care of my brother's debts for him."

Niall supposed that *could* be the reason. But a more likely one was that Payne had used his brother to pay off business debts with counterfeit notes, knowing that if the notes were discovered, Sir Oswald would be blamed. And if they weren't discovered, then Payne would make a tidy sum.

"If he was doing all of this from France, why

did he decide to come visit you?" Niall asked. "Just to make sure you were . . . er . . . paying his business debts properly?"

"Or to torment me about putting the family property up to let. Who knows, with him? But I'm done with him after this." He stared at Niall. "And you should be, too, if you know what's good for you. After he found out how badly we lost last night, he went off in a huff to talk my daughter out of marrying you."

That sparked Niall's temper. "What?"

"Said he heard some rumors about you and other women. I told him it was probably the usual nonsense, but he's on his way over there right now to give her a lecture."

"The hell he is." Niall doubted that Bree would be swayed by her uncle, but if the bastard *was* the counterfeiter, Niall didn't want him anywhere near Bree.

"I have to go," he said, turning for the door. There was no telling what Payne really intended to do. Especially if he had any suspicion that Niall was trying to unmask him.

"Give my brother what for. I'm tired of his nonsense." Sir Oswald downed some more brandy.

He wasn't the only one. Payne had essentially separated Bree from Niall years ago, and for that alone, Niall would make the man pay.

Now he could only pray that Payne's reason for going to speak with her was merely to talk her out of marrying Niall. Because if there was more to it than that, if Payne had figured out that Niall was in league with Lord Fulkham, and was intending to use her to get back at the men who were threatening his criminal enterprise ... .

Then God help him, Niall would tear him limb from limb.

Twenty

Brilliana was in the drawing room drinking coffee and refining her design for Wedgwood when Aunt Agatha's footman came to tell her she had a visitor.

"Now?" It was awfully early for formal calls. Which meant her visitor was probably Niall. And she still wasn't ready to give him his answer. "If it's Lord Margrave—"

"No, ma'am. He says he's your uncle. A Mr. Toby Payne?"

"Oh," she said, inexplicably disappointed. "Please show him in."

As the footman went to fetch Uncle Toby, she rose. How odd that he would come here to visit. Then again, he'd seemed very glad to see her the other day, and in truth, she'd been glad to see him.

When he entered, she went to greet him with a kiss on the cheek, then bade him sit down.

"Would you like some coffee? Or I can send for tea."

"Nothing for me, thank you."

She dismissed the servant, then resumed her place on the settee, setting aside her sketchbook and pencils.

"You still draw, do you?" he asked, leaning forward to look at what she'd been working on.

"Yes." She couldn't keep the pride from her voice as she added, "Wedgwood is considering one of my designs."

"Ah. Very wise of them."

An awkward silence fell between them.

At last he cleared his throat. "I know you're probably wondering why I've come."

"I assumed you just wanted to see your favorite niece," she teased.

When he didn't even smile, it gave her pause.

"Actually," he said, "I . . . er . . . came to speak to you about your fiancé."

That put her instantly on her guard. "Lord Margrave? Why?"

There was something decidedly different about Uncle Toby today. He looked agitated, even wary. How strange. She'd always thought of him as an amiable sort, unruffled by life's troubles.

Yet his eyes darted nervously about the room. "Where's Lady Pensworth this morning?"

"No doubt she went out for her morning walk. She likes to get that out of the way while Silas is having his breakfast and such, so she can enjoy watching him play later." She smiled. "Despite her gruff manner, she does love her great-nephew."

"Ah, of course." He stared at her. "I forgot that your boy's name is Silas. May I see him?"

The request shouldn't have struck her as odd, coming from her son's great-uncle, but it did. Every instinct told her to keep her son away from the man just now. And though it made no sense to her, she always heeded her instincts. "Not at present, I'm afraid. He's . . . er . . . having his morning bath."

"Right." Uncle Toby drummed his fingers on his knees. "I tend to forget how the English have made a religion of cleanliness. The French aren't as industrious about such matters."

"True." Why the devil was he here? What was going on? "So," she said primly, smoothing her skirts, "you said you wanted to speak to me about Lord Margrave?"

Her uncle nodded. "He's not lurking about here anywhere, is he?"

"At this hour? Of course not." Though she began to wish he *was*.

"Good, good." He steadied his gaze on her. "I'll be frank with you, niece. I don't approve of his courting you. I fear he cannot be trusted."

She began to fear that her *uncle* could not be trusted, though that remained to be seen. "Oh? And why not?"

"For one thing, he has a reputation as a roué. People say he fought a duel over a woman, probably some light-skirt. That's not the sort of man you wish to marry, is it?"

Now that she knew why the duel had really been fought, it pained her to hear such gossip. It took all her will to force a smile for her uncle's benefit. "Honestly, Uncle, I don't care *what* he did back then as long as he's attentive to *me* now. Which he is."

What she *wanted* to say was that it was none of his concern whom she married, but she wouldn't keep her temper if she got into that.

With a scowl, Uncle Toby sat back against the chair. "And what about Margrave's gambling? Surely you don't want to marry another fellow like your father."

That gave her pause. Niall had told her of unearthing a counterfeit note only yesterday, and now her uncle was suddenly trying to talk her out of marriage due to Niall's "gambling." That couldn't be a coincidence.

"I doubt his lordship would ever be so foolish as to behave like Papa," she said blithely.

"It wouldn't surprise *me*." He leaned close with a confidential air. "He lost a great deal at the tables only last night. And you're not even married yet."

She lifted her eyes heavenward. "It's only a bit of card-playing. I'm sure once we're wed and settled in the country, he'll be more careful."

A fierce light shone in her uncle's eyes. "You don't want to involve yourself with this man, I tell you. You already had one arranged marriage with a gambler that didn't end well. How can you even be thinking of going into another?"

His words arrested her. "You *knew* that my first marriage was arranged?"

The guilty flush spreading over his cheeks showed he was aware of far more than she'd initially thought. "I . . . um . . . heard of it from your father, yes. *Recently.* After your visit the other day."

He was lying. So she should be cautious with him and not let on that she'd spotted his falsehood. "Oh, of course." She pasted a smile to her lips. "Though I'm surprised he told you. It paints him in a very poor light."

Uncle Toby tapped his fingers on his knee. "Yes, well, he was desperate. Your father is . . . often indiscreet when he's desperate." His voice hardened. "But that's precisely what I'm talking about. It's his gambling that drives him to despair, and I can see the earl following in his footsteps if you're foolish enough to marry the man."

What in heaven's name? Uncle Toby's persistence in this vein was bordering on the absurd. Did this have anything to do with the counterfeiting or not? She tried another tack. "But I told you before, I *like* Lord Margrave. He's handsome and charming and—"

"You're not listening, damn it!" he cried.

She blinked. This became odder by the moment. "Calm yourself, Uncle. I can't imagine why you are so concerned about my engagement." The faintest bitterness crept into her tone. "You never cared so much about my affairs before."

As if realizing he was giving away his agitation, he said nothing for a long moment while he apparently fought to rein in his emotions.

Then he steadied his shoulders. "Very well, you force me to tell you the truth. It pains me to say this, niece, but I have a more pressing reason for meddling in your affairs." He stared her down. "What if I was to tell you that I think your fiancé is trying to frame my brother for a crime he didn't commit?"

Her breath dried up in her throat. Oh no. If Uncle Toby had some inkling of what Niall was trying to discover . . . "I would say you're quite mad. What reason could Lord Margrave possibly have for doing so?"

"To weasel his way back into the good graces of the government. They pardoned him for killing that fellow, you know. Perhaps they did it in exchange for his help framing your father."

Oh, Lord, she couldn't breathe. How had he figured out so much? From Papa, perhaps? Did that mean Papa truly *was* guilty and was once again turning to his brother for help?

But somehow she couldn't see her uncle

believing any lies Papa might tell about being "framed" for a crime. Unless . . .

Unless Uncle Toby *knew* Papa wasn't being "framed," because he, too, was involved in the scheme.

Her heart stumbled. That made far more sense. Uncle Toby wouldn't go so far as to risk his own reputation to help Papa. But to keep *himself* from getting caught . . .

"Framing my father for what?" she asked. "Being a terrible gambler is hardly illegal."

"I don't want to say until I'm sure, but it's serious. Something that would . . . send your father to the gallows."

It took all her meager skills of dissembling to look shocked. "The devil you say!"

"I suspect that Margrave is in league with Baron Fulkham. That's the *real* reason Margrave has been courting you. Not because he wants to marry you, but so he can sniff around your father's friends and . . . pin some nonsense on my brother that Fulkham has cooked up."

That was a bit too close to the truth for comfort—which made her wonder all the more if Uncle Toby was the real culprit. She couldn't let on that she knew anything, especially since he refused to tell her exactly what "nonsense" Lord Fulkham had "cooked up." It was paramount that she play dumb.

Forcing herself to look concerned, she leaned forward. "Are you sure about this? I mean, Lord

Margrave and Lord Fulkham have certainly met in society a time or two, but I had no idea that they were *particular* friends."

He snorted. "They're members of the same club, you know. It would give them ample opportunity to hatch their plan to paint your father as a criminal."

"But why?"

"I'm not sure yet. I'm trying to figure out what their game is. All you need to know is that they're attempting it."

She stared at him, her mind racing. Somehow she had to find out what had roused his suspicions without revealing her part in everything. More information was more ammunition, and Niall was going to need that.

"I can't imagine that Lord Margrave would do such a thing," she said, hoping her uncle would elaborate.

He huffed out a breath. "Look, you are a lovely woman, my dear, whom any man would be lucky to marry. But you said it yourself the last time we spoke—you're a widow with a son, and your dowry, while attractive, is hardly enough to entice an earl to marry you. Not when he could have any heiress in the city. I tell you, Margrave has an ulterior motive for his attentions to you. And Fulkham is the one providing it to him."

She shook her head as if unconvinced. "Even if that's true, what do you suggest I do about it?"

"Break off the engagement, of course. Tell him you don't like his gambling. That should be enough to convince him."

"And then I will gain a reputation for being a jilt," she pointed out.

Her uncle waved his hand dismissively. "A woman as pretty as you can get away with refusing a man for any reason."

He wasn't even bothering to make sense anymore.

"Weren't you just pointing out that I'm a widow with a son and a *very* small dowry?" she said dryly. "Jilting an earl is hardly going to enhance my appeal." When he shot her a suspicious glance, she continued, "I'm just saying that breaking the engagement is sure to have consequences."

"And letting this man get your father hanged will have consequences as well!" He clenched his hands into fists on his knees. "Surely you don't want to do anything that would hurt your father."

"Of course not," she said.

"Besides, Margrave has no intention of actually marrying you, anyway. Not after he's proved that your father—" He caught himself most tellingly. "Or rather, has made it *look* as if your father is guilty. Why would he marry the daughter of a criminal?"

Because he loves me.

The thought flashed into her mind with such clarity and truth that it shone a light on all her fears about marrying Niall, showing them to be as foolish as he had claimed.

He was trying to uncover the counterfeiters precisely because he wanted to ensure their future happiness, to free himself of Lord Fulkham's machinations so they could live in peace. He knew that the scandal could damage his own reputation and that of his family, but he didn't care. He'd offered to save her father if that was what she wanted. He'd even defied Edwin to tell her the truth about the duel, knowing full well he was risking a great deal to trust her with it. What kind of man did that?

A steady one. Who would be there for her . . . and Silas and their children, the way he'd been there for his sister. If she would only let him.

"Are you listening to me, niece?" her uncle asked sharply.

She blinked. "Oh. Sorry. I'm just . . . trying to figure out how best to refuse Lord Margrave—if you are absolutely certain about what you have told me. Are you sure you want me to jilt him right away? If I continued the engagement, I could find out more information for you." She flashed him a bland smile. "Although you would have to explain what they're trying to frame Papa for, so I'd know what questions to ask."

The alarm in his eyes was unmistakable. "No, indeed, I do not want you involved. You just jilt the man, and let me take care of the rest. I'll have no trouble convincing your father to stop playing cards with Margrave once the two of you are no longer engaged."

Ah, so that *was* why he was so desperate to end this. Because of the card-playing. Had he somehow figured out that Niall had put his hands on a counterfeit note last night?

Whatever the reason, she needed to get Uncle Toby out of here before either her aunt returned or Niall arrived. She had to warn Niall about this.

She rose. "Well then, Uncle, I suppose I have no choice but to end my engagement with Lord Margrave. I'll let you know once I've had the chance to speak with him—"

"I do need to discuss one more thing with you," he said, remaining seated.

Stifling her irritation, she sank back onto the settee. "And what is that?"

Uncle Toby rose and came to sit beside her on the settee. "It so happens I have need of your talent as an artist." With a furtive glance at the door, he drew a sheet of paper from his pocket and laid it on her lap.

She stared at the document. It looked vaguely official, something that might be presented at a government office or bank. Unfortunately, it was in French, and French was not her strong suit. "What is this?"

"Something that will exonerate your father— *if* you can copy it exactly, down to the image stamped on the corner. But you'd have to make minor changes to a name and a few numbers. Do you think you could manage that? I would pay you to do it."

Her mind raced. He wanted her to fake a document to "exonerate" her father—right. "I could copy it easily, of course. But how exactly will it exonerate Papa?"

He flashed her a thin smile. "Oh, it's much too complicated to explain at present. But it would help a great deal. If you're sure you're willing to do it."

She should probably agree, if only to see what he was up to. Then she could show it to Niall, who could figure out what was going on. "Anything to help Papa, of course."

At that moment, her aunt's footman entered the room. "Lord Margrave is here to see you, ma'am."

Oh no, she needed more time to get Uncle Toby out of here!

Her uncle leaned close. "You should admit him, niece. No better time than the present to send him packing. That way, if he gives you any trouble, I'm here to support you."

When she hesitated, her mind sorting through all the choices, he rose and said to the footman, "Send him in, will you? My niece and I wish to speak to him together."

The footman nodded and walked out.

She jumped to her feet. "Uncle! I don't know if I'm ready for this. I have to think about how—"

"Nonsense. It's a simple matter." He stuffed

the document into his pocket. "Tell him you know all about his gambling, and you can't abide marrying such a man after what happened with your father and late husband." He took her rather forcefully by the arm. "You can't let him send my brother to prison, girl."

"Of course not." Drat the man. He would *not* leave until she sent Niall away, and she had to go along or risk his suspecting that she and Niall were working together. "But you must let *me* tell Lord Margrave or—"

"Tell me what?" Niall asked as he walked in. He dropped his gaze to her uncle's hand on her arm, and his lips tightened. "Forgive me, sweeting, I was unaware you had company."

Uncle Toby squeezed her arm.

She none too subtly tugged it free of his grip. "I'm afraid I have a delicate matter to discuss with you, sir."

"Oh?" Niall searched her face, and she put as much emotion into her gaze as she could manage, hoping he read her mind as well as he usually did.

Crossing her hands over her waist, she drew herself up. "When I agreed to marry you, I had no idea of your . . . deplorable tendency to gamble every night away. But you've spent the last two evenings at the tables and I find that intolerable."

His eyes narrowed. "Intolerable? Two nights at the tables?"

She couldn't look at him, afraid she would

burst out with the words *I love you*. Which would rather defeat the purpose of jilting him. Or worse, she might say, *My uncle could be one of the counterfeiters*, though she had no firm evidence of that.

"It's the timing of those nights that's problematic," she said. "If you can't stay away from gambling now, when we've just become engaged, how can I believe you'll stay away from it later?" Deliberately, she turned to meet his gaze. "Once we're an old married couple, I mean?"

Something warm flickered in his eyes, leading her to hope he understood what she was trying to tell him. That she trusted him, loved him . . . wanted to be *married* to him.

"I had not expected you to get cold feet so soon, Mrs. Trevor," he said, matching her formal tone. "But if you insist upon ending this—"

"She does!" Uncle Toby burst in. "And I, for one, say good riddance."

When Niall's expression turned deadly, Brilliana cried, "Uncle! Do not be rude."

Niall fixed Uncle Toby with a black look. "So, whose idea was it to end the engagement? Yours, sir? Or my fiancée's?"

"Mine, of course," Brilliana broke in. She had to get Niall out of here before he broke Uncle Toby's nose or something equally dreadful, which at the moment he looked liable to do. And that would *not* help their situation. "Please, my lord, I am very sorry to disappoint you, but I find that we would not suit, after all. So it's probably best that you leave."

After casting her a lingering look, he nodded and turned for the door. "Please pay my respects to your aunt, madam," he said in chilly tones. "Good day."

Once he'd departed, she wanted to collapse into the nearest chair, but she had to remain standing, if only to get her uncle to depart, too, so she could find Niall and tell him what she knew.

"You see?" Uncle Toby said. "That wasn't so difficult, was it?"

"I do hope you know what you're doing, Uncle. I may never find such a fine suitor again."

"I doubt that," he said amiably, all smiles now that she'd done as he asked.

"Well, I should go look in on Silas—" she began.

"Not yet. He has a nurse, right?"

Her heart faltered. "Yes. Why?"

"Because I need you to copy that document for me *now*. It needs to be on a special kind of paper, which I have in my rooms at your father's. I was hoping you'd come there with me, so we can get the matter taken care of right away."

Alarm tightened a vise about her heart. Could Uncle Toby be dangerous? A week ago she would have said he'd never hurt her, but now she wasn't so sure. Of course, if they were at Papa's, there would be other people around. He'd have trouble doing anything to her with Jenkins and Papa . . . Unless Papa was guilty, too. Or even Jenkins.

Then it dawned on her that if she went with him, she could get the evidence of counterfeiting that they needed! She'd have two copies of a government document and whatever else she could find in his rooms.

Why, she could hand everything over to Niall and Fulkham, all tied up with pretty pink ribbon, and be *done* with this. No more subterfuge, no more lying to Aunt Agatha, no more worrying about who knew what. And she and Niall could *finally* be together.

That was surely worth the risk of her uncle's trying to hurt her.

"Of course," she said brightly. "Just let me get my coat."

Twenty-One

Niall stood in the garden across the street, waiting for Toby Payne to leave so he could talk to Bree. He wasn't sure what was going on, but he did know one thing—Bree would never jilt him over his supposed penchant for gambling. Something was up with her uncle, and he meant to find out what.

And dared he believe that her words about their being an "old married couple" were intended to reassure him about their future together? God, he hoped so.

The door opened and he held his breath. When he saw Bree being urged down the stairs by her uncle, a cold rage seized him. Payne was carrying her off somewhere, damn it!

Though apparently not against her will. They seemed awfully comfortable together as Payne motioned to a waiting hackney and helped her in. Then he heard Payne order the driver to take them to the address of Sir Oswald's town house.

As the coach drove off, Niall considered how to proceed. He could go to Sir Oswald's after them, but once there, what could he do? He had no concrete evidence of Payne's involvement, let alone the power to order an arrest. So the last thing he needed was to put Payne on his guard by accusing the man.

He could go to St. George's instead and meet with Fulkham as planned, to report on what he'd learned so far and see if Fulkham had more information. If they'd gathered enough to build a case against Payne, Niall would urge Fulkham to strike now. Because instinct told him Payne had a reason for convincing Bree to jilt Niall so summarily, not to mention for persuading her to go off with him. Niall just hadn't figured out what the reason was yet.

The only problem with heading for St. George's was that it meant leaving Bree with Payne for a while, which didn't sit well with him. He couldn't be entirely sure that she was safe with her uncle. And while her father did seem to care about her, would he make any attempt to protect her?

After all, he *had* allowed his brother to talk him into brokering that marriage. And Sir Oswald might just be desperate enough for cash that he would do whatever Payne demanded of him.

But Bree wasn't some simpering miss. She could handle her relations. Hell, she'd already handled a great deal more than Niall had realized. Perhaps it was time to trust her to look after herself. Because if she'd wanted him to "save" her just now, she would have said so. She was no fool.

Besides, if after all they'd been through with this scheme, Niall ruined everything by blundering in too soon, she would bloody well kill him.

His mind made up, he emerged from the garden into the street, only to be nearly mown down by a woman walking at a brisk speed toward him.

"Margrave!" Lady Pensworth cried. "What are you doing here?" With a disapproving frown, she peered into the garden. "Is Brilliana with you?"

"I'm afraid not. She left here a few moments ago with her uncle."

"Toby Payne? How peculiar. She told me he was in London, but I had no idea they were so friendly. Why on earth would she go off with *him*? And why are you lurking about out here in the garden?"

He had no time for this. "Forgive me, Lady Pensworth, but I need to—"

"Do you know where they were going? How long she intends to be gone? Why he fetched her?" She shoved her spectacles up her nose. "This is most distressing. It's not like Brilliana to go running off without telling me where she's headed, if only because of Silas. I wonder if she left a note with the servant. I do not like this at all. It sounds entirely too havey-cavey."

Her concern and outrage gave him pause. "It does indeed."

And in that moment, he made a decision. He needed to be in two places at once, which he couldn't manage without help. Why not enlist Lady Pensworth?

She, too, was a clever woman capable of handling herself in a difficult situation. She had Bree's best interests at heart, and she was perfectly capable of creating a believable distraction. Not to mention that she despised Sir Oswald for what he'd done to his daughter.

And Bree had always been bothered by the necessity of keeping the truth from her. So by including Lady Pensworth in the scheme, he'd be doing Bree a favor.

Best of all, the baroness owned an equipage. "Lady Pensworth, if you'd be willing to carry me in your coach to St. George's, I will explain exactly what's going on with Bree and her uncle, to the extent that I know it. When I'm done, I hope you'll agree to assist me in my attempt to save my fiancée from a criminal who may wish her ill."

"A criminal? Hmm." She eyed him over the top of her spectacles. "Will you also reveal the truth about why you and Brilliana are engaged to be married? And none of that fustian you told me the night of your announcement, mind you. I want the real reason."

A clever woman, indeed. Rather scarily so. "Yes, that would be part of the explanation."

She cast him a cool nod. "Well then, sir. Let us call for my carriage."

Lady Pensworth's landau halted just outside St. George's Club. Niall had given the baroness a succinct explanation of how he and Bree had ended up betrothed as part of Fulkham's scheme. Then he had explained that it had turned into something more. Fortunately, the harridan possessed a talent for grasping particulars and had also deduced some of the truth about him and Bree on her own.

He wasn't able to reveal the details concerning the duel, but she'd seemed content to accept that it was none of her concern. She'd been far more interested in determining whether he and Brilliana did intend to marry. And he'd told her he hoped so, since he was in love with the blasted woman.

That had seemed to satisfy her at last, leaving him free to explain what he wanted of her. Which he'd just finished doing.

He laid his hand on the door to the carriage. "So, you understand your mission, right?"

"I'm to go to Sir Oswald's and engage in a

subterfuge to delay and thwart the gentlemen in their criminal enterprises until you arrive with reinforcements."

"Precisely. But you mustn't behave so obviously or outrageously that either man grows suspicious of your appearance there."

"Of course." The gleam in her eyes told him she was looking forward to her part in the plot. "I should hope I am perfectly capable of managing the likes of Sir Oswald and his scurrilous brother."

Niall rather thought she was. "I shouldn't be long. Fulkham will already be waiting for me with more information. If he won't act on it, I will. I'll go find what I need in that house by hook or by crook." His heart caught in his throat. "Just make sure Bree is all right until I can do so."

Hiding her concern for Bree behind a sniff, she opened the carriage door. "For pity's sake, go do your part. *I* will look after my niece."

"Thank you. You won't regret this."

"I'm sure I won't. A lady needs an intricate scheme now and again to stimulate her constitution and keep her brain sharp."

Taking her by surprise, he kissed her papery cheek before jumping out and shutting the door.

"Such a rogue," she muttered, but a faint pink rose up her neck as she ordered her driver to go on.

Niall found Fulkham in the deserted reading room, and Fulkham immediately slid the counterfeit note across the table at him. "This is identical to the others we had. And you're sure it came directly from Sir Oswald?"

"I am. But there have been new developments." He explained his suspicion that Toby Payne might be involved in the scheme and why.

When Niall was done, Fulkham muttered a low curse. "That does clarify something the new French ambassador told me. It seems that our Mr. Payne has been having financial difficulties in Paris, what with the recent overthrow of the government—again—in France. The new regime isn't as amenable to British merchants, so he's been scrambling to pay his various creditors."

"With counterfeit notes."

Fulkham frowned. "We can't prove that. Sir Oswald is the only one passing them along so far, so only he can be charged with a crime."

Niall had expected this. "I know in my bones that Payne is guilty. What if I can guarantee that there's proof in Sir Oswald's house of Payne's involvement? Would that be enough to search it?"

Fulkham eyed him suspiciously. "Can you?"

"Not half an hour ago, Payne coerced Bree into jilting me. After he thought I was gone, he carried her off to her father's house. He wants her there for *some* reason. And given that he's been framing her father for the counterfeiting, it's conceivable that he needs her help for that."

"How?" Fulkham scoffed.

"I don't know, but why else make her go with him? For that matter, why make her jilt me at all?"

"Unless he didn't make her. Perhaps she just jilted you all on her own, because she's had it with our machinations. Perhaps the fact that her uncle was visiting had nothing at all to do with why she jilted you. For all we know, her deep love for her uncle made her rethink her willingness to help get her father arrested."

"Oh?" Niall crossed his arms over his chest. "Then why did she give my incessant gambling as her reason for jilting me, instead of our more personal issues? Payne was coaching her on what to say—that much I *am* sure of."

Niall hardened his tone. "And now he has her in his power, for no apparent reason other than something criminal. So if you *don't* go in there now with constables and officers to search the place, *I'm* going to go there myself, if only to make certain she's all right. Which will probably ruin your investigation and make it impossible to charge the real culprit. Is that what you want?"

Fulkham leaned back to assess him. "If you do that, I can have you jailed for interfering with a criminal investigation."

"I don't care. If I lose her because her uncle does something to hurt her or her father, I might as well be in gaol." His heart twisting in his chest, he gazed out the window. "As it turns out, you were right—the course of true love never does run smooth. But it's the only course worth running. So if I lose the race before I even finish the course, nothing you can do to me will compare to the hell my life will be from now on without her."

That seemed to take Fulkham aback. "She means that much to you."

"And more." He released a shaky breath. "I lost her once. I can't lose her again."

"You do realize that if we go in there with all the power of the magistrate's office and we find nothing, we've squandered our chance to capture the bastard."

Niall fixed him with a fierce look. "Have I ever let you down before? Sent you on any wild-goose chases? Given you bad information?"

Fulkham rubbed his temples, then let out a vile oath. "No, but you can be a bloody pain in the arse sometimes."

"I learned that from a master," Niall quipped.

"Fine," Fulkham grumbled. "But it will take me an hour or two to get my men together. Are you comfortable with that?"

Now that he'd convinced Fulkham, he was comfortable with anything. "Don't worry. I have a trick up my sleeve, in the form of a very annoying female. Payne won't be going anywhere for a while—even if he wants to."

Twenty-Two

Brilliana and her uncle sat in the upstairs parlor at Papa's house, which no one seemed to use anymore, judging from the thick layer of dust on the mantel and the lack of coal in the grate.

Now that she'd had a chance to examine more closely the paper Uncle Toby wanted her to copy, she thought it was a French bill of exchange. She couldn't be sure, but it certainly looked like the English ones she'd dealt with in running Camden Hall.

How stupid did he think she was, assuming that she'd believed his absurd story about the document's exonerating Papa? That was downright insulting. Clearly, he wanted the name and some numbers changed so he could turn a legitimate bill of exchange belonging to someone else into one *he* could gain cash with.

"Niece, this is taking an inordinate amount

of time," he complained as he peered over her shoulder.

"Do you want it to look right or not?"

She needed to get him away from her. If she could alter her copy in a spot that *didn't* typically change, then if she was accused of anything later, she could point to her deliberate error to prove that she hadn't had any fraudulent intent. It had to be subtle enough to escape his detection, but clear enough that a bank would notice it.

Perhaps a change to the fancy artwork at the top—would he notice that?

"Would you please stop looking over my shoulder?" she complained. "I can't work with you making me so dreadfully nervous."

"Fine," he muttered, and rose to go look out the window.

Thank goodness. Swiftly, she considered the artwork. What about the griffin? It seemed to be part of the bank's emblem, so surely the bank would notice if it were changed into a dragon.

No, that was too like. A winged stallion, like Pegasus?

Yes. Perhaps that would work.

While her uncle was away from the table, she toiled over her altered copy of the image. But the longer she worked on the paper meant to "exonerate" Papa, the angrier she got. How dared Uncle Toby try to drag her into his criminal enterprise?

He left the window to pace the room. Why was he so fidgety? What more was he planning?

At least one good thing had come out of this. Since her uncle had insisted on sneaking into the house so Papa and Jenkins wouldn't know they were around, she had to believe that Papa wasn't part of the counterfeiting scheme.

Unfortunately, with no one knowing she was in the house, even if Niall thought to come here looking for her, Jenkins would turn him away.

She worked in silence, taking as much time as she dared. Uncle Toby had just turned toward her, obviously annoyed, when a sound wafted up from the floor below.

"I need to see my niece, blast you!"

Aunt Agatha? What the devil? How had she known to come here?

There was a long silence, during which Brilliana could imagine Jenkins trying to dissuade Aunt Agatha.

It clearly didn't work, for the bellowing voice continued. "What fustian! I know she's here, sir. I must see her. *Now*."

"Why has she come?" Uncle Toby hissed.

"I have no idea. But if you don't let me go talk to her, she will make a ruckus until you do. Or worse yet, search every room until she finds me."

As if her aunt had read her mind, the woman shouted, "Brilliana? Where are you? I must speak to you at once!"

"Well?" Brilliana asked her uncle. "Shall I go down?"

Uncle Toby scowled. "Only if you can get rid of the woman."

"I shall try." Thank goodness for Aunt Agatha. She had an uncanny ability to recognize when something was amiss.

Her noncommittal answer seemed to give him pause. "I'll go with you, my dear."

His insistence on accompanying her would have distressed her if not for one thing. Uncle Toby was no match for Aunt Agatha. No one ever was.

Brilliana waited until his back was turned, then surreptitiously grabbed the paper she'd been copying, as well as the half copy she'd already made, and slid them into her apron pocket.

Then she let him hurry her out into the hall. "I'm up here, Aunt Agatha! What do you need?"

Her aunt started up the stairs, shouting to Brilliana all the while. "Margrave told my servant that you jilted him!"

Somehow Brilliana doubted that, but she played along. "That is true."

"What? Have you lost your mind?"

With an eye to her uncle, who was avidly listening, Brilliana cried, "I don't think that's any of your concern, Aunt!"

"I daresay it is. I'm providing you with a dowry—and that is enough to give me a say in your choice." Aunt Agatha reached the top of the stairs to confront Brilliana. "What in heaven's name are you thinking, to be jilting a man of Margrave's consequence?"

Uncle Toby stepped in. "Margrave is a gambler. Who cares about his consequence?" He eyed her closely. "And what are you doing here, anyway? Who told you to come here?"

Brilliana held her breath, hoping her aunt could allay his suspicions.

"Not that it's any of *your* concern, sir," Aunt Agatha said in her most imperious voice, "but as I was walking home I saw the two of you pass by in a hackney. When I questioned my footman about it, he told me that my niece had gone off with her uncle, and that you had given your brother's house as your destination."

"You saw us drive by?" he said. "I noticed no one passing us on your street."

"Brilliana clearly spotted me," Aunt Agatha said blithely. "She waved to me. Didn't you, Brilliana?"

Aunt Agatha must have some reason for the lie. "Of course. I'm sorry, Aunt, but there was no time to stop and tell you of my change in plans for the day."

She waved off the apology. "It doesn't matter. But I *was* alarmed when the footman told me of your falling-out with Margrave. Have you gone mad? He's an earl, for pity's sake. How could you jilt an earl?"

Brilliana's father came up the stairs, clearly drawn by the commotion. "What is this?" he said, glancing from Aunt Agatha to her. "What are you doing here, daughter?"

"She jilted Lord Margrave!" Aunt Agatha said, as if that explained everything.

"What?" Papa said. "*Why?*"

Uncle Toby gritted his teeth. "Because he's an inveterate gambler."

"What does *that* signify?" Papa asked. "Half the men in London are inveterate gamblers. Including her father."

"Which is precisely why she shouldn't marry such a man," Uncle Toby said.

"Nonsense," Aunt Agatha said. "Sir Oswald is right. His gambling is naught to worry about."

"You see, Toby? Best to stay out of these matters with the young people."

As her uncle faced her father in a fury, Aunt Agatha winked at her. Winked! Brilliana had been unaware that the baroness even knew *how* to wink.

"You may stay out of it, Oswald," her uncle said. "But I care about her too much to allow it."

Brilliana had to stifle a snort.

"So go back to your cards and your ridiculous friends," Uncle Toby went on. Then he glared at Aunt Agatha. "And forgive me, Lady Pensworth, but your niece has made up her mind, so there's no point to your haranguing her further."

"Haranguing her!" her aunt cried, with a gleam in her eyes. "How *dare* you, sir? I will have you know that I have taken that woman into my bosom, yet she has chosen to insult my charity by refusing a perfectly good gentleman. It will not be borne, sir. It will not be borne, I say!"

From there, the matter deteriorated into a melee. Uncle Toby argued with Aunt Agatha, Papa put in his own opinions here and there but was gainsaid at every turn, and Brilliana did her best to stir up trouble wherever she could, because she had a sneaking suspicion that there was a method to Aunt Agatha's madness—though she had no idea what it was.

Until the sound of pounding on the door downstairs brought the melee to an abrupt halt. "Open this door in the name of His Majesty, William IV!" cried a loud, official-sounding voice.

Brilliana's mouth fell open. And when she shot her aunt a quizzical glance, Aunt Agatha winked at her again. Good Lord.

Papa seemed genuinely surprised to hear visitors at the door, and immediately headed off down the stairs to see what was afoot. Uncle Toby, however, blanched and darted off to the parlor.

Brilliana hurried after him. Whatever was going on, she would not give him the chance to dispose of any evidence that might be in the house. She entered the parlor to find him frantically searching the room.

He rounded on her. "Where are they, niece?"

As she heard sounds of booted feet tramping up the stairs, she cast him a look of pure innocence. "Where are what?"

"The papers, damn it! The one you were copying and the copy!"

She peered over at the table. "Are they not there?"

"You can see that they're—" He held out his hand. "Give them to me. Now!"

"I don't have them. Perhaps they fell on the floor," she said sweetly. "Did you look there?"

He advanced on her with a look of such rage in his eyes that she stepped back, but then Niall walked in. Brilliana could have wept with relief.

"Are you all right, sweeting?" he asked with concern.

She beamed at him, and threw herself into his arms. "Perfectly fine, now that you are here."

He gave her a brief buss on the lips, which reassured her that he hadn't thought she was really jilting him earlier.

Her uncle said, "What in God's name are you doing here, Margrave?" but she no longer cared about Uncle Toby. She had Niall, and that was all that mattered.

Papa burst through the door next, looking as if his entire world had just shattered. "Toby, the officers are saying you've been counterfeiting banknotes! They're looking at all the money you've given me over the past few months. Go tell them that it's a mistake." His voice grew frantic. "It can't be true!"

"Of course it's not true," Uncle Toby said soothingly. "It's a simple misunderstanding."

"Hardly that, sir," said a triumphant voice from the door. Lord Fulkham entered the tiny parlor, waving a sheaf of notes in his hand. "We found these among your funds, Sir Oswald. At least a quarter of them are fake."

"So it's true?" Papa asked his brother, clearly shocked. "You've been giving me counterfeited money to spread around town, you bloody arse?"

Assuming an expression of outrage, Uncle Toby turned to Lord Fulkham. "I don't know what he's talking about. I haven't given him a damned thing. If there are counterfeit notes in his possession, they did not come from me."

Lord Fulkham's smile of satisfaction didn't dim. "Ah, but these did." He opened an apparently empty valise, then removed its false bottom to reveal more banknotes. "*These* we found in *your* rooms."

Though the color had drained from Uncle Toby's face, he shook his head resolutely. "My brother must have planted that valise in my bedchamber to implicate me in his scheme." He ignored Papa's roar of anger to add, "I'll have you know, sir, that I'm a respectable merchant. Why would I break the law?"

"I don't know the *why*," Brilliana put in, "but you were certainly attempting it." Drawing the document and its copy out of her pocket, she handed them to Fulkham. "I can't be sure, but I think this is a French bill of exchange my uncle was trying to get me to forge a copy of."

As Lord Fulkham looked over the two papers, Uncle Toby shot her a murderous look. "Don't you see what is happening here, Lord Fulkham? My brother and my niece are in league to blame their crimes on *me*. I am not the one with the bill of exchange in my possession—*she* is. And I am not the one with artistic abilities. *She* is."

As Papa cast Brilliana a frantic look, Niall stiffened beside her, but she squeezed his arm reassuringly.

She was just about to explain how she'd changed the art to keep the bill from being used fraudulently, when Papa told Lord Fulkham, "Don't listen to him, sir." He drew himself up with a heavy sigh. "My daughter is just trying to protect me. *She* did not do anything. That copy was made by me."

Surprise flickered over Uncle Toby's face, but he masked it quickly. "You see? They're in it together."

"No, *we're* in it together, Toby," Papa bit out. "The jig is up." Facing Lord Fulkham, he held out his wrists in an expression of resignation. "I will tell you everything, sir. Just take us both away, and leave my daughter be."

Oh, for goodness' sake, Papa chose *now* to show he cared about her? "Lord Fulkham, my father had naught to do with—"

"Be quiet for a moment, Mrs. Trevor," Fulkham ordered before turning to her father. "If that is so, sir, then tell me this." He held up the original bill of exchange. "What sort of mythical creature appears in the emblem on this paper?"

As relief coursed through Brilliana, Papa blinked. "Mythical creature? What the bloody hell do you mean?"

"The artwork contains a mythical creature. The artwork of *both* contains a mythical creature. What particular mythical creature is on this piece of paper?"

Papa looked as if he might faint right there. "Mythical . . . hmm . . . A dragon?"

Thank goodness she hadn't chosen the dragon.

Smirking, Lord Fulkham turned to her. "And what would *you* say is on there, Mrs. Trevor?"

She grinned. "A griffin on the original. The copy has a winged horse."

Lord Fulkham nodded. "Very clever of you, my dear. It seems you are not so bad at subterfuge, after all."

"You . . . you *altered* it, you damned bitch?" her uncle cried.

She glowered at him. Now his true colors came out. "That's what you ordered me to do, isn't it? I seem to recall your saying that I needed to make only a few changes. So I did."

As if realizing he'd given himself away, her uncle began to sputter, "This is not . . . I have friends, *good* friends in the government, who will not tolerate—"

"Take this scoundrel away, will you?" Lord Fulkham called to some men in the hall. As the officers entered to seize Uncle Toby, Fulkham added, "Judging from what Mrs. Trevor *was* able to copy, you were planning to run, weren't you? With a few simple changes to the name and the amounts, a 'respectable man of business' like you would have easily been able to get some foreign bank to honor the bill of exchange."

Uncle Toby's expression showed nothing. "I have no idea what you're talking about, my lord."

"Doesn't matter," Lord Fulkham said. "Thanks to your niece and her fiancé, we have plenty of evidence against you." As they took Uncle Toby out, Lord Fulkham smiled at her. "A pity that you have no interest in this sort of work, Mrs. Trevor. I could use a woman like you."

Niall tugged her close. "Over my dead body."

"I will overlook your impertinences, Margrave," Lord Fulkham drawled, "since this turned out well. But it could easily have gone wrong, Lady Pensworth's help notwithstanding."

"I *knew* something was up when she arrived," Brilliana said. "She was behaving very oddly."

"You can thank Margrave for that," Lord Fulkham said. "He sent her here to distract Payne and make sure he didn't harm you, while Margrave and I marshaled our resources."

She gazed fondly up at Niall. "How very clever of you."

"Yes, but thanks to his insistence on acting now," Lord Fulkham grumbled, "we still don't have the men who did the forgeries for Payne."

"If I hadn't acted now," Niall pointed out, "Payne would have fled. And you know it."

"Probably. I daresay your father's losing that one note to you made Payne nervous enough to fear he was on the verge of capture." Fulkham sighed. "Besides, I'm not sure we ever *can* apprehend his cohorts, given that they're likely in France. We'll have to work with the French authorities on that."

"What will happen to Papa now?" Brilliana asked.

"Since he had no intent to defraud, I can make a good case for not charging him at all. Especially once I tell the magistrate how you and Niall assisted in your uncle's capture."

Papa gaped at her. "You . . . you knew about the counterfeits this whole time?"

She nodded. "Lord Fulkham said that if I wanted to keep you from being hanged, I needed to find out what was really going on. And he enlisted Niall to help me."

Her father clutched his cane. "You did that for me?"

"I couldn't see you hanged, Papa," she said softly.

He digested that a moment, then turned to Lord Fulkham. "Is that what will happen to my brother? Is he going to hang?"

"I'll do my best to see that he only receives transportation, sir. After all, I owe your daughter for catching him."

"Don't spare him on *my* account," she said

with a sniff. "He tried to frame my father for counterfeiting. I can never forgive him for that."

Fulkham nodded. "We'll talk more about it later. But for now, I must go oversee the men who are gathering evidence."

As he went out, Aunt Agatha pushed her way in.

Brilliana rushed over to hug her. "Oh, Aunt, I do adore you," she said. "Thank you for being here for me."

"If something had happened to you, my dear," Aunt Agatha murmured, "I don't know what I would have done. You are essential to me. Do you understand?"

"Yes. And I feel the same about you."

Drawing back to blot her eyes with a handkerchief, Lady Pensworth took a deep, steadying breath. "Enough of that now." She shot Papa a furtive glance. "I am happy to be the *one* relation who hasn't let you down."

"To be fair," Niall broke in, "Sir Oswald wasn't entirely to blame for brokering Bree's marriage to Trevor. Payne had a part in that, too."

"What!" Brilliana and Aunt Agatha exclaimed in unison.

Niall smiled at Brilliana. "Your father asked your uncle to help him pay off the debt to Captain Trevor, so you didn't *have* to marry anyone you didn't want, but your uncle refused to lift one finger on your behalf. In fact, he urged your father to accept Captain Trevor's suggestion of an arranged marriage."

"Why, that . . . that lying weasel!" she cried. "Now I *really* hope he hangs!"

Her father stepped forward. "Ah, but it wasn't his fault in the end, daughter. I could have refused the captain's offer, come hell or high water. Instead, I made you feel you had no choice but to accept it." He hung his head. "And I have never regretted anything so much in my life. Do you think you can ever forgive me?"

She stared at him, her heart twisting in her chest. She'd never expected to hear such words come from his mouth. He was still a negligent wastrel, but in light of recent revelations, she couldn't think quite as ill of him as before. Especially after what he'd just attempted to do for her.

"You offered to go to prison for me, Papa," she said softly. "I'd be an ungrateful daughter indeed to stay angry with you after that. So, yes, I forgive you."

"Well," he said in a relieved voice, "it was the least I could do, considering that you married Reynold Trevor to keep *me* out of prison." He cast her a rheumy smile. "So, does that mean you'll let me see my grandson at last?"

"It does." She cast Niall a teasing glance. "But it may have to wait until after the wedding, since I believe that will be occurring soon."

"*Quite* soon, if I have my way, sweeting," Niall said.

"I beg your pardon?" Aunt Agatha exclaimed.

"After everything I have put up with from you two, I believe I've earned the right to see my niece wed in a grand ceremony befitting a future countess. She deserves it, and I can afford to pay for it. So *that* is what we'll do."

Brilliana appealed to her fiancé. "Niall, do tell her—"

"Who am I to gainsay your aunt? If she wants a grand ceremony, she can have one." He took her hands in his. "As long as I'm the groom, I don't care when or how we marry, my love."

She stared into his eyes, her heart so full she could hardly bear it.

Aunt Agatha cleared her throat. "Come, Sir Oswald." She took Papa by the arm. "Let's go see if we can find some tea in this place. I am positively *parched*."

As they walked out, Papa muttered, "So am I, but it ain't for tea."

"Come to think of it," her aunt said, "a bit of brandy in the tea wouldn't be amiss."

She closed the door, and Brilliana and Niall burst into laughter.

Then it dawned on both of them that at last they were alone . . . or as alone as they could be with men tramping about the house. And suddenly she didn't know quite what to say to him.

She remembered only too well how they'd left things last night, and all she seemed able to do was stare down at her hands as she gathered her thoughts.

"Please tell me you're not planning to jilt me again," he drawled. "I can only endure one jilting per day."

"Niall, don't tease. I have something very serious to say to you."

With a squeeze of his hands, she met his gaze. Her heart broke to see the uncertainty in the beautiful hazel eyes she loved so well. She had put that uncertainty there with her fears.

And now she would banish it for good. "Last night, you were right when you said I was afraid to trust my heart. But in my defense, once a body's heart is broken, even after it mends you feel as if it's too fragile ever to be taxed again. So you coddle it and keep it wrapped up in wool, so it won't get scarred or torn or even scratched."

Tears welled in her eyes that she swallowed ruthlessly. "But this morning, when I sat there listening to Uncle Toby's idiocy about jilting you, I realized that my heart is stronger than I thought. It believed in you when I couldn't, it waited for you when I couldn't. And it loved you even when I couldn't."

She smiled tremulously. "As it turns out, it didn't need protecting after all. It just needed me to take it out of the wool and let it breathe. And now it's doing precisely what it always wanted: loving you. Freely. As apparently I always have."

A smile broke over his face more beautiful than any sunrise, and he bent to touch his forehead to hers. "That's the nice thing about hearts.

They're stubborn as the very devil. Since mine has been longing for you all these years, too, what do you say we give them what they want?"

She nodded, so full of happiness and joy that she could hardly speak.

Niall kissed her with the sweet, deep love of a man who knew her, body and soul, and then he kissed her again for good measure.

When finally he drew back, he wore that rakish smile she adored. "So, no more jiltings?"

"Never again, my love. You're stuck with me now."

With a chuckle, he took her arm in his and led her toward the door. "It's about damned time."

Epilogue

Margrave Manor
Twelfth Night, 1831

When they cut the cake, Niall got the piece containing the bean, which meant he was king for Twelfth Night. Brilliana couldn't help but laugh. The last thing her husband needed was a crown to make him more self-assured.

Fittingly, his sister Clarissa received the piece of cake containing the pea, thus making her queen for the night. Many jokes about the reign of the Lindsey siblings ensued, all in good fun, and Brilliana smiled at the sight of her husband marching about the ballroom, paper scepter in hand.

Wearing her own paper crown, Clarissa came up to stand next to Brilliana. "You have no idea how pleased I am to finally be at a party. I thought I would go mad, cooped up in the country for three months."

"I can well imagine," Brilliana said with a smile. "And how *is* little Horatio?"

Clarissa beamed at her. "He's adorable! I know every mother says the same, but he is the cleverest lad. At only two weeks, he smiles!"

"Of course he does." Brilliana wouldn't tell her that many infants appeared to smile at that age. "I do hope we can see him soon."

"You shall, as soon as I can convince Edwin that it's safe." Clarissa rolled her eyes. "I love my husband, but he must be the most overprotective man in all Christendom."

"I think it's rather sweet," Brilliana said.

"Sweet, yes. And sometimes very trying." Clarissa turned serious. "I . . . um . . . understand that my brother told you why he had to go into exile."

"Yes." Brilliana reached over to squeeze her friend's hand. "And it made me admire you even more. You are incredibly strong to have survived that so well."

"Thank you. In truth, I hadn't survived it nearly as well as I thought. Then Edwin came along, and he showed me that . . ." She smiled. "Anyway, I wanted to speak to you about it because Edwin finally told me how keeping my secret was the cause of your separation from Niall. I am *so* very sorry that—"

"Please, don't be concerned. You couldn't stop what was done to you, any more than we could have stopped how we reacted. Niall and I have found each other again, and that's what's important."

"Very true, and I'm delighted for you both."

Clarissa hugged her. "I am *so* very glad to have you as a sister."

Brilliana's eyes welled with tears. "Me too."

Then her other sister-in-law, Delia, appeared. "What's this? Clarissa, are you making my sister cry?"

"She's *my* sister now, too," Clarissa said blithely. "So you must share her."

Delia chuckled. "Happily. One can never have too many sisters."

The three of them hugged and laughed, and were well on their way to having a jolly good cry, when Niall appeared. "By God, what is going on? Is my queen consorting with my wife?" He frowned. "That sounds odd, doesn't it?"

Clarissa laughed. "Yes, but it's all right. You're king tonight. You can say anything you please."

"Then I will say that I wish to have my wife to myself for a while, ladies."

"I understand entirely." With a knowing smile, Clarissa drew Delia off with her.

Niall grinned. "There are some advantages to being the Bean King."

"Don't get cocky," Brilliana teased. "You are only king for the evening."

"That's long enough to suit me—I don't wish to rule *this* lot. They are completely unmanageable."

With a laugh, Brilliana glanced about. Warren was sneaking brandy into the punch bowl. Jeremy, another member of St. George's, was trying to convince a portly old gentleman to pose for one of his outrageous paintings. Aunt Agatha was whirling Silas about the room in her arms as he laughingly trailed ribbons through the air. And Papa—

"Good Lord," Brilliana said. "My father just brought a glass of punch to your mother."

Niall followed her gaze, then groaned. "Can you imagine those two together?"

"We mustn't allow it to go beyond this party. God forbid they were to marry. Why, they would always be in arrears."

"Between my mother's spending and your father's gambling . . ."

They watched the couple talk for a few minutes. They did seem rather animated. Brilliana rarely saw her grouchy father laugh, but the dowager Lady Margrave caused him to do so several times.

"He *has* become a bit better with his gambling," Brilliana pointed out. "I think that Uncle Toby's downfall frightened him into reconsidering his way of life. A bit. I don't know if it will last."

"Well, nothing would prompt my mother to become more responsible," Niall said. "She's entirely too old to change."

And too featherbrained, Brilliana thought, but it wasn't as if Papa was any sort of scholar. The two of them were matched evenly there.

A frightening thought.

"Speaking of your uncle," Niall said, "how do you feel about the sentence imposed upon him?"

She sighed. "I confess that I'm relieved he only got transportation. I know what he did was wrong, but—"

"I understand. And our laws are absurdly draconian with regard to such matters, anyway." Niall shook his head. "No one should have to hang for counterfeiting."

"I agree." She smiled up at him. "Thank you for convincing Lord Fulkham to be lenient with him."

"Only because I knew you would wish it. I was none too happy when I realized your uncle was trying to embroil you in his scheme." Niall slid his arm about her waist.

Aunt Agatha came up to them holding Silas by the hand. The minute Silas saw Niall, he cried, "Jack, Jack!"

When Niall grinned and reached into his pocket, Aunt Agatha said, "Margrave! You wouldn't!"

"It's not *that* watch. It's a perfectly respectable image of ladies dancing in a wood." Niall wound the music-box portion of the pocket watch, then held it out to her. "Here, see for yourself."

Aunt Agatha examined it while Silas tugged on her arm, trying to get his plaything. "I suppose that's all right." She handed it to Silas, who stared at it entranced as the music tinkled away. "But couldn't you get him one with puppies or something?"

"They don't make them with puppies," Brilliana said dryly. "Trust me, I checked."

Her aunt rolled her eyes. "Well, at least the dancing ladies are fully clothed. That's something to be thankful for."

"Of course they are," Niall said irritably. "How much of a rogue do you think I am, anyway?"

Aunt Agatha stared at him over her spectacles. "Enough to capture my niece's heart, when I thought no one could."

When Niall blinked at that compliment, Brilliana laughed and slid her hand into the crook of his arm. "He does have a way about him, doesn't he?"

"Jack! Jack!" Silas cried, and held the watch up to Niall. "Papa! Fix Jack!"

The soft look that crossed Niall's face touched Brilliana's heart. Silas had recently taken to calling Niall "Papa," and every time he did, Niall looked so pleased that she wanted to kiss them both.

He wound the watch again and handed it to Silas. This time the boy toddled off to show it to Grandpapa Payne, who was now flirting most decidedly with Grandmama Margrave. Lord help them all.

"I'd best make sure the boy doesn't get into any trouble," Aunt Agatha said. She paused a moment. "Though I know it's too early for this, since you only got married a month ago, I do hope to see more children running about your house soon. Silas needs someone to play with."

It was all Brilliana could do to keep a straight face. "He does, indeed."

As soon as her aunt was out of hearing, she and Niall burst into laughter.

Placing her hand on her belly, Brilliana whispered, "How on earth are we going to convince her that our child was conceived on the right side of the blanket?"

"Dr. Worth will never tell. And honestly, eight-month babes are rather thick on the ground in London."

"But this may be a seven-month babe." Brilliana worried her lower lip with her teeth. "Perhaps we should go away to have it."

"Since it's the Earl of Margrave's heir, no one will be counting the days."

"And if it's a girl?" she said tartly. "Children do come in two flavors, you know."

He smirked at her. "Then she'll be the spitting image of her mother, and people will be so blinded by her beauty that they won't even think to count."

"You are such a rogue!" When he frowned, she added softly, "Truly, Niall, I mean that as a compliment. You will always be a wild rogue to me, even when you're a respectable old married man with children and grandchildren and a penchant for port. Because the part of your roguery that I love is the part that makes me feel young and free and full of life."

"Ah. The part that is Lady Rebel."

She grinned. "Exactly."

With a gleam of mischief in his eyes, he leaned close. "Well, since I'm king for a night, I command you, Lady Rebel, to join me in the library, after all our guests leave, for a glass of port. And perhaps a few other . . . endeavors. Whatever your little rebel heart desires."

"In the library? No trees involved?"

"It's too cold outside to involve trees. Will bookshelves do?"

"Or the rug by the fire?"

Slyly, he slid his hand down to pat her behind. "That would be just about right for certain . . . pleasures."

"Port and the pleasures of passion. Sounds perfect." She flashed him her best sultry glance. "I am your subject for the night, sir. Do with me as you will."

"In that case, why wait until our guests leave?"

Though she gave a shocked laugh, she went unresisting as he tugged her toward the door. Because once in a while, a woman just had to play the rebel to her rogue.

At St. George's Club, guardians conspire

to keep their unattached sisters and wards

out of the clutches of sinful suitors.

Which works fine…

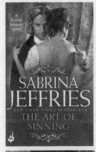 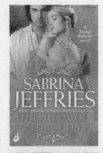

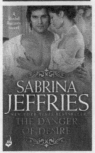 

…except when the sinful suitors are members.

Don't be shy.
Meet the Sinful Suitors.

Available now from

Do you dare to encounter the
Hellions of Halstead Hall?

They're the scandalous Sharpes,
five hell-raising siblings tainted by a shocking family legacy.

Meet Lord Oliver, Lord Jarret, Lady Minerva,
Lord Gabriel and Lady Celia.

Expect secrets, shenanigans and sensuous romance.

Available now from

HEADLINE
ETERNAL